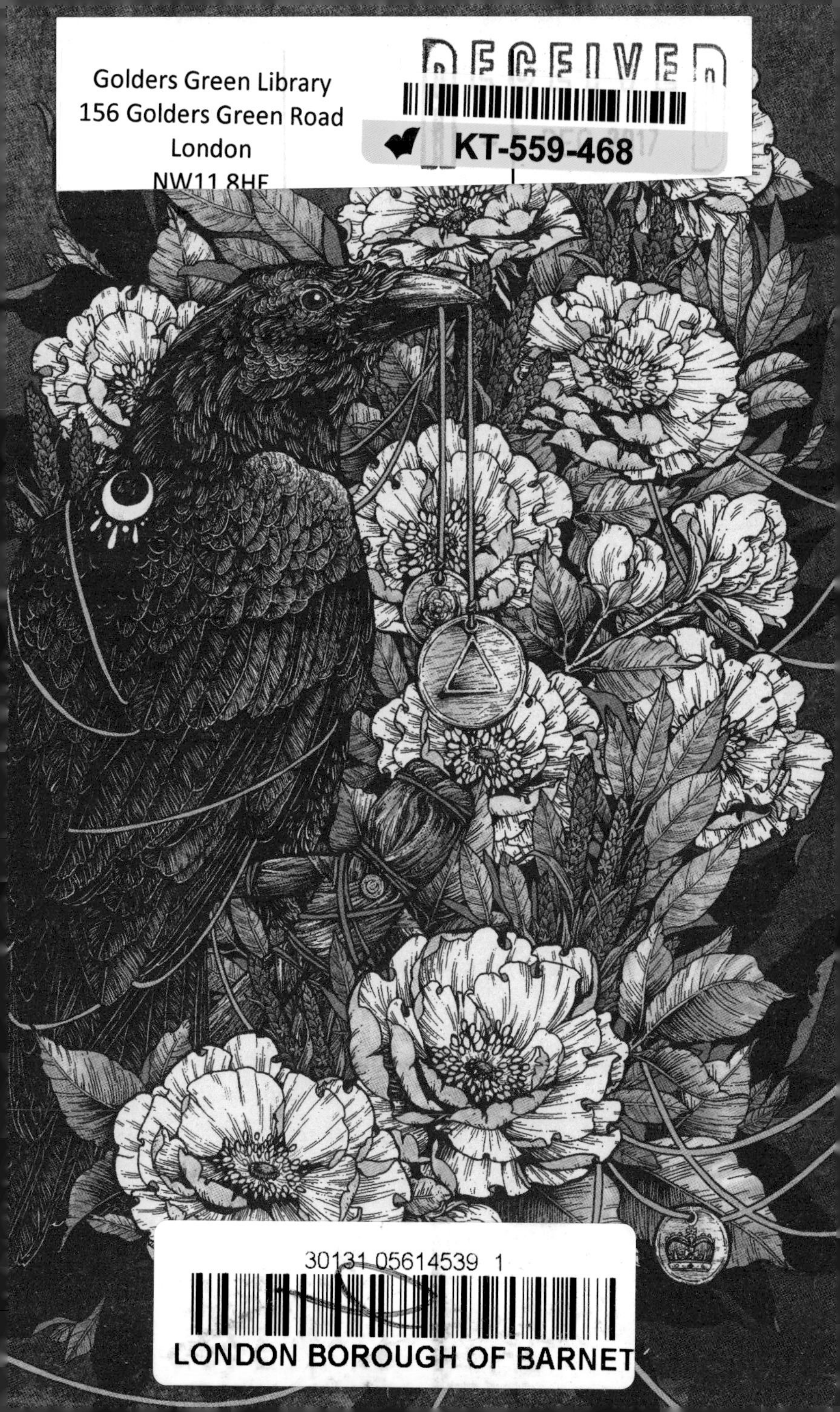

Wow. Here's something truly special: I was *totally* gripped, almost strangled, sometimes terrified by Nicholas Bowling's debut. This shadowy, clever, intricate tale takes place in a world you *think* sounds familiar. Here you'll find warring queens, court intrigues, sorcery, actors, witches and madness – not to mention the restless dead. Read this book and be bewitched: I dare you.

BARRY CUNNINGHAM
Publisher
Chicken House

WITCH BORN

NICHOLAS BOWLING

2 PALMER STREET, FROME, SOMERSET BA11 1DS

WWW.CHICKENHOUSEBOOKS.COM

Text © Nicholas Bowling 2017
Illustration © Erica Williams 2017

First published in Great Britain in 2017
Chicken House
2 Palmer Street
Frome, Somerset BA11 1DS
United Kingdom
www.chickenhousebooks.com

Cover design and interior design by Steve Wells
Typeset by Dorchester Typesetting Group Ltd
Printed and bound in Great Britain by CPI Group (UK) Ltd, Croydon, CR0 4YY

The paper used in this Chicken House book is made from wood grown in sustainable forests.

1 3 5 7 9 10 8 6 4 2

British Library Cataloguing in Publication data available.

ISBN 978-1-911077-25-1
eISBN 978-1-911077-26-8

For Mum and Dad

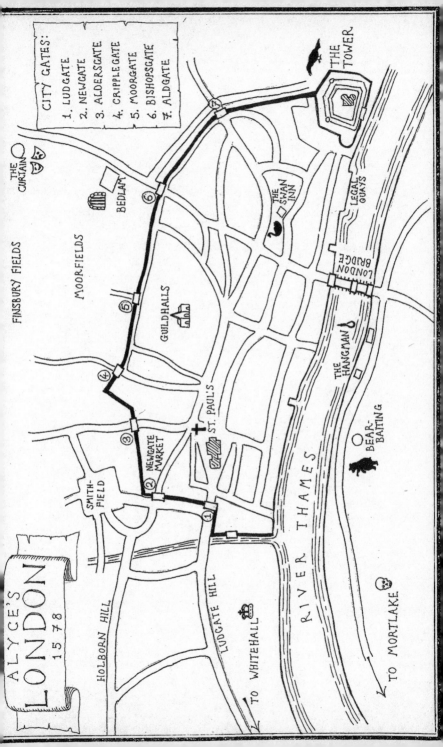

ALYCE'S
LONDON
1578

CITY GATES:
1. LUDGATE
2. NEWGATE
3. ALDERSGATE
4. CRIPPLEGATE
5. MOORGATE
6. BISHOPSGATE
7. ALDGATE

FINSBURY FIELDS

THE CURTAIN

MOORFIELDS

BEDLAM

GUILDHALLS

THE SWAN INN

THE TOWER

LONDON BRIDGE

LEGAL QUAYS

SMITH-FIELD

NEWGATE MARKET

ST. PAUL'S

THE HANGMAN

HOLBORN HILL

LUDGATE HILL

RIVER THAMES

BEAR-BAITING

TO WHITEHALL

TO MORTLAKE

The Witch's MOMMET is a most cunning Piece of Sympathetick Magick, by which She may both harme and heal. With such materialls as her Craft allowes, the Witch shall make a figure in the shape of Man or Woman, and thence shall binde it to a livinge Soul through some vitall Matter; that being, some Hair, or Skin, or Spittel, or Blood, &c. In such wyse, whatsoever the Witch may perform upon the MOMMET, this will also bee performed upon the Soul to which it is bounde.

Full many a Witch may choose to craft a MOMMET in her very own Likenesse, and take such Care of this as to safeguard her own Life.

The Arcana, 'On Sympathie'

FORDHAM, ESSEX
20 November 1577

The knocking came harder this time. Ellen could clearly hear two voices just outside the cottage's window, and behind them a low sea-swell of agitated muttering. It sounded like they had brought the whole village with them.

The house shuddered. She looked at the door, then down at the cooking pot slung over the fire in front of her, and then back to the door again. It wouldn't take much for them to break it down, but it might buy her a little time while they tried.

Hastily, Ellen gathered up the last remaining objects from around the hearth – dried herbs, stones, figures of straw and bone – and threw them all into the pot, poking each one under the surface of the broth with a wooden spoon as she went. Then she heaved the whole concoction out of the fire and left it steaming on the earthen floor.

'*OPEN THE DOOR, CRONE!*'

Again, the frame of the tiny cottage shook. Ellen sighed.

'Crone?' she murmured to herself, fishing a bonnet from the back of a chair, and stuffing her masses of brown curls underneath. 'I don't look *that* old . . .'

She stood up straight, smoothed out her smock and roughly tightened the laces in her bodice. Her appearance probably wouldn't count for much once she had opened the door to her visitors, but she wasn't going to make their job easier for them. She glanced at the two beds in the corner of the room, one so small it could have been a cot, and a shadow passed over her face.

I hope she remembers what to do.

More pounding. The door seemed to be coming off its hinges.

I hope she'll be safe.

Ellen took a deep breath, and went to open it. Pale light and cold air, rich with the damp smells of late autumn, flooded the cottage.

The sight that greeted her on the other side gave her a thrill of surprise more than fear. The man in front of her had a quite impossibly handsome face. His high cheekbones, arched eyebrows and pointed beard gave him a slightly devilish aspect that Ellen found rather appealing. Those features were framed by a vast ruff and tall black hat, its huge feathers nodding like the plume of some Greek warrior. And at the centre of it all were his eyes – the kind of eyes that seemed to be all pupil, cold and black as forest pools. He smiled at her.

'Good day, sirs,' said Ellen calmly. At the shoulder of the handsome man stood a taller, thinner companion. In one hand he was clutching a Bible. In the other a noose. Behind them both were the dirty, ugly, absurd faces of the villagers, pressed in a ring around her cottage.

The handsome man cleared his throat and spoke. His voice sounded like a hammer striking an anvil.

'Ellen Greenliefe. By the authority of the *Malleus Maleficarum*, you stand accused of the practice of witchcraft, denying Almighty God and his son Jesus Christ, of sealing a covenant with the Devil, and performing diverse crimes of sorcery and necromancy with which you have cursed and afflicted the good villagers of Fordham.'

There were subdued noises of agreement from the onlookers. Ellen did her best to look underwhelmed, and smiled back at the man.

'Forgive me, gentlemen, but I suspect you've had a wasted journey. I am a poor housewife, no more. I spin. I weave.' She gestured to a broken spinning wheel that was leant against the outside wall of the cottage.

The handsome man laughed. 'Ay, I can believe that. It is a web of *lies* and *deceit* that you have been weaving, and most subtly too.'

His smugness showed so plainly on his face, Ellen thought for a moment he might take a bow. A couple of villagers took heart from his reply and cried their approval.

'She ain't never been to church!'

'She turned all our milk sour!'

Ellen sighed, and replied over the handsome man's shoulder. 'That's a matter you should discuss with your cows, Master Garrard, not me.' There was a titter from one of the children in the crowd. 'Come, sirs, it is a long journey back to London. Stay awhile and have something to eat, and I'll see you on your way. I have just made a fresh stew.'

'She's lying!' shouted another of the peasants. 'It's *poison*!'

'I'll admit I'm not the most talented cook, but that's a little unkind . . . At least come inside and rest your feet.'

The handsome man continued to smile, although one of his eyes twitched with impatience. He waited for the villagers' baiting to die down.

'How very gracious of you,' he said quietly, his eyes now a pair of black storms. 'We will be coming into your house, but that is not to say we will be accepting your hospitality.'

Ellen's face hardened. 'If it's evidence of witchcraft you are looking for, I am afraid you will be disappointed.'

'Yes, of course,' said the man, drawing close to her. His eyes roamed greedily over her, as though searching for something on her person. 'No doubt the Devil has taught you most cunning ways of concealing your art.'

Ellen let out a cold laugh. 'So, if you find what you are looking for, I am damned. And if you don't find it, I am damned for concealing it? How clever! And I thought I was meant to be the tricksy one.'

The handsome man's face split into a grin, revealing a set of perfectly white teeth. He was inches away now. He smelt of iron and woodsmoke. 'You may be able to conceal your apparatus, witch, but you cannot conceal your own body.' Suddenly he grabbed her wrist in a gloved hand, pulled her on to the doorstep, and tore a sleeve from her arm. Her skin prickled in the cold breeze. The crowd gasped.

'Look upon this, gentlefolk!' crowed the handsome man, dragging her from the doorway and thrusting her arm up into the air. 'The witch's poisonous teat, with which she has been feeding her familiar! Who is to say how many more of these she has upon her vile body?'

Ellen looked at the two little pink lumps a few inches up from her wrist. They still hadn't healed after an accident with a toasting fork. Searching the faces of the villagers she found nothing but hatred and ignorance, and she turned back to the man who held her.

'This is madness! That's a *burn*, you fool, can't you see? Show me a wife in this village who doesn't have any imperfections like this!'

'Still she denies it, when the evidence is clear as day! Lies, wicked lies!'

The villagers roared. Some began to pelt Ellen and her house with stones and mud and manure. The handsome man basked in their wild indignation, and spoke to the man at his shoulder.

'Master Caxton, bind her while I search her lodgings.' Then he turned to address his frenzied audience. 'There are yet more unholy discoveries within, too foul for your eyes to look upon.'

'The girl!' a woman screeched. 'She's hiding the girl!'

Ellen stared at the handsome man, whose back was to her now. The noise of the crowd had become overwhelming, and seemed to suck her underneath it like the waves of an incoming tide. Even while he faced away, she still heard his words. They seemed to blossom from inside her own head.

'Yes,' he said. 'The girl.'

Then, without looking at her, he disappeared into the darkness of the cottage.

With practised efficiency, the taller man yanked her arms behind her back and began tying them tightly together at the wrist. Ellen was thinking too hard to feel the rope bite into her flesh, to notice the hotness, the stickiness of her hands and fingers.

The taller man spun her around again, pulled her upright and attempted to force the noose down over her head. Up close she saw his features were nothing like his superior's — they were blank and sallow, expressing precisely nothing. Behind him the villagers' howling faces rippled like a mirage, and beyond them she glimpsed the cool, inviting foliage of the beech woods.

I should have run away with her, she thought. *As soon as I saw them I should have run.*

The witchfinder's extravagant hat bobbed and emerged into daylight again. His smile still hadn't faded, although there was something more predatory about it now as he marched towards her. His tall, blank companion tightened the noose a little.

'Where is she?' the witchfinder said.

Ellen stared at him. He took another step forward, and nodded to the man holding the noose. It pressed against her windpipe.

'Speak,' he said.

She cocked her head. Tighter still.

'Speak.'

She could feel her pulse behind her eyes.

'*Speak, witch.*'

After the third time, she turned her attention to the man holding the rope. She opened her mouth as if she were trying to form words, and he leant in to listen. When he was close enough for her to feel his sour breath on her face, she lurched forward and kissed him.

The handsome man roared with laughter. 'I'm afraid your womanly charms, considerable as they are, will not distract us from our duty, Miss Greenliefe. But I'm sure Master Caxton appreciates the gesture.'

Ellen drew herself back, whispering softly as she did. Caxton struck her with the back of his hand, knocking her to the ground. The crowd whooped with delight.

Then, for the first time, an expression registered on his pale face. Something between fear and surprise. It looked like he was trying to spit on her, but couldn't. His lips purpled and blistered. In his panic he tried to speak, but something was obviously lodged in his throat. He gurgled, then heaved, then spat; and when he did, he saw his tongue, blackened and decayed, fall whole from his mouth and land in the dirt between his feet.

The handsome man looked at his whimpering companion for a moment, then at Ellen. He took a couple of steps forward, bent down, and plucked the tongue off the floor with his gloved thumb and forefinger. The villagers were silent now, save for a flutter of whispered prayers.

'This woman and her child,' he announced, 'are a plague. They will infect us all. And as any physician will tell you, gentlefolk, there is only one sure way to prevent the spread of contagion.' He looked from one face to the next, his eyes sparkling. 'Fire.'

Fordham was all ash and smoke. It had started raining an hour ago, but the remains of the bonfire still smouldered and the cloying, acrid smell of charred wood and flesh clung to the houses. It was the villagers' own fault – they'd got carried away, and the fire had been far too large. Most were returning, exhausted, to their homes, but some could still be heard tramping through the woods and hollering to each other in search of the girl. A wraith-like sun hovered on the horizon.

Two men remained at the edge of the ashes, staring at the spot where the stake had been. Despite the drizzle, John Hopkins stood with his tall, black hat in his hands and smoothed its feathers absent-mindedly. His pearl-studded, velvet doublet was soaked through by now, as was his hair, but he didn't seem to have noticed. Just behind him was the village parson, an old man slow in mind and body, who kept coughing and spluttering as the wind blew grey flakes into his face.

'I thank God you came, sir,' he said, bowing his head slightly.

'Hmmm?'

'I–I thank God. For sending you to us.'

Hopkins didn't reply.

'And I shall pray for your companion,' he continued. 'That God may comfort him in his . . . affliction.'

'As you wish.'

The parson looked up, confused. He tried to blink the ash out of his watery eyes. Hopkins' eyes were still fixed on the smouldering stake.

'Stubborn old thing, wasn't she?' he said, drumming his jewelled fingers on the top of his hat.

'Beg pardon, sir?'

'The hag. Usually the flames haven't even reached the soles of their feet before they're confessing.' He was talking mostly to himself, and for once his lips weren't curled into a smile. 'But this one . . . Didn't want to give us anything, did she?'

'No, sir. Must've been thick with the Devil for him to stick with her till the end.' He crossed himself.

Hopkins' jaw twitched. He'd hoped that burning the woman would have brought the child out of hiding. Or that she would have revealed where the girl was, once she was tied to the stake. But neither of those things had happened. And now Ellen Greenliefe was gone.

He suddenly whirled round, and the parson audibly cringed. 'The girl. Did she have any friends in the village?'

'No, sir. Kept themselves to themselves, the pair of them. Never came to church. Not even after the fines. Never left that cursed house.'

Hopkins regarded the old man in silence for a moment, and then looked over the top of his bald head to Ellen Greenliefe's house, perched on a hill overlooking the rest of the village.

'Never left the house,' he muttered.

Without another word, he set his hat upon his head

and marched away from the parson up the hillside. Rain was falling more heavily now, and the rutted pathway he was following quickly becoming a muddy torrent. The sky was bruise-black.

When he reached the cottage, the door was still wide open and inside was as dark and empty as they had left it earlier. Tiny though the place was, the gloom gave it an unexpected air of menace. He would have to tread carefully; he didn't want a repeat of the business in Norfolk. Thunder began to murmur overhead, and the beech trees sighed in the mustering storm.

Hopkins stepped inside and shook the rain from his cloak. In the dying light, he could just make out the beds in one corner of the room, and in the other the feebly glowing embers of the cook-fire. A pot of cold stew still rested on the floor.

He waited for his eyes to adjust to the darkness and moved over to the two beds. Something crunched underfoot, and he saw that the floor was scattered with little figures of animals and people, woven from straw and twigs. He placed one of them carefully in his palm and examined it in the dim firelight. Then he tucked it into the folds of his doublet and began to pace the room, scowling. The place was too small to have a false wall or a priest hole or any cavity for concealing a man. Or a child. But he must have missed something.

The thunder rumbled again, closer now, within the cottage walls, within his own ears, low like the growling of a cornered dog. It was suddenly much darker, too, a deep, oppressive darkness that seemed to creep into his nose and mouth when he tried to breathe.

Groping through the shadows, he stubbed his toe on something hard and immovable. When he'd finished cursing, he knelt down and brushed the dirt away from the offending object. It was an iron ring, cold and furred with rust. Strange that he hadn't seen it earlier.

Hopkins squatted and heaved twice at the handle. On the third attempt, he was able to straighten his legs, and the trapdoor opened and fell heavily backwards. A steady orange furnace-glow filled the cottage from beneath. He basked in the light, standing triumphantly over the entrance to the witch's cellar, hands on hips.

That was the moment she chose to stab him.

The knife she used was so sharp he didn't even realize what had happened until he looked down and saw its handle protruding from below his ribs. He staggered forward and fell halfway down the stairs, twisting awkwardly to catch a glimpse of his killer as she stepped over his body. He saw her face, surrounded by curls that seemed to burn with a fire of their own, and for once he stopped smiling.

It was true. All of it was true.

He never heard her leave. She was somewhere behind him, her breath slow and steady as his own grew shallower and more uneven. He felt a strange numbness creeping in from his fingers and toes.

The girl was still watching when the darkness finally claimed him.

LONDON
One month later

Alyce slowly uncurled herself and sat upright on the flagstones. Instinctively, her hand went to the top of her head. Every time she woke up she did this; every time she knew exactly what she would find; and every time her heart sank a little lower when her fingers felt the coarse, uneven bristles where her hair used to be.

She missed her hair, especially when the nights were as cold as this. She'd never cut it, not once in fourteen years, and it had been long and thick enough to wrap around her like a blanket. Her mother had loved it. The governors had removed it all in one go.

Next, she stuck a finger in her ear, and scooped out the candle wax she had stuffed in there earlier that evening. For a couple of weeks now she had taken to collecting the little white blobs that dripped on to the floor from the governors' candles, and used them to block out the laughing, crying and screaming that echoed sporadically through the passageways. It always got worse at night.

Her cell looked strangely pretty in the moonlight, frozen into a delicate, white stillness. The floor had been swept, the bucket in the corner had disappeared, and she had been given a bundle of fresh straw to make her bed in, as though she were a prize cow. Above the straw hung a pair of manacles, which the governors had not used. They had tried, but her hands and wrists were too thin and kept slipping out. Nonetheless, they still served as a bleak reminder that she was a prisoner.

A prisoner, not a patient. 'Bethlem Royal Hospital' read the inscription above the gate, but she had realized the truth of it very quickly. Bedlam, as they called it, was no hospital, and she wasn't here to be nursed back to health.

Alyce padded over to the window, her feet as hard and icy as the stones underneath them, and looked through the bars of her cell. A huge, ragged raven was perched on the gables of the governors' lodgings. It flapped noisily across the courtyard, then glided over the gatehouse and out into the street.

It wasn't the other prisoners that kept her from sleeping as much as her own memories. They made a terrifying noise of their own, inside her head, that couldn't be blocked out. Those last moments of panic: the fear in her mother's eyes, the grip of her fingers on Alyce's shoulders, so tight it had left bruises. Then the sight of the carriage pulling into the village at the bottom of the hill, her mother scrawling and sealing the letter, and bundling Alyce into the cellar underneath the cottage.

Make for Bankside, she'd said. *Find the hangman John Dee. Give him this letter.*

The trapdoor closing, and after that…

Alyce's frozen face became flushed and hot. *Don't think about it*, she scolded herself. Her eyes stung. She thought she could smell burning. *Nothing to think about. There's nothing to be done.*

All the way to London, Alyce had muttered her mother's words, over and over until they seemed to lose all meaning: *Bankside. The Hangman. John Dee. Bankside. The Hangman. John Dee.* She'd still been chanting when Master Makepiece had found her in the ditch, wrapped up in her wet, filthy hair and half dead from exposure. It was no wonder he'd thought Bedlam the best place for her. She must have seemed quite out of her mind. And maybe she was.

When he'd first taken her in, she was only supposed to have stayed for a few days. There were endless arguments outside her cell about her upkeep, and how she had no one to pay for her, and how she should be thrown out to make way for an inmate who could bring in some much-needed funds. But her sponsor had stuck by her, despite the objections of his fellow governors, and it was now several weeks since she'd made this stinking cell her home.

Suddenly, she heard the sound of a key rattling in the lock behind her. She hurriedly wiped the tears from her eyes.

Let it be the nice one. Please, please, let it be the nice one.

It wasn't the nice one. It was the other one. The fat one. The one who shouted at her, and scolded her, and told her she had been cast out by God, that the Devil was in her, and plunged her into baths of ice to cure her of her ill humour. Despite the cold, his face was red and sweating, with thin strands of straw-coloured hair slapped down on to his forehead. He was still panting from climbing the single set of stairs up to Alyce's cell.

'Hello, my dove,' he slurred. Drunk, again. She shivered. 'Cold one tonight. Everyone's getting something to keep 'em warm, Master Makepiece's orders.' He spoke the name with barely disguised venom, and held out a bowl of porridge.

Alyce crept forward and took it, keeping her eyes fixed on the governor's glistening face. The bowl was freezing.

He watched her as she retreated into the corner and lifted a spoonful of the grey slop to her lips.

'Alyce!' he said, frowning in mock outrage, and wagging his finger. 'Good Christians say grace before a meal.'

He had played this game before, and she always lost. She didn't know what 'grace' was, and even if she had done, speaking was not something that came easily to her any more. Sometimes Master Makepiece coaxed a few words out of her, but she had never said a thing to this Master Kemp. In her silent world, she heard them talk about her. *Melancholic*, Makepiece had said. Kemp, on the other hand . . . well, his descriptions of her were a bit more imaginative.

'If you can't thank God for the food in front of you, girl, I'm not sure I can let you eat it in good faith.' The governor reached out a hand to reclaim the bowl, and Alyce flinched. 'Repeat after me: *benedic nobis, Domine deus* . . .'

Alyce said nothing. She just stared.

'Repeat after *me*,' said Kemp, nourishing his frustration, allowing it to bloom across his face. His jowls wobbled. '*Benedic nobis* . . .'

Again he was met with silence. In one motion, he stepped forward and grabbed Alyce's chin in his stubby little fingers, and then began working her jaw up and down as though she were a puppet he might force to speak.

Alyce grew hot with shame, which quickly turned to anger. She gripped the edge of the bowl, and hurled its contents at him. The porridge struck him square in the face with a deeply satisfying *slap*.

There was a strange pause. Master Kemp peered at her through his lumpy, gelatinous mask. Oats clung to his eyebrows and dripped from his chin. Alyce wanted to laugh, for the first time in what felt like years. But then the moment passed. He wiped a sleeve over his eyes and roared into life, seizing her by the throat and pouring curses upon her.

'Edmund!'

The second voice surprised her. It was low and warm, but weary. Over Kemp's shoulder she saw another man standing in the open doorway. It was Master Makepiece, the one who'd found her in the first place, and the only governor who shown her the slightest kindness. Kemp released her from his grip, and turned with a sharp sigh.

'*What?*'

'She is even less likely to speak with your stinking breath in her face. Leave her be.'

Master Kemp snorted. 'She refuses to accept the Lord, Thomas! How can she ever hope for salvation if she cannot pray?'

'Not all prayers need be spoken aloud, Edmund. God knows this child's thoughts better than we do.'

Master Kemp looked back at her. Alyce kept her face perfectly still.

'It's not right. She should be shouting her faith from the rooftops. Calling to Him, begging Him for forgiveness.'

'She is not allowed on the rooftops,' Master Makepiece said calmly.

Master Kemp looked at him coolly, and then hiccoughed, ruining his composure. 'All of the others, for all their caterwauling, they can still say a few words of prayer. They still know the power of the cross when they see it. But this one . . .' He shoved his finger in her face.

Master Makepiece allowed Master Kemp to trail off, and waited for quiet. 'It hardly matters now, anyway. She is leaving. Tonight.'

'Leaving?' said Kemp.

Leaving? thought Alyce.

'Yes. They are waiting for her downstairs.'

'They?' It took a moment before Kemp realized who Master Makepiece was referring to. Then Alyce watched his sagging face split into a grotesque smile. 'You *see!* I was *right*!' He turned back to her. 'You'd better get learning those prayers now, girl. I *knew* it!'

Makepiece ignored him. 'Come child. There is somebody to see you.'

Alyce came forward, one cold foot settling in the spilt porridge as she went. She gave Kemp a wide berth, his grin like a carved, exaggerated mask in the moonlight. Once outside in the passageway, the air thrummed with the wailing and laughing and demented chattering of the other inmates. She wanted to plug her ears again.

Master Makepiece placed a hand gently on her shoulder, and she looked up at him. His features were somehow soft and hard at the same time – as though the years had worn then down into an expression of resolved, immutable kindness. But tonight they looked sadder than usual. He peered at her from under his heavy eyebrows.

'I'm so sorry, Alyce,' he said, and led her down the stairs.

II

Without Master Makepiece saying anything, Alyce knew who was waiting for her down in Bedlam's gatehouse. Of course the witchfinders had found her. Who else would it be? As she passed the other cells, white faces stared out through the tiny square windows, men and women, eyes wild and unblinking.

Her stomach was too empty to feel sick. She just felt hollow, thin, like a sheet on a washing line. She started to sweat; boiling underneath her skin, freezing on top of it.

'Though I do not agree with Master Kemp's methods,' said Thomas quietly as they walked in the echoing darkness, 'he may be right about the need for prayer. When you are taken from here . . .' He paused. Alyce stared at her feet. 'When you are taken, you may find that you have few friends apart from God. Remember He will always listen to you.'

I wouldn't put money on that, thought Alyce. Her mother

had hardly ever spoken about God. The other villagers did, though, and apparently He didn't think very highly of either her or her mother.

When they reached the gatehouse, it was bathed in the dull, rust-coloured light of a dying fire, giving it a slightly infernal feel. From a corner behind the fireplace emerged two shadows, more substantial than the others, as though the darkness itself had gathered itself together to give them form and motion.

Curious, thought Alyce. These two looked very different from the men who had come for her mother. The fellow with the hat she saw in her dreams most nights. He had been confident, brazen, swaggering around in his pearls. This pair looked much more furtive, nervous even, both in black, rough-spun travelling cloaks with hoods over their heads. They also had swathes of material pulled up over their faces, so she could only see their eyes – and even those were blank and glassy in the firelight.

'Alyce,' said one of them. Strange, again. A woman's voice, but the figure that spoke did not look at all feminine. The other man – or maybe he was a woman too – turned to look at his companion, as though he were just as surprised as Alyce was. 'Please come with us.'

Alyce swallowed. They must have tracked her all the way from her home. How was that even possible?

'This is not right,' said Master Makepiece, his hands on Alyce's shoulders. His tone suggested he'd made this same speech before, and had never been listened to. 'It is not Christian. How many winters do you think she has seen?

Thirteen? Fourteen? I found her in a ditch. She has no one to pay her upkeep. Is there no room in your hearts for forgiveness of one so young?'

The man stared at him, but didn't reply. Then he turned to whisper something in his partner's ear.

The woman had not made any movements either, except to cock her head while she scrutinized Alyce. 'Where are her effects?' she asked. 'What did she have on her person when you took her in?'

'Only the clothes she was wearing,' said Makepiece.

'Fetch them.'

The governor sighed. 'It is our custom to give our patients' apparel to almshouses, to clothe the poor.'

'And have you done that?' asked the man, who still had one eye on his companion.

Thomas shook his head slowly. 'Not yet.'

'Then give them to us.'

Alyce was suddenly very alert, poised between Master Makepiece and the two figures standing in front of her. The governor's words had kindled a small, hopeful flame in her belly, which she fed and protected, holding her hands over her navel as though physically trying to keep it from going out.

If they still had her smock, there was every chance the letter would still be stashed in a pocket. If she could reclaim that bit of parchment, escape Bedlam, get to Bankside — wherever that was . . .

The hope inside her guttered and spat. She was so weak, so hungry, her nerves taut and brittle as ice. Maybe she wasn't meant to escape, anyway. Perhaps that was her fate: that she was meant to be plucked out of existence just like her mother had been, an inconvenience to the smooth running of the world, a thorn in the side of the cosmos. Perhaps she deserved it, too, after what she'd done.

Master Makepiece left her alone in the gatehouse with her captors, and shuffled out of the back door to whatever dank corner of the hospital they had stored her clothes in. Alyce shifted uncomfortably from one foot to the other.

'You're going to kill me, aren't you?' she murmured.

Neither of them answered.

'You know what I did. You know who I am.'

'We know who you are,' the woman said. The fabric concealing her face rippled under her breath. 'Do you?'

The oddness of the question caught Alyce unawares. Was this woman toying with her? She could taste bile in the back of her mouth, as though she was about to be sick. She hated her. She hated them. More than anything.

'Your mother never told you, did she? Before she died?'

Alyce swallowed, and clenched her fists into two stony balls. 'I'll tell you what my mother said, before you burnt her.'

'Listen, child—'

'She said: "If they catch you, you have to kill them."'

The pair looked at each other.

'If I were you, I wouldn't try,' Alyce said, pointing a thin, dirty finger at them both. 'Because I've already had some practice, and it turns out I'm pretty good at it.'

She dashed to the door. Beyond it, the darkness and mist

that had settled into the courtyard waited to embrace her. The woman shouted, lurching forwards, and just as Alyce got a foot upon the threshold, she felt the man's huge hands clasp around her waist and haul her back. She tried to prise his fingers off her, but each one was buried firm as tree roots into her skin. Flailing, she jabbed him in the groin with a sharp elbow, and a muffled grunt escaped from the scarf covering his mouth.

She was just squirming free of him when the woman grabbed one of her wrists, but that only gave Alyce more momentum as she whirled round and raked a handful of filthy nails across her face. The woman's hood fell back from her head. Her features were deathly pale, angular, almost skull-like, and the dirty red glow of the fire only made them look more ghoulish.

At the same time, she heard shouting and footsteps from the passageway. Master Makepiece was returning. The woman hurriedly rearranged the cowl and the layers of material over her face, while the man clutched at his manhood and whimpered. Alyce considered waiting for Makepiece. Her clothes. The letter. No, there was no time. She seized a tankard from the gatehouse table, swung it into the man's temple for good measure, and then ran out into the courtyard.

The main gate was shut. She would have to escape out of the back of the hospital buildings, past the remains of the chapel, through the graveyard. Her feet slapped against the flagstones as she ran, the madmen and madwomen peering sadly at her through the bars of their cells.

When she reached the chapel wall, she stopped, panting. Moonlight filtered down between the branches of the yew trees, casting pale shapes and figures that twisted with the breeze. The place was alive with ghosts. She thought of her mother again, and physically shook the memory from her head. *Think later. Just run.*

The woman's voice echoed somewhere behind her, and Alyce leapt over the wall, into the graveyard. She ducked and weaved from one headstone to the next, among the poor, mad, buried souls of Bedlam's past, feet crunching on the frosted earth. Behind the chapel ruins, another low wall, and a ditch, which she skidded to the bottom of, only just keeping her balance, until she planted her feet in six inches of dirty, freezing water.

And then she was out, free, running across Moor Fields under the moon with the grass whipping her calves and breath exploding from her in hot, glistening clouds.

The feeling of triumph didn't last. She had no idea where she was going. But she didn't stop. Couldn't stop. Twice she thought she heard a man's gruff voice carried on the wind, and each time she found another ounce of energy to drive her legs a hundred paces further. There was another sound, too – it was like the loose flapping of her own smock, a few yards behind her, above her head. Beating wings, she could have sworn. She only had the courage to glance behind her once, and when she did everything seemed swallowed up by the vastness of the midnight sky.

She ran until she was at the foot of London's city walls, and she followed them around until she was met by one of the great turreted gatehouses. The portcullis was down. The city was closed.

Alyce's tired legs buckled under her, and she crawled on all fours down into a corner where the wall met the tower. A variety of animals had marked their territory here, but there was a breeze, and after the stench of Bedlam she didn't find it particularly bothersome.

She got cold quickly, now she wasn't moving. Her memories caught up with her too, as though she had momentarily outpaced them in her escape. She looked out over the open fields, and found the world an empty, lonely place.

What am I doing here?

Thinking of home – though she hardly wanted to – something occurred to her. She tucked her heels under her thighs and raked through the dirt for what she needed to keep her safe through the night.

Straw. Sticks. Feathers. Bone.

She twisted and wove them together, her hands moving deftly despite the cold, until they began to form a recognizably human figure. She could almost hear her mother's voice, over her shoulder, encouraging her, helping her to get things right. Then she realized that, for the mommet to be anything other than completely useless, it would need some of her hair. There was nothing to be done with the horrible bristles that poked out of her scalp at the moment.

Alyce sighed and curled up like a dog. She hugged her knees closer to her body, clutching the straw figure tightly, shivering too much to sleep.

III

She must have managed to drop off somehow, because the next thing she knew she was surrounded by chattering voices and thumping feet. She heard the croak of birds too, poking around in the dirt by her head.

'Shoo! Get out of here!' said a reedy, unpleasant voice, and suddenly there was an explosion of feathers, throwing dust and straw into the air.

Alyce opened her eyes like a pair of newly healed wounds, and glimpsed a black silhouette fly to safety atop the city walls. She scowled at the whiteness of the day, and placed a hand on the top of her head. No, it hadn't grown back.

The city gate was now packed with bodies, men and women trudging into London with livestock and produce. A little further up the road a cart had overturned, spilling its load of root vegetables, and a crowd had gathered to watch the owner screaming obscenities at the tired, bony horse who was still straining on the harness. A sea of grubby faces, pink from the cold, surged past her, shouting, laughing, coughing, spitting great lumps of phlegm at her feet.

There were so many of them. More human beings than she had ever seen in her life. Two, three times the number of villagers in Fordham, and that was just on this side of the gate.

I know them, she thought, shivering. *I've seen all these people before.*

They looked just like the faces that had hollered and cursed at her when she'd left her house, when she'd gone to the well, when she'd tried to talk to their sons and daughters. These sorts of faces had jeered while her mother burned. Unfriendly, intolerant faces. Just because they didn't know her here didn't make her feel any safer.

Her frozen muscles screamed into life as she got to her feet. As she swayed and staggered, she saw an unshaven, unfed young man standing beside a handcart full of oysters, staring straight at her.

'Excuse me,' she began, her tongue feeling fat and sticky. 'Where might I—'

'I was talking to you too. Get out of here.' It was the same voice as before. The hot stench of leeks and onions flooded over her, accompanied by a few flecks of spittle. 'I know it's called Cripplegate, but this ain't a meeting place for cripples.' He shoved her roughly to the ground, and went back to hawking his wares.

The flow of townsfolk continued to swell. Alyce picked herself up out of the dirt as a dozen piglets swarmed around her, chased by a flustered boy much younger than her, trying desperately to herd them through the archway. The smell, the noise, the whole thing was unbearable.

Bankside. That was what her mother had said. With or without the letter, she needed to find the river.

She held her mommet tightly, concealed in the front pocket of her smock, and set off towards the gate. All around her, the other bodies parted slightly, their eyes glancing at her just long enough to decide that they definitely didn't want to rub shoulders with her. She felt as though she were carrying the plague.

Within the city walls, London seemed to have been designed and built by a drunkard. He'd carelessly erected row after row of tottering buildings, sprawling over the northern bank of the Thames in a bewildering maze of avenues and alleyways, and then, swollen with his triumph, had proceeded to claim this shambolic metropolis as his own by urinating on each and every street corner. The whole place stank.

Alyce had only wandered a few hundred yards before realizing that, unless she ate something, she wouldn't even make it to the river. She was so hungry. The savoury whiff of the man's breath outside the gate had actually made her mouth water.

The problem was, even if she'd had a single groat to her name, no one would have allowed her anywhere near their shop to spend it. Fishwives shooed her away with their baskets, grocers and bakers jeered and cursed, hounding her from alleyway to alleyway, until she staggered into an inn yard and collapsed in the damp straw of the stables. She had just managed to gulp down two mouthfuls of brackish water from the horses' trough before an expensive pair of riding boots was kicking her back into the sludge of the main street.

The only thing that stopped her from passing out was a new scent that reached her nostrils – something sweet and spiced. Ahead, on whatever thoroughfare she had found herself, a huge bear of a man was selling hot codlings, his stall piled high with steaming, baked apples. The man's back was turned.

You shouldn't steal, said a quiet voice, as though her conscience were trapped in a well at the bottom of her mind.

You've done worse, said another one, loud, urgent, ravenous.

Alyce faltered.

Do it.

The shopkeeper was still talking to another customer in loud, coarse tones – he was either telling them a joke or telling them off, it was difficult to know which. She crept through the mud, her wisp of a body slipping between the loitering men and women, and laid a hand on one of the apples.

She hadn't counted on the flesh of the fruit being as hot as molten lead. It scalded her palm, and she yelped. The huge stallkeeper whirled around, far too quickly for a man with so much blubber, and grabbed her by the wrist.

'So,' he roared, 'thought you'd 'ave one o' my codlings for *free*, did you?'

He snatched the ruined apple from her hand and hit her

across the face. Her jaw felt like it was a few feet away from the rest of her head.

'You're no better than a rat. You hear me? A *rat*!'

Through her blurred vision, she saw him raise his hand again. She winced, but suddenly heard another voice, loud and clear among the muttering onlookers.

'Oh, come now,' it said, 'I hardly think the rats would stoop so low as to eat from your stall. There's far better stuff in the gutter.'

There was a nervous titter from the crowd, which had doubled since the man had started shouting.

'Who's this then? The rat's 'usband? Lovely couple, rat like 'er and a poxy little ferret like you!'

The stallkeeper didn't get the laugh he was looking for from his audience, and that only seemed to make him angrier. Alyce's saviour stepped forwards and put an arm under her shoulder. He wasn't quite a man yet, with only a hint of a beard on his chin and upper lip, and was rather gangly, too. Under a thatch of crow-black hair — a little greasy — his eyes were surrounded by dark, purple rings. He looked like he needed a year's worth of sleep.

'It will be Christmas Day in two days' time,' the boy said, hoisting her off the ground like a half full sack of onions. 'Call me a Puritan, but I don't believe the best way to mark the occasion is by beating and starving the poor and the needy.'

'The *needy*? Who's *needy*? I've got a wife and children to feed!' He thumbed to the window behind him, where an equally large woman was bustling around an oven in her apron, preparing more baked codlings to bring out to the stall. 'How's that going to 'appen if I just go 'anding these out to stray dogs?'

The boy looked over the shopkeeper's shoulder. 'Zounds! Is that your wife? To be honest, I'm not sure she needs any more feeding.'

The man's face turned to thunder, and he moved to swing a great hairy arm at him. The boy skipped around, back to the stall laden with fruit, and pelted him with two apples, covering his broad, bristling face with steaming pulp.

The giant cried out as though he had been blinded. The boy danced past him again, surprisingly nimble for someone with such long limbs, and took Alyce by the hand.

'Come on, I know somewhere we can take you.'

Alyce stumbled though, still weak, her head and face throbbing from being struck by the stallkeeper. The boy gathered her up in his arms, and half walked, half ran away from the scene of chaos he had just created.

She drifted in and out of consciousness, her head lolling and rocking in time with his footsteps. The half-timbered faces of buildings marched past her, their roofs jutting into the white sky like rows of jagged, disordered teeth. When she felt she was going to disappear from the land of the living completely, the sounds of drinking and merrymaking forced her eyes open again. They were outside a building taller than the others, and overhead she glimpsed a painted swan hanging above the door.

The boy stepped inside. In the front room, the laughter

of drinkers came to an abrupt halt. 'Where is Mrs Thomson?'

'She's over here,' a voice boomed from the kitchen. A stocky, middle-aged woman appeared in the opposite door. The two of them faced each other across the common room as though preparing for a duel. 'Brought me a present, have you, Solomon? Very kind of you!' She bustled forward heavily, and the drinkers tentatively resumed their conversations. 'Usually when the dogs bring me some dead animal, they at least leave it on the doorstep instead of bringing it inside.'

'I found her in the street. She needs something to eat and drink, and some warm clothes.'

'Any particular reason why I should be feeding beggar children out of my own pocket?'

'Thought you might offer a little Christian charity.'

'Heavens above,' the woman said hoarsely, and Alyce felt a rough hand on her forehead. 'Look what they done to you, poor child. She's half dead, Solomon. Bring her out back.'

In the sudden warmth and noise of the inn, everything took on a delirious, dreamlike quality. Cradled in the boy's arms, Alyce seemed to float through to the kitchen, past the maids and the cooks, into another, smaller room, where she was laid carefully in a chair.

The innkeeper surveyed her in the candlelight, and her red, leathery brow creased into a frown.

'I reckon I got something for her,' she was saying. The boy named Solomon swam in and out of focus. 'But we need to keep her awake.'

She heard rustling, and the crunch of a pestle and mortar.

'Keep her *awake*, Solomon! Talk to her, do something!'

'It's all right,' he said, looming over her. 'You'll be all right.' Then he leant in until he was right beside her ear. 'I'll keep it safe,' he whispered.

Keep what safe? The effort to speak was too great. Alyce parted her lips, then promptly passed out.

HOPKINS

There was no shelter in the graveyard. Perched on the top of an ancient tumulus, the wind and rain had scoured it mercilessly, wearing away the headstones' inscriptions and leaving them bleached and faceless. The graves hadn't been arranged in any particular order, it seemed – some leant at impossible angles, others were being reclaimed by the boggy ground, grey crowns of stone still just visible above the surface, gasping for air.

A graveyard, not a churchyard. There was no church to be seen. Just the earth, the sky, and the dead.

There were two figures among the graves that night, one a man, the other something different. They waited patiently in the cold, perfectly still, a rime of frost forming on their cloaks.

'Don't know why she couldn't have just met us at a tavern,' muttered John Hopkins. 'I'm going to lose a finger out here.' He closed and opened his hand, rings clacking under his gloves.

The creature who had once been Caxton made a creaking noise, and pointed his long, leather crow beak at Hopkins. He stared at him with blank, perfectly circular glass eyes. He was completely silent. Hopkins couldn't even hear him breathing.

He spoke again. 'When she arrives – *if* she ever arrives – let me do the talking, won't you?' He permitted himself a laugh. The silent creature stared at him a moment longer, and then turned his grotesque birdlike head back to the centre of the hill.

Hopkins twisted uncomfortably, feeling the numb, tugging sensation around his wound. It was like that cursed girl's knife was still in there. Sometimes the phantom blade seemed to nudge the base of his spine, sending pain shooting up to his neck and back down again. Dead flesh healed slowly. Still, it was probably nothing compared to the agonies Caxton was suffering.

The Doctor had lived up to his reputation in the miracles he had performed, but he'd taken his time about it. While Hopkins had been able to sew himself together like a ragdoll, Caxton's affliction had needed more attention. In the cellar of some godforsaken crossroads tavern, the Doctor had worked day and night to contain Ellen Greenliefe's curse, which had already spread beyond the man's lips – but the 'cure' had taken longer than expected and the Doctor's techniques had left Caxton, well, somewhat *changed*. Now they were days behind the girl, and this unexpected meeting with his mistress would only delay them further. Still, to deny her an audience would have been unwise.

It was midnight when she came.

They glimpsed her face first, passing among the headstones like a full moon behind clouds. For several minutes, it seemed to hover disembodied, a pale will-o'-the-wisp threading its way through the darkness, until she emerged into the clearing in front of them. Her features became more distinct, and might even have been called beautiful, were it not for the black emptiness of her eyes.

'Your Majesty,' said Hopkins, bowing fractionally.

'You lost her, then.' The sound of her voice somehow made the air colder still. It started to snow.

'I wouldn't say lost. Lost suggests that we had her in the first place.'

'You lost her, and then you demanded the Doctor come and tend to your wounds.'

'Your Majesty, I demanded nothing. Caxton sent word to the palace—'

'Do you know how difficult it is,' she interrupted, 'for the Doctor to leave the Court in secret? Without raising suspicion? Do you know the risks *I* am taking, coming before you like this?'

Hopkins was silent. Caxton lowered his head.

'You disappoint me,' she continued. 'You have spent your whole life hunting and murdering witches with such masterful skill, and now you are outwitted by a single girl. It wasn't for this that I saved your life, John Hopkins. You are meant to be *helping* us now, not leaving our plans in tatters.'

A bitter, empty laugh rang through Hopkins. *Saved your life.* He'd had no life to save, not by the time she'd bartered for his services.

The nightmare had begun a year or so back, and he'd never woken up from it. It should have been simple, routine. A gaggle of crones in Norfolk – witches, all of them. But there had been more than expected, and he'd been careless, let himself get captured. For weeks they had kept him prisoner, cursing his mind and body, reducing him to a living death. His flesh had turned cold. Justice, the crones had called it. They wanted him to feel, in the marrow of his bones, the death of every woman he'd ever tried and executed. And all the while his God, whose work he had faithfully performed for so long, looked on and did nothing.

Instead, this woman had come to his rescue. He still remembered the first time he saw her, bizarre, dreamlike – a phantom, like now, standing regally before him amidst the bones and the filth in the crones' hovel. Not just a woman. A queen. Mary Stuart, Queen of Scots, come to claim him as her servant. At the time he thought he had lost his mind.

'Perhaps,' she continued, as he tried to banish the memories, 'you are failing on purpose? Perhaps you still find the idea of serving a witch distasteful? If that is the case, then I can always send you back to Norfolk. I am sure I can recruit another witchfinder – less skilled, maybe, but more willing.'

Hopkins' jaw twitched as he ground his teeth. 'That will not be necessary, Your Majesty,' he said. 'Besides, all is not lost.'

She glared at him. Her eyes looked like holes in her head.

'Firstly,' he continued, when she did not reply, 'Ellen Greenliefe is dead. Which means your enemies are one fewer.'

'Ellen Greenliefe was a simpleton. There was no need to kill her. She could have been turned. But go on.'

Hopkins took a couple of breaths to calm himself.

'Secondly,' he said, 'the girl's trail has been easy to follow. She stopped in every village on the way to London. It is regretful that our injuries set us back, yes, but once we reach the capital, she will be trapped.'

Mary Stuart breathed in deeply, and the whole graveyard seemed to shudder.

'London.'

'Ay, Your Majesty.'

'Queen Elizabeth is in London. What then?'

'I hardly think—'

'What happens when they find each other? She might put her in a ship bound for the Continent. Exactly how big is this "trap" you speak of?'

'They will *not* find each other.'

'Make sure of it. If the girl escapes, all is lost.'

She paused, flurries of snowflakes gusting around them.

'I am weak,' she sighed. For a moment, her oddly translucent features seemed to disappear completely. 'I shall contact the good Doctor again. We may need his help, if the girl gets too close to Elizabeth. If she slips through your fingers again.'

'I assure you, Your Majesty, she will not.'

'I hope so, for your sake, John Hopkins. If events fall as planned, I shall be able to oversee your progress in person very shortly.'

One of Hopkins' eyes twitched. 'In person?'

'In the flesh. And I expect the girl to be in our hands by then, to help with my succession to Elizabeth's throne.'

'Yes, Your Majesty,' he said. 'I understand.' He bowed slowly.

'Very well. Then do not fail me. Remember that your life belongs to me now. It will give me great pleasure to drag out your miserable existence until your debt is paid.' She extended a thin, spectral finger towards him. 'Think on your sins, John Hopkins.'

Then Mary Queen of Scots turned and drifted back through the gravestones, leaving no footprints in the snowfall.

IV

The innkeeper had taken Alyce to The Swan's smallest room, up in the gables, and she'd slept right through Christmas Eve and Christmas morning. Her dreams had been troubling. Visions of Bedlam, of the witchfinders, of her mother, came and went in a leering parade. She had imagined a giant black bird, too, watching her through the window, her memory of it so vivid she couldn't even be sure it *was* a dream.

In the evening of Christmas Day, she had been woken by the sounds of singing and dancing and the roaring of the Master of Revels, and Mrs Thomson had brought her bread and some fatty soup, which she had barely managed to keep down. There had also appeared a little slice of spiced mince pie the following evening, which the innkeeper had saved specially for her. Alyce felt sad to leave it untouched, and in the morning it had disappeared from the bowl at her bedside.

She felt a little stronger now. It had been four days since her arrival, and she had been asleep for most of them. The stubbled, sorry mess of her hair had not yet grown out, but her cuts and bruises showed signs of healing, and when she looked in the dresser's dirty mirror, her eyes seemed less sunken and her cheeks a fraction fuller. And since her first bath, she smelt a good deal better too.

It was midday, and the sun was trying to fight its way through the thick, grime-encrusted windows at the foot of her bed. The room was desperately cold, and barely large enough for her to stand up in. She suspected nobody had stayed up here for years, and the dust and mould was just thick enough to stop the place feeling homely. Still, it was warm enough under the blankets, and Mrs Thomson had left a pie on the side table, crammed with rich goose meat and aromatic herbs that set Alyce's senses reeling.

She chewed on the last mouthful while she tried to make sense of last few days. Abruptly she stopped, and swallowed.

The mommet, she thought. *Where is it?*

She flung the bedclothes off, the flesh on her legs rising in goose pimples, and went in search of her smock. The mommet itself was incomplete and essentially useless, but her mother had warned her about letting other people see the things she made. They wouldn't understand them.

As she rummaged in a chest of drawers, the stairs outside her room creaked to herald the return of Mrs Thomson. She whirled around to face her as the door opened.

'Good God, child! It's a good thing to see you out of your bed, but you're in nought but a nightdress! You'll catch your death of cold, you will, after all I done to nurse you back to health!' Mrs Thomson was not a slim woman, and she lumbered awkwardly over to Alyce to manhandle her back into bed. Alyce stood her ground.

'Where is my smock?' she asked quietly, teeth chattering.

'That old thing? Martha's giving it a good old scrub. Filthy it was! Full of lice too. Why would you be wanting that, my love? Got you a lovely warm nightdress there. That was mine when I was a girl. I was a little bigger than you, mind,' she chuckled.

'I need it,' Alyce croaked. Mrs Thomson's smile faded. 'Not the smock. But there was something in the pocket. You took it, didn't you?'

Mrs Thomson rested her small, scarred hands on her hips, and a lifetime of wrinkles appeared on her brow. She sighed through the great caverns of her nose.

'I've been accused of many things in my time, Alyce. Some gentlemen think I water down me ale. Some think I short-change them. On St Stephen's Day, heaven help us, a lady thought I was putting rat meat in me pies. But I ain't never been called a common thief.' She paused. 'You don't trust nobody, and I don't blame you. But I swear 'pon this inn, and every one of the barrels in my cellar, that I ain't stolen nothing of yours.'

Alyce looked at the floor, and then back at Mrs Thomson. 'Perhaps the maid has it?'

'Martha? Maybe. I'll ask.'

'No,' said Alyce, more forcefully than she meant to. Mrs Thomson's eyebrows went up. 'I mean, I would rather ask myself. I don't want to put you to the trouble.'

'Very well. Down we go. Wrap yourself up warm and we'll go and speak to her. But keep yourself out of sight, mind. Inn's a place for loose talk, and I got my reputation to think of.'

Mrs Thomson roughly wrapped Alyce's shoulders in a blanket so heavy and uncomfortable that it may as well have been a coat of mail, but it kept off the chill. She quickly made up the bed, and spied the empty platter as she did so.

'Well, at least you're eating. Good to see. Enjoy the pie, did you?'

Alyce nodded. 'Very much.'

'That'll be the herbs then. You need to know your herbs. Much more to it than just adding savour. Settle your humours, they will.'

With that, she picked up the platter and stomped out of the room. Alyce followed nervously – upon leaving her room her head spun, but when it became clear that Mrs Thomson was not going to wait for her, she forced herself dizzily down the stairs, clutching the bannister.

It was only the second day of Yuletide, and The Swan was positively glowing with talk and song and drunken jests, and the rich scents of warm ale and roasted meat. Every beam and bannister was wreathed in holly and holm oak, which Mrs Thomson periodically stopped to rearrange as she passed. It actually wasn't so different to the midwinter festival that Alyce celebrated with her mother back in Fordham, although it was a bit more raucous. She took a waxy holly leaf between her fingers and smelt it, the scent and the memory bittersweet. Perhaps she was still in time to see the sacrifice, to take her cup of lamb's blood. Maybe they'd let her wear the horns of the hunter god.

No, that probably isn't the way they do things here.

Mrs Thomson led Alyce down the back staircase into the kitchen, and by the time they had reached the ground floor the heat from the ovens and the crowds of revellers was already causing them both to sweat profusely.

Alyce found the bustle overwhelming, and was buffeted this way and that by cooks and maids who cursed with words and oaths she had never heard before. She was relieved when Mrs Thomson took her straight through the kitchens and out into a narrow alley that led off the inn yard, where Martha, the buck-toothed serving girl, was busy scrubbing clothes in a tub of dirty, icy water. Her hands were blue, her nose red – it was dripping, too, and as they approached she paused to wipe it on a dress she was supposed to be washing. For all her discomfort, though, she was humming to herself.

'Martha, you remember Alyce.' Mrs Thomson brusquely introduced them. 'You want to ask, Alyce, you go ahead and ask. I got customers to attend to.' There was an almighty uproar from the front of the inn, that was somewhere between outrage and hilarity. 'If I don't go calm that game of Hot Cockles, there'll be blood running in the streets before long . . .'

Her last few words were lost as she charged back into the kitchen to avert disaster. Alyce stood, feet frozen, and pulled her blanket up around her.

'How now, loon,' Martha said, without looking up from her work.

Alyce was not quite prepared for that. She cleared her throat. 'Good day.'

Martha continued scrubbing and humming. Alyce shifted from one foot to the other, and coughed again. 'I think . . . I think you are washing my smock.'

'Yes.'

That was all. Alyce pressed ahead.

'There was something in the pocket. A . . .' She paused. 'Something I made. Do you have it?'

'I do not.'

She tried a different tack. 'I am not a loon,' she said quietly.

Martha dropped her bundle of washing into the water with a great splash. 'Is that so? Got yourself locked up in Bedlam for japes, then?'

'How did you know . . .?'

'It's hardly a secret!' Martha cackled. 'Look at you! Your hair, your face. If you weren't mad before you went in, you must be by now. Must've kept some fine company in there, fine company . . .'

'Listen to me.' Alyce began to feel her choler rising. 'I am not a lunatic.' But the statement did not sound as confident as she had hoped.

'Them's the only folk that go to Bedlam. Them that's gone mad on their own. Or . . .' Martha held up a finger, and her face brightened. Alyce suspected the whole convoluted exchange had been leading to this point. 'Or them that's been *driven* mad by the Devil.'

Alyce felt a rush of hot blood to her face.

'If you aren't a lunatic, must be you're a w—'

'*That's enough out of you.*' Mrs Thomson had returned, and was standing behind them with her hands on her hips, an immovable colossus in the kitchen doorway. 'Why do you always got to bait our guests, Martha? Don't listen to her, child. Leave her be. There's someone else here to see you. Won't get any nasty words from him, that's for sure.'

Alyce didn't move for a moment. She stared at Martha, who had gone back to sloshing the water around with a grin. Her heart was rattling uncomfortably behind her ribs.

'Alyce?' the innkeeper said again. She blinked herself back into the real world, and turned around to see the boy, Solomon, standing awkwardly at Mrs Thomson's shoulder.

He slipped his frame past Mrs Thomson's bulk like some huge spider. His midnight-blue doublet looked rather fetching from a distance, but as he advanced she noticed his sleeves were rather too short, and the waist of his breeches was too large, crumpled and cinched with a belt that he had forced extra holes into so it would be snug around his skinny hips. Over one shoulder hung a well-used leather satchel.

'My lady,' he mumbled, with a neat little bow.

She could have wept. After all the scorn, all the disgrace heaped upon her, those two words seemed to give her the strength of twenty women. She straightened up. *My lady!*

Behind her, Martha snorted with derision.

'My lord,' Alyce replied, the only thing she could think of. They stared at each other, the full stupidity of their exchange dawning on them, and then both lapsed into nervous laughter. 'Thank you,' she added at last. 'For helping me. In the street. I thought he was going to finish me off, that man. Over a baked apple.'

'Didn't just help you in the street!' chipped in Mrs Thomson. 'He's been back at your bedside nearly every day, I reckon. Cooling your fever and whatnot.'

Alyce was touched. She tried to smile at Solomon, but he wasn't looking at her.

'Um,' he said. He scratched at something non-existent on the back of his hand. 'I just wanted to make sure you were getting better, that was all. You look well.'

'No I don't.'

Solomon cocked his head, and his mouth twitched with amusement. 'No. You don't. You look terrible. I just didn't know what else to say.'

Alyce laughed again. The sound took her quite by surprise.

'Did you find what you wanted?' asked Mrs Thomson. Alyce's smile faltered, and she shook her head. 'Not to worry. Come inside, the both of you, get yourselves warm and fed. Solomon here's an actor with Sussex's Men, he don't get many hot dinners.' She chuckled to herself.

'We're doing very well at the moment, I'll have you know,' said Solomon, trying to puff himself up a little. 'We're playing at Court for the next few weeks.'

Mrs Thomson whistled. 'You hear that, Alyce? Our Solomon, a courtier!'

'That doesn't actually make me a courtier . . .'

'Well, come on then! What's the latest news? How's our

Queen Bess?'

Solomon sighed. 'I knew you'd ask. I don't know her personally, Mrs Thomson. I just get rumours.'

'Well?' Mrs Thomson was undeterred. 'What are they?'

'Just that she's tired. And angry.'

'Oh,' said Mrs Thomson, her face falling. 'And why's that?'

'Story goes,' said Solomon, with sudden relish, 'the Queen of Scots is smuggling messages out of prison.'

'Mary Stuart?' Mrs Thomson crossed herself. 'She's no good, that one.'

'Apparently, Mary's gaolers are making her a bit too comfortable. Letting her have the run of the place. Bess is furious.'

'The devils! And?'

'And what? That's just what I heard the other night. I have to wait until the courtiers are drunk before they start letting things slip. And then when they get *too* drunk they stop making any sense. It's quite a delicate art, actually.'

Alyce smiled, and she saw Solomon *see* her smile.

Mrs Thomson tutted. 'It's a wonder this country's still in one piece. It's a wonder Queen Bess is still in one piece, for that matter. Bet Mary Stuart's got her spies all over the place.'

She looked at Alyce as though expecting some response, but Alyce didn't have a clue what they were talking about. Queen Bess, Queen Mary – the names meant nothing to her. The only queens she'd ever known had been in stories. There was the Wolf Queen and the Queen of the Dead,

Queens of the East and Queens of the Sea.

She thought of a hundred questions but none of them left her lips.

'Are you just going to stand there talking all day?' piped up Martha. 'Or can I get on with my washing?'

'Well! You're a saucy one, aren't you?' Mrs Thomson clipped her round the ear. 'We'll be out of your hair, *Your Majesty*,' she said, giving her a mocking curtsy. 'Come on you two. We got other things to talk about besides politics.'

Once inside, they went into the same back room that Alyce dimly remembered being carried to when she had first arrived. It seemed to serve half as a storeroom, half as a makeshift office for Mrs Thomson. There were sacks of grain, bunches of dried herbs hung on the walls and piled on shelves, and in the centre were two stools and a desk, covered with spilt ink and sheaves of parchment. While Alyce was trying to read what was written on them, the innkeeper settled herself into a creaking chair on the other side of the desk, and swept them away from prying eyes.

'There'll be some fresh pie for you soon. Frumenty too, if you fancy,' she said, making a pile of the parchment on the corner closest to her. 'Sit down, both of you. You know my favourite thing about Yuletide? Everyone telling stories. No one tells a good story in the summer, don't know why that is. But come winter, when you got your roaring fire, and your belly full of beer and wine, and your tongue's good and loose, *everyone's* got a story to tell.' She let that observation hang in the stuffy air for a moment. Alyce and Solomon looked at each other. 'But I reckon, of all the tall tales that are getting passed around out there –' she waved in the direction of the common room – 'there aren't many that will compare with yours, Alyce. So, now you've had a bit of rest, how about you tell us your story, and let's see if we can't find a place for you here.'

Alyce frowned, and rubbed the top of her head, feeling suddenly self-conscious. She wanted nothing more than to tell them everything, to pour out all the contents of her tired heart, but a month of silence in Bedlam had left its mark. The old Alyce had talked a lot – too much, her mother had always said. But perhaps the old Alyce was gone for good.

She looked at Mrs Thomson's kindly, expectant face, then into Solomon's dark eyes. Where to begin? What to say? More importantly, what *not* to say?

She took a deep breath, found her first words, and fumbled on from there.

'**W**itches!'

Once Alyce had finished her story, Mrs Thomson heaved herself out of the chair, skirted around her and checked that the door was fully closed behind them. Alyce couldn't quite gauge her tone – she was half expecting the innkeeper to go out into the kitchen and round up an angry mob.

'There ain't no such *thing* as witches, girl. Ain't that the truth of it, Solly?'

Solomon silently rolled the stalks of something he'd found on the table between his finger and thumb.

'*Witches*,' she muttered again under her breath. 'It's all just a lot of folk with no manners, poking their noses into women's business. They don't *understand* what we do, or they think we're *different*, and they don't *like* it, so they call us "witches".' She turned to see the comprehension dawning on Alyce's face. 'Oh yes, girl, they called me that too. Lot of uses for herbs beyond just flavouring meat pies. Been learning all my life. Won't find another herbalist in London with half my skill. But they don't like that I know something that they don't. So it *must* be black magic, and I *must* be learning from Lucifer Himself.' She spat. '*Witches*. They ain't nothing but faerie stories. And all over England women getting killed. Just cos they *know* things.' At this she whirled around, her apron catching the parchment she had tidied and sweeping it on to the floor.

Alyce dared not move or speak. She sensed Mrs Thomson was not quite spent. Solomon was staring at the buckles on his shoes like a chastised schoolboy.

'That's why they came for your poor mother, Alyce,' she continued. 'I'm sorry to say it. That's why they came for his mother too.' She pointed a stubby finger at Solomon, who glanced up at Alyce with something that looked like an apologetic smile. 'My best customer. And a better friend. They need to control us, Alyce, see? They don't like what they don't understand. They don't like it if you ain't doing and saying what they want. Now, may well be you're just as strange as your mother . . . but as if a girl like you might be talking with the Devil!' She crossed herself again.

'Um—'

'That's what people will think, mark my words. Most folk in this city would have tied you up like an animal and hanged you, if they heard the things you're saying. Saw the way you look. But not me, i'faith, no. I been on the end of that sort of slander too often, and I'll make sure no one around here speaks ill of you. You ain't the first so-called witch I've had under this roof, and I dare say you won't be the last.'

Mrs Thomson suddenly looked a little embarrassed at how loudly she had been speaking. She smoothed out her apron, pushed her explosion of grey frizz back under her bonnet, and sat back down in her chair. She was perspiring a little.

'Now. What's done is done.'

You don't know the half of 'what's done', thought Alyce.

'You got any relatives who might give you a helping hand?'

Alyce paused for a moment, again weighing up how much she should tell these two, who, kindly as they seemed, were still perfect strangers.

'I need to get to Bankside.'

'Bankside? Who's there?'

'John Dee.'

Solomon and Mrs Thomson looked at each other.

'I take it you don't mean Doctor John Dee,' the innkeeper chuckled. 'Then you really would be moving up in the world!'

'Why?' asked Alyce.

'He's an advisor to Queen Elizabeth,' said Solomon.

'Is she the same as Queen Bess?'

Solomon and Mrs Thomson looked at each other. She'd obviously said something stupid.

'Bess. Elizabeth. She's the Queen,' said Solomon. 'And John Dee is part of her inner circle. I see him at Court sometimes. He's a bit of an odd one.'

Alyce shook her head. 'I don't think that's him. This John Dee's a hangman.'

'Why in God's name would you be wanting to go see a *hangman*?'

'My mother told me to.'

Alyce could feel herself tensing up. Now she was saying it out loud, it really didn't seem to make sense. Her memories were so confused now, she wondered whether she'd made the whole thing up.

'So,' said Mrs Thomson, confusion plain on her face. 'When you find the hangman John Dee, then what?'

'I have to give him a letter.'

'What letter?'

'The one my mother gave me.'

'Well . . . let's have a look at it, then!'

'That's the problem,' sighed Alyce. 'I don't have it any more. The governors took it from me when I was at Bedlam. It was in the dress I was wearing when I arrived.'

'Ah. That isn't good news.'

'They might still have it, though. The governor said he hadn't sent it to the almshouse yet.'

'Strange that they didn't return it to you when they let you out,' piped up Solomon.

'Let me out?' Alyce swallowed. 'Oh. Yes, let me out.'

Solomon frowned.

'Ay, it is strange,' said Mrs Thomson. 'Well, p'raps you and I can go back there and see if they'll hand over the dress, and we'll cross our fingers the letter's still there. That would be best, don't you think?'

'*No*,' said Alyce, much louder and firmer than she was expecting to. If she went back, it would have to be in secret. After her escape, what would happen when the governors saw her again? Master Makepiece had seemed nice enough, but was timid, and had crumpled unimpressively when the hooded man and the woman had come to snatch her away. Master Kemp's allegiances were obvious. What if her pursuers were still there? Or had left spies to see if she returned?

'I mean,' she said, making an effort to speak softly, 'I don't want to put you to any trouble.'

Solomon's thick eyebrows were far too agitated to suggest that he was completely convinced by Alyce and her story.

'Really, no trouble at all, my pet . . .' continued Mrs Thomson.

'I'd like a little more time to rest, anyway.'

'Yes, course you do. No need to think about it right now. In the meantime, though, you can stay here and help me with the inn. Then Solomon knows where to find you too,' she said, her tiny black eyes almost disappearing into the wrinkles of her grin.

Alyce smiled back, but felt uneasy. Trapped, even. All she said was: 'Thank you.'

'I'm employing you too, mind,' she said, wagging a fat finger. 'How's about you go upstairs and get ready, and I'll show you what you can do in the kitchen. Go on, get yourself dressed.'

'I'll come,' said Solomon.

Alyce couldn't help giving a spluttering laugh.

'That's very thoughtful of you,' she said, 'but usually I manage to get dressed all by myself.'

'No, not that, I didn't mean . . . You know what I mean.' The slightest hint of warmth could be seen creeping across his pale cheeks. 'I meant to Bedlam. I'll come with you to Bedlam. It's on Bishopsgate Street Without, same road as the Theatre and the Curtain. I'm up there a lot with the company. If you want me to, that is. I just thought . . . Well, it's up to you, isn't it.' He trailed off, embarrassed by his own embarrassment, tugging at his ruff as though he had found something important stuck in its folds.

'Thank you,' said Alyce. 'Like I said, I think I'll wait until I feel a little stronger. At least until my hair has grown back a bit.' She scratched her head and then coughed. 'I'm going to go now.'

She scurried from the storeroom to the back stairs, and began hiking up them two at time, her head swimming. That was the most she had spoken to anyone in months. That was the most she had *ever* spoken to anyone who wasn't her mother. The urge to be alone drove her quickly to the top floor, away from the warm vapours of soups and stews and baking pies.

As kind and as tolerant as Mrs Thomson seemed, something didn't feel right. *No such thing as witches*, she'd said. *Yes there are*, thought Alyce. *And they can do a lot more than just sprinkle a few herbs around.* Mrs Thomson was half right: Alyce *wasn't* in conversation with Lucifer. God and the Devil were, as her mother had put it, 'just a distraction from the real work'. A sideshow. But she wondered how Mrs Thomson would have reacted if Alyce had told her the full story. The *true* story. Fires in the woods. Prayers to the moon. Long, dark nights speaking with the dead.

No, her place wasn't here.

Her hand came to rest on the cold handle of the bedroom door as her name floated up the stairs.

'Alyce?'

She turned and saw Solomon loitering on the stairs under a holly bough. He started up after her, pricking the top of his head on the dry, sharp leaves, and cursing under his breath. She wondered how he bore himself on stage, if this was how clumsy he was in real life – but then remembered how deftly he had dealt with the apple seller in the street. She couldn't quite make sense of him.

'Really, Master . . .' She didn't know his surname. 'Master Solomon. I have dressed myself many, many times. I know what goes where.'

'I think Mrs Thomson has mocked me enough today, don't you join in as well. I have something of yours.'

Alyce paused on the threshold, raised an eyebrow, and came halfway down to the landing below.

He chewed his lip, and opened up the satchel that was slung over his shoulder. Inside, Alyce could see a few tatty pieces of parchment, and, poking out from between them, the looped, twisted head of her mommet. He fished it out, and held it in front of him in both hands, tenderly, as though it were a real child.

Alyce took it without saying anything. There was something about Solomon seeing and touching the mommet that made her anxious. Unpleasant, uncomfortable truths could be altered, hidden in words. But here was the thing itself: her and her mother's craft, in a curled, distorted, grotesque little figure. It looked all the more otherworldly now, in the harsh, accusatory light of the day.

'I used to have one of those,' said Solomon, as she hid it self-consciously behind her back. The sweat from her palms was starting to make the mommet go limp.

'Really?'

'Yes. My mother showed me how to make them too. Before she left. It's a good luck charm, isn't it?'

Alyce ignored his question. 'Why did you take it?'

'I don't know. Reminded me of her, I suppose. I haven't seen one in so long . . . I wanted to see if I could remember how to make them. I tried to copy that one, but it ended up looking more like a worm. A worm with a human head. Horrifying, really.'

'If your parents taught you anything, you should know that its bad luck to steal someone else's mommet.'

'My *mother*. Not my parents. My father would have taught me that I was going straight to Hell for making false idols. Frequently *did*, in fact. Anyway, like I said, it was with the best intentions. They were going to wash your smock, I took it before Martha could get her hands on it. Or Mrs Thomson. She's got a good heart, and I'm forever in her debt, but . . .'

'But what?'

'She doesn't really know what she's talking about.'

'And you do?' she said.

He frowned and the rings around his eyes turned an even deeper shade of purple. But he didn't reply.

Alyce brought the mommet out again from behind her back.

'Thank you,' she said. 'For this. For everything.'

'It was my pleasure.' His face lit up a little. 'And I meant what I said about Bedlam. I know the area well.'

Alyce studied him. Dressed head to toe in ink-coloured velvet, head concealed under a heap of black hair, a slender shadow of a boy – he could make the perfect thief. And if they were caught, she thought, looking at his pale, tired face and slightly bulging eyes, he could happily pass for a lunatic.

'Whenever you're ready, of course,' he said, filling the silence she had left. 'If you need to rest—'

'I don't need to rest,' said Alyce, shaking her head.

'But you said—'

'I've had nothing but rest and sleep and fattening food for the last four days. The governors won't hold on to my dress for ever.' She toyed with the strange straw figure between her fingers. It felt good to have it back, even if it was still unfinished. She felt a little more composed. And she was happier talking to Solomon on his own than when he was with Mrs Thomson.

Yes, she could say it.

'You can come with me to Bedlam, Solomon. But we are going there tonight.'

HOPKINS

John Hopkins stood in Bedlam's gatehouse, staring at the governor's slender fingers interlaced on his belly and thinking about how easy it would be to break them. He'd probably let Caxton have the pleasure.

'This is an amusing fiction, Master Makepiece, and I recognize that in your line of work you must take any opportunity to entertain yourself. But come. A little cooperation.'

'I *am* cooperating, sir. They have already taken her. A man and a woman. They were *your* people. Witchfinders.'

'A woman? There are no women in our line of work, for reasons I am sure you can understand.'

'There is no mistake. Unless you employ eunuchs? I know what a woman's voice sounds like.'

'Then they were imposters.'

'If you say so.'

'But who would wish to impersonate a witchfinder, Master Makepiece? We do the Lord's work. Who would be so deceitful?'

'I wouldn't care to say.'

Hopkins sat back and regarded the little man across the table, narrowing his eyes.

'Two of them?'

The governor nodded.

'In black cloaks, you say?'

'Their faces were covered. Hooded. Not like your friend here, though.'

Hopkins turned to look at Caxton, looming masked and motionless in the corner of the hospital gatehouse. His appearance had made interrogation an almost boringly easy affair in every village they had stopped at. Most assumed that the beaked creature who trailed in Hopkins' shadow was some spectre, some demon, conjured by black arts to wreak vengeance on their wrongdoing. And, really, that wasn't so far from the truth. But they were in London now, not some rural backwater ruled by superstition. The governor seemed to be made of sterner, more rational stuff.

'Why does he wear this costume?' asked Master Makepiece. 'Some sort of mummer's trick? Are you not getting as many confessions as you would like?'

'Master Caxton was grievously injured,' said Hopkins, turning back to him and affecting a face of deep concern. 'The mask contains a poultice, a mixture of herbs to aid in his recovery.'

'I am sorry to hear it,' said the governor, not sounding sorry at all. There was something almost admirable about his insolence. 'I shall pray for him.'

Hopkins laughed. 'Of course you will. Your prayers are gratefully received.'

'Then are we finished?' said Master Makepiece, pushing back his chair over the flagstones and getting to his feet. 'I'm sorry I cannot be more helpful. If you'll excuse me, my charges will be getting restless.'

Hopkins remained where he was, reclining a little, one knee crossed over the other. 'I'm afraid we are not finished. And I'm afraid you'll simply *have* to be more helpful. You see, governor, it's not me who wants the girl. It is the Queen.'

'The Queen? What would Elizabeth want with her? What would Elizabeth want with *you*, for that matter—'

'Who said anything about Elizabeth?'

Hopkins smiled, watching the governor's face contort with confusion, and then realization. Queen Mary would probably not appreciate him revealing their connection, but these small triumphs were one of the few things that still gave him pleasure. And besides, Caxton would make sure the governor stayed silent.

'You're working for *her*, aren't you?' said Master Makepiece. '*Traitors.*'

'That is very much a question of perspective. I'm sure Her Majesty will reward you handsomely in return for your help reclaiming what is rightfully hers.'

'Rightfully?' the governor spat. 'What does the Queen

of Scots want with that poor girl?'

'I don't think you understand how an interrogation works,' said Hopkins, laughing. 'You are the one who needs to give *us* information.'

'But I'm telling you, I don't *know* anything else.'

'I think you'd be surprised what you can find, with a bit of digging. Caxton?'

There was the creak of leather from behind him.

'Help Master Makepiece into his seat.'

Even Hopkins shivered a little as the tall crow-like figure stalked past him and took the governor's hand in his own.

VI

The light was already failing when Alyce and Solomon set out for Bedlam, and the sky was the colour of Martha's dirty washing water. The streets of the city were still busy, but most had finished their day's work, and everyone gave off a collective glow of exhaustion as they made their way to their homes, or their taverns, or other, darker corners of London.

Alyce went forth in another of Mrs Thomson's old dresses, blowing and snapping around her skinny frame like a galleon's sails, a plain cloak on her shoulders and one of the maid's bonnets pulled over her ears to hide her shaven head. The wind seemed to slip between her ribs and around her heart, gnawing at her resolve. The plan had seemed so much easier in the warmth of the inn.

What if the hospital gate was closed? What if it was open, but she couldn't find the letter? What if she got herself caught before she could even look for it? The prospect of returning to her tiny, filthy cell was too dreadful to contemplate. The noise, the stench, the delightful company of Master Kemp — memories that had receded into vagueness suddenly took on their old, hard, painful shapes. She focused on simply on putting one foot in front of the other.

Alyce had spent most of the afternoon in the kitchens, helping Mrs Thomson prepare her pies and soups. She had taken special care, though, to burn the pastry just a little too much, and to drop one too many spoons into the bottom of the saucepan, until the innkeeper was forced to think of other, more useful errands she might run. Perhaps, suggested Alyce innocently, she should go out and buy some more flour, after she had wasted so much on her failed experiments in baking (she apologized again).

Mrs Thomson had not needed much convincing, but had insisted that Solomon accompany her. Alyce hadn't argued with that.

And now here they were, on their way out of the city again, walking with quick and deliberate strides. It was a race against the sunset, when the city gates would close, but Alyce did not want to draw attention and so restrained herself from running.

Solomon tried to orientate her as best he could, pointing out particularly important buildings, and naming the streets when he knew them. He led her along Little East Cheap, before turning right on to Grace Church Street. Alyce shivered a little more violently as they passed the spot where the codling seller had beaten her. Thankfully he'd shut up shop for the day.

'Why did you save me?' she asked suddenly, when they were past it.

Solomon's eyes went round with surprise, making them look even more amphibious. 'Why wouldn't I?'

'Why *would* you? No one else in the whole city wanted to help.'

'I don't know. Just got a feeling about you. I thought we had something in common.' He looked away. 'I don't know,' he said again.

'Something in common?' Alyce snorted, but knew she was protesting too much. She understood exactly what he meant. 'The only thing we have in common is that we both need to eat more.'

'I saw your mommet.' He formed a few different words with his lips before he spoke again. 'You reminded me of someone.'

'Who? Your mother?'

He shrugged.

'Why?'

'She was strange, like you.'

'Strange how?'

'I'm not going to say out loud.'

'Why not?'

'Because we're in earshot of everyone.'

'What happened to her?'

'God's bodkins, Alyce!' Solomon stopped at another crossroads. A gentleman glared at him for his blasphemy. 'Can we call a halt on the inquisition? I don't recall trying to fill in all the gaps in your story.' He raised his eyebrows meaningfully.

She stiffened, suddenly aware of how ignorant she was, how inexperienced when it came to talking to city folk. Talking to anyone, for that matter. She had no idea when she was overstepping the mark. Or where the mark was. Or what the mark even looked like. When she was at home, her mother had always encouraged her to ask questions. But she wasn't at home any more. And her mother was dead.

They crossed over the brown mire of the intersection and continued walking in silence. Alyce felt the muddy water soaking up the hem of her borrowed dress.

'Forgive me. I won't ask anything else,' she said eventually.

'You can ask questions. I just might not answer them.' Solomon kept striding ahead, and Alyce occasionally had to perform a little skip to keep pace with him. 'Honestly, there is nothing much to say about my mother. Nothing that you don't know about from your own experiences. She had some interests that were a little . . . unusual. Folk didn't like it – and when I say *folk*, I mean my father. He was the one who started whispering. Then one night she disappeared from the house and I never saw her again. The end. You can bet she ended up like your mother, but it's not as if I'm going to go looking for her. Or what's left of her.'

'What about your father?'

'No, not going to go looking for him, either. Haven't seen him for two years or more. And that's the way he wants it too. Bad enough that I was suckled by a devil, in his eyes, but now, shame upon shame, I'm an *actor* too. There's no coming back from that.' He smiled again, but this time it was thin and bitter, and it didn't reach his eyes.

Alyce couldn't gauge what Solomon wanted her to say, if anything. Maybe she should just laugh at his joke? Her indecision lulled her into silence again.

'Hum,' said Solomon, not looking at her. 'You didn't mention your father at all.'

That was true. But it was only because she knew virtually nothing about him. She could count the number of times her mother had spoken of him on one hand, and on those occasions always in the vaguest terms. There was never any hint of spite, or longing. He had arrived; they had been in love; he had left before Alyce was born. And since Alyce never knew him, she never missed him.

'No, I didn't,' she said, forestalling any further conversation.

'In fact, there were quite a few things you didn't mention.'

'Who's giving the inquisition now?'

'I'm not asking any questions. I'm just stating that I think there are things you're not telling me. That you're not telling anyone.'

By now they had reached Bishopsgate. To Alyce it looked very similar to Cripplegate in design – a large, arched portcullis in a square tower, flanked by two taller, thinner towers, each with its own postern gate. There was one difference, though. Illuminated by the last sullen rays of the sunset, a collection of four severed heads on spikes stood as watchmen, looking out over the battlements.

Alyce stopped and gulped. Solomon grinned.

'Pretty, aren't they? Criminals. When they first go up, some of the other actors in the company place bets on which head loses its eyes first.'

Criminals, thought Alyce, and she imagined her own head up there, feeding the birds. Then, as if bringing the daydream to life, she saw a raven circle the gate and come to perch on one of the spikes. It bristled, and then seemed to look straight at her.

Alyce lowered her eyes and pressed on.

Once they were free of the shadow of Bishopsgate, the air was immediately fresher. The broad road leading out of London was lined closely with black and white half-timbered houses and their gardens, some of them rather grand, but on either side the landscape was broad and flat and green. Despite the gathering dusk, a handful of gentlemen were still congregating in the fields to practise their archery.

Alyce recognized the scenery. Bedlam was not far away. Her stomach lurched as she spotted the roof of the Great House.

'Where's the playhouse, then?' she asked.

'Further up. Two of them, actually. We can probably hide out there afterwards, if we need to.'

Alyce nodded. Even if they didn't need a hiding place, they would still need a roof over their heads. Chances were, the city gates would be closed by the time they were finished. The last of the daylight was an orange, slitted eye glowering on the horizon.

'Why is it all the way out here? Why not inside the city

walls where more people can see you put on your plays?'

'Really?' He stopped in the middle of the road, and looked at her steadily.

'Really what?'

'I just assumed you'd know. I am an outcast, Alyce. An exile. We all are. Players have been expelled from the city for a couple of years now – we can only perform outside the walls, or if we have been invited to private residences. Like the palace.'

'Oh.'

'Bad apples, the lot of us, so we have to be chucked out of the barrel. The Devil's servants, that's all players are, corrupting good Christian morals.' He pointed between Alyce and himself. 'See, Alyce? We have *plenty* in common.'

Then he resumed his loping walk, and it was a few moments before Alyce snapped out of her reverie and ran to catch up.

They soon saw the bleak, grey buildings of Bedlam hospital huddled on their left-hand side. The infirmary and the tenements were set back from the road behind a high wall and a gatehouse, looking to any casual observer like they had been abandoned – not the faintest light could be seen coming from any of the tiny black windows. But Alyce could feel the hum of crazed, fractured lives imprisoned behind the bars.

'Do you have a plan for getting in?' asked Solomon.

'Not really,' confessed Alyce. She squinted. 'But maybe we won't need one. Look.'

Outside Bedlam's gate, a sleek, black carriage was drawn

up, apparently unattended, its horses puffing great clouds of steam into the cold evening air. And the gate itself was wide open.

Alyce stepped into the shadows beside the wall. 'We should go in now . . .' she whispered.

'But what are we going to do? Or say? I thought we were going to talk through some sort of strategy. And don't you need a disguise or something? You'll stand out like the Queen herself in that great white sheet you're wearing.'

'We might not get another chance. The gates aren't often left open like that.'

'But—'

'*I'm* going in now. You can do what you like.'

While Solomon silently protested, Alyce crept forward as far as the horses' noses, keeping her shoulder pressed against the damp stones. Something about that empty carriage made her feel horribly uneasy, as though there were something watching her from within, unseen. The back of her neck prickled, and urged her to keep moving.

As the last slivers of sunlight disappeared from the rooftops, Alyce slipped through the gate, and into the hospital's mad labyrinth.

VII

After her time at The Swan, Alyce found the sight and
the smell of Bedlam unbearably sad. It was a hopeless place. The squat, bleak infirmary sat at the centre
of a cobbled yard, surrounded by the tenements and, un-
believably, some private residences. The governors' Great
House was on the Bishopsgate side, but looked no more
hospitable than the patients' accommodation. Every building was in desperate need of repair.

She and Solomon squatted in the dirt and looked at each
other, muscles stiffening in the cold. Evening mist had
shrouded the world, dampening every sound, but from time
to time the peace was rent apart by howling from one of
Bedlam's inmates. It set them both even more on edge than
they already were.

Alyce was suddenly aware of how little she had thought
this through. Solomon looked nervous too.

'I always have a dream,' he hissed, 'where I walk out on

stage and realize I don't know any of my lines. Where I don't even know what play it is I'm performing in. This feels like that.'

Alyce ignored him, and tried to remember the layout of the buildings' interiors, for any hints as to where the governors might have kept her possessions. She'd seen Master Makepiece go out of the back door of the gatehouse to fetch them, but that meant nothing. He could have gone in any number of directions after that.

Inside the gatehouse, two men were talking. Or was it three? She couldn't quite hear. One of the voices sounded weak, and the other speaker kept interrupting him. Sometimes the second voice laughed an odd, humourless laugh that made Alyce's skin crawl. She turned to Solomon.

'You should go and talk to them.'

Solomon didn't even answer. He simply pointed at himself, and his eyes bulged again.

'You're the actor,' she whispered. 'You could pretend you have some questions. Say you have someone you want to admit to the hospital. Ask for a tour. Just keep them occupied while I search for my things.'

'Just because I'm an actor doesn't mean I can act *any* part whenever anyone asks for it.' His voice was loud with agitation.

'Hush!' She looked at him desperately. 'Please, Solomon. I can't be caught here. Not again. Just talk to them for a few minutes. I'll see you outside when I've finished looking.'

'And if they lock the gates?'

She looked behind her at the wrought-iron bars and her

heart skipped several beats. She couldn't, she *wouldn't* end up imprisoned here again. 'Then I'll just have to escape the way I did last time. Through the churchyard and over the ditch.'

Alyce stopped herself, knowing she had said too much.

'Escape?' said Solomon, the edge of his lips curling. 'I thought you said they'd let you out?'

Alyce turned red, and looked back at the door of the gatehouse.

'Very well,' said Solomon, with mock solemnity. 'I'll go and ply my trade, and hope they are easily gulled. On the condition that you tell me the *true* version of your story. Afterwards.'

'Fine,' said Alyce with a single short, hot sigh. 'Just go and give the best performance of your life.'

Solomon raised himself from his haunches, knees popping. He dusted down his doublet, arranged his ruff, breathed deeply, and went into the gatehouse.

The two men stopped speaking instantly, and Alyce could almost feel the heat of their annoyance radiating out of the doorway. She heard Solomon clear his throat tentatively, before the louder of the two voices snapped at him.

'What is it, boy?'

'Um. I wondered if I might speak with the master of this fine . . . institution.'

Alyce skirted the threshold, treading as lightly as if the ground were silk, and passed under the window beyond. Inside, Solomon was hardly warming to his character. In fact, he sounded downright terrified.

'It's my aunt, you see, she's not . . . quite right. Um. You look busy, perhaps I should come back.'

It was so awkward she was tempted to step in and save him. Or throttle him. One of the two.

Ideally, she would have searched the gatehouse first but since that was impossible, she decided to head for the infirmary. That was where she had been disrobed and shorn when she'd first arrived. Perhaps her clothes had not been moved since then. She left Solomon blabbering, and set off across the yard to where the patients brooded in their darkened cells. There was no moon. All their lunatic thoughts, hopes and fears were concealed by the night.

The door into the lower ward was not locked, and opened easily. Straight away the rank smell of sickness and decay and unemptied slop buckets curled itself into Alyce's nose and throat, and she fought to keep her stomach from rising. Somehow, she had endured this air for a month or more – she had sat in her cell while it had pooled around her like warm soup. Now, she felt like she couldn't take a single breath without being sick.

She forced her feet forwards. Immediately ahead of her, an aged wooden staircase climbed to the ward above, and a passageway extended to her left, lined with cell doors on either side. The patients rustled in the shadows. She could hear their ragged breathing.

Her heart leapt when she saw a row of smocks hanging on hooks underneath the stairs, but once her eyes had adjusted to the darkness and she had searched through their folds it became clear that these were the sad garments that the governors gave their patients on arrival, all identically shapeless and uncomfortable. A peal of laughter sounded from somewhere down the passageway, as though mocking her disappointment, then swelled uncontrollably and descended into weeping. The sound was just as pitiable and terrifying now as it had been on the first night she'd been here. Alyce made her way to the floor above, hauling her cold, leaden heart with her.

The search of the infirmary was fruitless. Upstairs and downstairs, all she found was rows of cells and their inhabitants. Most of them were women, at least those whose ghostly features hovered in the small, square windows of the cell doors. They weren't raving and muttering, but just looked sad and lost. Alyce wondered how many of them were like her, abandoned in the hospital to be cured of something that nobody — least of all they themselves — really understood.

The only other room — if it could be called that — was the overflowing cesspit on the ground floor, referred to simply as the 'Great Vault'. Opening that door just a crack was all that was needed to convince her to escape the infirmary and try elsewhere.

As she walked back along the passageway, a frail, icy voice suddenly cut through the gloom.

'Is that you?'

Alyce stiffened.

'It is you, isn't it?'

It was coming from one of the cells. Alyce tried to reply, but her lungs were numb from the cold.

'Did you bring my books? Did he give them to you?' The voice drew a long, fluttering breath. There was a scratching noise too, as though something were being inscribed on stone in one of the cells. 'So hard to see without them.'

'I don't – I don't know what you mean . . .' said Alyce. She groped through the darkness, unable to pinpoint where the sound was coming from.

'Not the black one. Burn the black one. Cast it in the pit! Black book. Black book. Black book. Black book.'

The words drifted and swirled through the corridor in fragments. They lapped like waves. Alyce crept from one cell to another, but whenever she thought she had found the source of the voice, it would echo from behind or above her and she would spin on the spot, disorientated. Madness, she remembered from her time here, is infectious.

'Oh.' The woman in the cell groaned.

'What is it?' Alyce whispered.

More scratching.

'Oh my. Why did you bring them here?'

'Who?'

'Black book. Black book. Black book.'

Alyce stopped and shivered.

'She's looking for both of us, you know. I won't go back. Let me out, and we'll run away to the woods, the three of us, three country mice. Not *him* though, no, not him.'

'I'm sorry . . .' muttered Alyce.

'Please let me out.'

'I–I can't . . . I don't have the key.'

'Please.'

'I'm *sorry*.'

'Please.'

Alyce frantically searched from one cell to the next but saw only darkness. The echo of their conversation had roused more patients, and the passageway began to fill with their confused chattering.

'They're here. The dogs are here.'

Alyce could hear voices outside the door. The only door. It was the men from the gatehouse. She cursed. *Solomon, you are useless! You've led them straight to me!*

The hinges groaned, and yellow torchlight licked its way across the floor. Alyce backed up, panicking. She'd reached the far end of the passageway. Dead end. If the governors came even halfway down the ward, the torch would reveal her, cowering in the corner. There was only one place to hide, one place where nobody would ever think to look for her.

Silently, she opened the door to the Great Vault, and slipped inside.

The hospital's cesspit looked like it hadn't been tended to in several decades. Alyce didn't want to think about how deep the pool of filth was – and however deep it was, it was overflowing, rolling in little peaks and troughs and spilling on to the narrow walkway around the outside. The smell seemed to manhandle her like a physical force, but she managed to shuffle along one side, hugging the wall, her feet occasionally coming to rest in a pool of something soft and wet. She held her breath, and listened.

'Start nearest her cell and work down.'

'Please, sir, these poor souls need rest.'

'These poor souls might have seen what happened to the girl.'

'But they are *distracted*. They see all sorts of things, most of them pure fantasy. And your friend here . . .' There was a pause. Alyce pressed her ear against the crack of the door. 'Your friend will only unsettle them further.'

'They can't all be as mad as you say. What about the girl herself? You said she was curiously lucid.'

'Yes, but—'

'I won't be taking any chances, Master Makepiece. If there is even one of them who has the faintest recollection of what happened that night, I should very much like to speak with them.'

Alyce hadn't realized it was the governor until they actually mentioned his name. His voice sounded different, like he couldn't pronounce his words properly. She hoped he would speak again, but all she heard was a creak and hollow thumping. They were going up the stairs.

Once the passageway was quiet again, Alyce pushed open the door. Her lungs were screaming at her. When she was sure the men were directly overhead, she ran for the exit, halting briefly to listen for the woman's voice, but it was lost in the babble of the other inmates. She slipped through the door, making sure the hinges didn't protest, and then tumbled out into the yard and scurried back across the cobbles.

When she arrived back at the gatehouse it was silent. She peered slowly round the door and found Solomon, alone, pacing around in the light of a single candle and wringing his hands.

'*Solomon!*' she hissed. 'What are you *doing*?'

He looked up, relieved.

'Thank God, you're all right! So they didn't see you?'

'No,' she said, glancing behind her and stepping into the gatehouse. 'But they're still in the infirmary. What happened to your captivating performance?'

'I'm sorry, I tried to stop them! They just ignored me, though. I said that—' He stopped suddenly and sniffed. 'Zounds, Alyce, what is that *smell*?'

'The cesspit, that's what.' She lifted the hem of her dress to show off her filthy ankles. 'I can't recommend it highly enough as a hiding place.'

'Oh. How vile. Still, at least they didn't find you. Terrible strange pair, those men. Did you see the—'

Alyce shook her head and pattered past him. 'Later, Solomon. We need to search this place before they come back.'

She didn't understand why she was being so curt when she was so pleased to see him. *What's wrong with you, you little harpy?* She took a candle from the table and went out of the passageway at the back of the gatehouse. Solomon followed without a word.

The building running alongside the courtyard was long and low and draughty, and three times the struggling candle almost went out completely. Alyce poked her head into each room as she went: a study, a damp wood-store, a larder that reeked of sour milk. Each got colder and smelt worse as she went along.

In the last room, a rat's eyes caught the light of the flame briefly before it scurried under a bundle of fabric in the corner.

'Look, Solomon,' she said. 'Clothes.'

Solomon was still nosing around further back down the passage. She delved into the pile up to her elbows, and three more sleek black shapes wriggled and squeaked into the darkness.

Here were the clothes of at least a dozen prisoners, and Alyce found that Bedlam hospital didn't discriminate. There were rich velvet doublets and colourful silk gowns mixed with dull woollen breeches and jerkins of material not much better than sackcloth. Mad was mad, however much money you had.

At the bottom, she found it. The yellowing smock that her mother had made for her, rolled into a ball. There was still some of the witchfinder's blood dried on the sleeve.

'You!' said a voice behind her, thick with saliva. 'You *devil*!'

Alyce couldn't see the man's face by the light of her candle, but she knew immediately who it was by his slurring, his panting, by the shape of his bulk slumped against the door frame. Her old friend. She shrunk at the sight of him, feeling that familiar cold surge of fear and shame. It was like she'd never left.

Master Kemp dropped his flagon on the floor and lumbered towards her. Alyce mustered her senses, snatched up her clothes and ducked, but he managed to grasp the back of her dress in his fat little fist. She tried to scream, but the neckline tightened around her throat to the point where she was on tiptoes, almost lifted clean off the floor. She couldn't breathe enough to shout for Solomon. The room purpled, her pulse loud in her ears, and with every kick and punch and scratch the dress bit more deeply into her neck.

'Your timing is impeccable, Alyce,' he said next to her ear. The last syllable of her name sent spittle spraying over the side of her face. 'They're here! Right now!' He giggled – actually *giggled* – in a way that Alyce hadn't done since she was a little girl. 'They came back for you! And you've walked right into their—'

It suddenly sounded like someone had stuffed his mouth, and she felt his grasp loosen. She squirmed around as Master Kemp made a wobbly pirouette and rolled on to the floor. Solomon was standing in the doorway behind him, looking triumphant.

'It's not like anyone would have eaten it,' he said.

'*What?*'

'It's gone bad.'

Alyce had no idea what he was talking about until she turned to look on Master Kemp, lying motionless among the pile of clothing with something on his head. Solomon, coming from the larder, had knocked the man unconscious with an entire wheel of cheese.

Together they ran back to Bedlam's east gate, and out into the street. As expected, Bishopsgate was closed, and Solomon took her to the playhouse a little further north. When the great whitewashed oval emerged out of the night, they got down on hands and knees and wriggled under its double doors. Inside, the yard was empty and completely dark – Alyce was glad when Solomon's groping hand found hers and led her up on to the stage and round to the tiring room out the back.

Even though she could barely see two feet in front of her face, she sat down on the hard wooden boards and unrolled her smock in her lap.

'Eurgh.'

'What?'

'Lice.'

She brushed their tiny crawling bodies on to the floor.

'Is it there?' asked Solomon.

She fumbled for a few agonizing moments, until her finger caught a blunt corner of parchment.

'It's there. A bit damp, but the seal's still intact.'

They were both out of breath, and took a moment to feel the coolness, the fullness of the air in their lungs.

'What was that?'

They both listened. There was a scratching sound, followed by an irregular flutter of wings. A bird nesting in the rafters of the upper circle.

'Just a pigeon or something,' said Alyce.

'Sounds bigger than a pigeon.'

'Well, it's not big enough to be anyone following us from Bedlam.'

'I hope not,' said Solomon, rubbing his arms. 'I was trying to tell you about those two men in the gatehouse earlier . . .'

'What about them?'

'Well.' She heard him swallow. 'The poor old governor looked like he'd been beaten black and blue. And the one with the mask—'

'The mask?'

'Like something from the pit, he was. Couldn't see any of his face. Horrible long beak—'

'*Beak?* Are you sure Master Kemp wasn't sharing his wine with you?'

'I swear! Didn't you see them?'

'No. I didn't. I heard them, though.' She fiddled with the smock. 'They were looking for me, Solomon.'

'Looking for you? What for?' She heard him clap a hand to his mouth in the darkness as he realized what she meant. 'God's teeth, that was a near miss!'

'They're like the people who came for my mother. I'm sure of it. Two others came looking for me before. Different ones. I wonder how many of them there are . . .'

'But why are they so obsessed? What's so important about you?'

Alyce turned the letter over in her hands. That question had been looming for a while now, and was getting too large to ignore.

'Nothing. There's nothing important about me. They're just angry.'

'Angry?'

'Because I killed one of them.'

HOPKINS

They found the woman sitting cross-legged in the middle of her cell, scratching a circle in the dirt around her. Her nails were white and bone-thick. A large open eye, drawn in the same way, stared up at the visitors from the ground beyond the threshold.

She was humming, or at least muttering something in a tuneful way, heavy curtains of grey, matted hair cascading over her face.

John Hopkins watched her swaying gently, as though buffeted by a draught. 'What devilry is this?'

'Ah, my husband! Come kiss me, my love!'

Hopkins ignored her, and gestured to the designs inscribed into the walls and floor of the cell. 'Master Makepiece, do you permit your patients to practise this kind of heresy openly?'

The governor mumbled something through his swollen lips, and the woman continued humming, or talking, or whatever it was she was doing.

'Perhaps we can count ourselves fortunate,' said Hopkins, turning to Caxton. He scuffed at the eye that had been drawn on the threshold. 'I'd wager this woman has seen a good deal more than her fellow prisoners.'

She barked, her breath momentarily parting the heavy shroud of her hair. 'She's gone she's gone. The both of them gone. The mice have scurried away, leaving their poor mother with the hounds!'

'You see,' said Master Makepiece. 'Her mind is broken. You'll get nothing from her.'

'Oh no,' said Hopkins, waving a black-velvet finger. 'This woman is one of ours. There is *plenty* she can give us. We just need to ask in the right way.'

'For pity's sake, sir—'

'Leave us,' he said, waving his hand dismissively. The governor opened his broken mouth again, but gave up and did as bidden.

'I saw them fly over the ocean,' said the woman. 'The two of them hand in hand.' She bent forwards, and began to draw a series of symbols around the interior of the circle she was sitting in. 'Over the ocean,' she repeated, nodding.

'That's enough,' said Hopkins. 'You can drop the act.'

'Act? Not an act. I'm no actor. He's the actor. Why, they're taking to the stage even now! They have quite a show for you. It is historical-pastoral, I believe. Or tragical-historical. Or tragical-comical-historical-pastoral.' She pointed at the two of them. 'You know your lines, I hope? No? Why, it is no matter – you may read

- 86 -

them in the black book.'

Hopkins closed his eyes and breathed deeply, summoning every ounce of his patience. Killing her wouldn't help. He'd made that mistake before, with Ellen Greenliefe.

He looked again at the eye, staring up at them from the dirt. 'You are a seer, aren't you?'

The woman paused in her symbol-drawing to shake her head. 'Me? No no no, I can't see a thing. Look at my hair! I can't see past my own nose.'

'Queen Mary would find a seer most useful. You could be a great asset to her. To us.'

The woman suddenly started laughing. '*Queen* Mary? This is new. Last time I saw her she was a librarian. She cursed me for getting my paw prints on her books. Ah, the wheel of fortune!'

'You will be Mary's subject soon enough, witch, and it would be wise to get on her right side. She can give you everything, or take it away just as easily.'

'I wouldn't want her to give me *everything*,' she giggled. 'Where would I put it all? This cell is so very small!'

'Very well,' said Hopkins, practically shaking with frustration. 'What would you ask for?'

'A kiss from your handsome friend,' she said, pointing at Caxton. 'What about you, John Hopkins? What have you asked of her?'

Hopkins paused. He hadn't told her his name. He'd

dealt with seers in the past, but the dark corners of their knowledge never became any less unsettling.

'I know what she's promised you,' she said sadly. Then a sharp intake of breath. 'Poor man. Poor, poor man. She will never let you go. She will punish and punish until there is nothing of you left.'

She knew. She knew what the crones had done to him, the bargain he'd struck with the Queen of Scots. He made a move to grab her, to silence her.

'Be careful, John Hopkins.' The woman's voice was suddenly deep and clear. She gestured around her. 'You cannot cross the circle.'

'Can I not?'

'It will be agony.'

'Agony?' said Hopkins. 'My dear, to feel anything at all would give me untold pleasure. I welcome agony. I long for it.'

He reached over the line of runes, and his flesh sang with pain. He could feel the skin of his arms blistering, but he didn't care. Was he gritting his teeth, or was he grinning? He didn't know himself.

He seized the witch by the hair, and dragged her out of the cell.

VIII

Alyce sat on the corner of her bed in The Swan, staring at the folded, slightly stained piece of parchment. Her fingers lightly traced the hard, lumpy circle of purple wax that kept its contents sealed away. Her mother had sealed this letter with her own hand. What was she trying to keep from her?

'Still haven't opened it, then?'

Alyce jumped up, dropped the letter, and turned to see Solomon hovering expectantly by the door to her bedroom. She folded her arms.

'You might have been a gentleman and knocked.'

'The door was open. Most respectable ladies lock their bedchambers.'

'Yes, well, I am not a respectable lady any more than you are a gentleman.'

'May I come in?'

'I suppose so.'

After their sleepless night at the Curtain, Alyce and Solomon had crept back into London through the morning mist, back to The Swan, like a pair of guilty lovers. And, predictably, Mrs Thomson had been waiting for them.

The innkeeper had slept just as little as they had, worrying herself sick, imagining increasingly grisly fates for poor Alyce, lost among London's dark, crooked alleys as she searched for a bag of flour. When they had stepped through the door, Mrs Thomson leapt off a stool next to the common room's fireplace, and pulled Alyce into a punishing bear hug. They'd told her at least a half truth: that Solomon had taken her to see the Curtain theatre and they'd been locked out of the city, and had to sleep backstage. Mrs Thomson had reprimanded her over a breakfast of eggs and freshly baked bread, and made a cast-iron pronouncement – Alyce was forbidden from leaving the inn until Mrs Thomson had decided she was well enough.

That had been over two weeks ago, and still the innkeeper would not heed Alyce's pleas. She was well-fed, well-rested – even her hair had grown back a bit, although it was so short and so red and so tightly curled it looked like she was wearing some sort of outlandish copper helmet. She'd finally been able to pluck a few hairs to add to her mommet too, and with the doll complete and tucked into her bed, that familiar feeling of warmth and well-being followed her everywhere. It almost felt like she was home.

But still, she was not allowed out into the city, and the innkeeper kept her busy enough with the cleaning and the cooking and the brewing that she would barely have had time to slip away if she wanted to. She had forgotten all about Alyce's letter, apparently, which Alyce was glad about.

No such thing as witches. That was better than *hating* witches, and wanting to see them burnt at the stake, Alyce supposed. But she still didn't feel like she could completely trust her. She didn't feel like she could trust anyone.

Apart from Solomon. He still came to visit. He seemed quite unruffled by the revelation that she was a murderer — in fact he had even gone so far as to suggest that she'd done the right thing. Even after that, she had expected him to disappear and never see her again, perhaps to inform one of the city's constables or watchmen of her crime and have her hauled off to the gallows, but he had returned the following day eager to continue the search for John Dee. Her secret, it seemed, was safe between the two of them.

'To answer your question, no, I haven't opened it.'

'Aren't you even curious?'

'Of *course* I'm curious. But it's not for me. It's for John Dee. I'll just have to wait until I'm allowed to go to Bankside.'

'Good luck with that. He'll be dead by the time Mrs Thomson lets you out on your own again. Zounds, *you'll* be dead, Alyce. Just have a quick look.'

'No! I'm not going to break the seal and ruin everything.'

'We can reseal it. Mrs Thomson has sealing wax in her study. You just have to be careful when you open it. Here, let me show you . . .'

Then Solomon was slipping his little finger under one

corner of the parchment, and Alyce was doing absolutely nothing to stop him. If she let him do it, she was without fault, wasn't she? Her conscience scoffed somewhere in the back of her head.

'Hum . . .' Solomon sighed through his nose. 'Do you have a hairpin?'

Alyce gave him a withering look. 'Do you really think *this*,' she said, pointing to the curling tufts on her head, 'needs hairpins?'

'No, I suppose not. Any sort of pins?'

'I think Mrs Thomson keeps some sewing materials in here,' she said, getting off the bed and opening a chest of drawers tucked under the room's one grimy window. After a little rummaging, she returned and presented him with a single needle pinched between her thumb and forefinger.

'Perfect.' He took it with a grin. Alyce watched him manoeuvre the sliver of metal under the edge of the letter, and realized she was rigid with excitement. She was barely breathing. Solomon worked slowly, delicately, his tongue poking out of the side of his mouth, until the seal popped unbroken from the front of the parchment, just leaving a small discoloured circle where it had been pressed into its surface. He picked up the wax and laid it carefully on the bedside table.

'Don't lose that,' he said. 'We can use it again if we need to reseal it. Here.' He handed the letter to Alyce. 'I don't think I should be the first one to read it.'

She unfolded it as though the whole thing might disintegrate if her fingers moved too quickly. Before she had even tried to read what was written inside, she was frowning.

EŁŁIIN ŴÍCCƎ TØ ÏOHᴧNUȘ ÐƐƐ ĻᴧRƎÓW
TWÉƏNÏENÐLIƆƆ ÞU HᴧRÊFN MÍFFIIÐE. ŴⱯRRȝST ᴧĿÛMPØN.
ᴮECYMEÞ FRĒO DÉᴧÞ NÉᴧÐHÆS. ᴧĿYƆȝ TØÞU ᴧȘÆNDIIÐE.
ᴧMᴧꞂ HÉᴧHLÛÞE ᴘÆDIꞂREȘ, OÞ TØ MOÐOꞂ HᴧMꞆYME.
ᴘØꞂꞠIEFƎDNĚȘE ᴮĚÐꞂƆE

The letter was nonsense. More than nonsense — indecipherable. Half of the symbols were from no alphabet she'd ever learnt. She remembered her mother inscribing them into stones and trees, sometimes into the earth, circles within circles around a fire or a grave. Now Alyce cursed herself for never asking what they meant.

'What is it?' asked Solomon. 'What does it say?'

Alyce shook her head. 'Nothing.'

'Nothing?'

'Nothing that I can understand, anyway.'

'Let me see.'

Alyce held one side of the letter, Solomon the other, and both of them stared blankly.

'I've seen these before,' Solomon said. 'When my mother was taken away, they found these all over our house. Under the beds. In my father's desk. Pages and pages of them stuffed in her clothes.'

'Do you think John Dee will be able to read them?'

'Well, if he's a hangman I wouldn't have thought he could read anything. Executioners aren't the brightest bunch, are they?'

Alyce shrugged. 'I don't know.' Abruptly, she turned to Solomon and gave him a penetrating look. 'So your mother definitely was a witch, then?'

'No such thing as witches, Alyce. Didn't you listen to Mrs Thomson?'

'Yes there are. We both know it. We were raised by them. You said it yourself, your mother had *unusual* interests.' She looked at the letter again. 'It's funny. I've spent my whole life thinking everyone *else* is unusual. I could never understand why they all went into that big building every Sunday and prayed to something they couldn't see, who never seemed to help them. They were always miserable. But the things my mother spoke to . . . the trees, the animals, the moon. The dead. They're real.'

She looked up to see that Solomon's face had become tense, the dark rings around his eyes suddenly more pronounced.

'The dead?'

'What?' Alyce had the creeping sensation she had said too much. Perhaps she'd been wrong to even trust Solomon. 'Didn't your mother ever speak to the dead?'

'I don't – I don't know.'

'The dead are everywhere. All the time. On the Other Side. Sometimes they come into our world, and it's up to witches to send them back again. Plug up the holes, as it were.'

Solomon looked at her curiously, as though wary she was making fun of him.

'The Other Side?'

'We never see it, but it's always there. Like a shadow of everything. But the shadow . . . is always cast directly behind the thing itself, however we look at it. So we can never see the shadow.' This was how her mother had put it, but Alyce could feel her own brow wrinkling even as she tried to explain it.

'Right. And the dead go there?'

'Yes. Go there and *come* from there.'

Again, Solomon seemed to choose his words carefully. 'So . . . is that where your mother is now?'

'I suppose so.' Alyce had never thought of it like that. But it was hardly reassuring. If anything it made her sadder to imagine her mother's spirit drifting through the darkness, forever out of reach. 'But she never taught me how to summon the dead. Let alone how to speak with any specific person. I was too young.'

'Oh.'

'Did your mother ever tell you how to do it?' Her sudden rush of excitement died before she even finished the sentence. He was shaking his head.

'No.'

'Didn't she even mention it?'

'*No.*'

'What *did* she teach you?'

'Nothing,' he said, sounding strangely prickly. 'She didn't teach me anything.' He gestured to the letter. 'This is all meaningless to me. Looks like you'll have to go to Bankside after all.' Alyce could feel him straining to move the conversation on to new ground, and she let the matter drop.

'Come on, we'll have to reseal it.'

He got up from the bed in a state of agitation, and rubbed his forehead furiously, as though trying to physically push the worries from his mind with the palm of his hand.

Alyce was confused. So was Solomon, it seemed – the boy was as eager as a puppy to explore the secret, strange, murky corners of *her* life, but as soon as he caught a glimpse of his own reflection in her story, he wanted to shut his eyes to the whole business.

'I'm sorry if I've upset you . . .' she said, trying to sound reasonable.

'We'll need a candle and sealing wax,' said Solomon, ignoring her completely and heading for the door. 'Mrs Thomson will be busy in the kitchen now, so I think we should be able to get into her study.'

And without looking at her, he took off down the stairs. On the floors below, the inn was still empty and silent, and Solomon's heavy footsteps thumped a solemn, irregular tattoo through every beam and floorboard.

Alyce shook her head in bafflement, and slowly got up to follow him.

IX

Downstairs, they heard Mrs Thomson engaged in a ferocious shouting competition with Martha.

'You think I'm blind, girl? These are filthier than when I gave them to you!'

They glimpsed her shaking a fistful of dirty bedsheets in her right hand, all of them blackened with something that looked like soot.

'Weren't like that when I hung them up to dry,' Martha protested. 'Dogs must have got in and torn them down.'

'Don't care what happened, you're washing them again!'

And so it raged on. While Mrs Thomson discharged her volleys of indignation, Alyce and Solomon crept into the study at the back of the kitchen and found the sealing wax among her papers.

'It's not as good quality as the stuff your mother used,' he said, pulling up a stool and hunching over a candle, 'but it will do.' He dripped a few blobs of Mrs Thomson's wax on to the parchment, then warmed the underside of the original seal that he had detached with the needle, and pressed them together. He blew on it so the wax would cool. 'There. Good as new.'

Alyce took the letter from him and inspected the workmanship. It was almost impossible to tell that it had been opened.

'Pickpocket, forger . . .' she said, shaking her head in mock disappointment. 'I'm starting to wonder if I should be keeping company with such a rascal.'

'I'm starting to wonder that too,' said Solomon. Alyce gave a half-hearted laugh, but was unsure of what he really meant. 'I need a drink.'

Without another word, he skirted around the desk and wandered out into the kitchen and beyond, as though he couldn't quite face being in the same room as her any more. Alyce was left perched on a stool, wondering what on earth was going through the boy's head.

The door slammed behind him, and the gust blew a sheaf of Mrs Thomson's parchment off the table and on to the floor. Alyce cursed under her breath and gathered the scattered pages, skimming over their contents as she tried to get them back into order. She stood up and laid them flat in the candlelight. It was soon clear that these were not the accounts of your average innkeeper.

They were covered with lists of strange names with numbers next to them:

1 goatweed
1 creeping willow
1 feverfew
1 nightshade

They were plants and herbs. Alyce's mother had taught them to her. She hadn't seen or heard them since she'd left home, and seeing the names again was like being reunited with old friends. A smile began to creep across her face, but was stopped short by the last item on the list. Nightshade? Wasn't that a poison? Surely that wasn't a special ingredient in one of Mrs Thomson's pies?

She was reading so intently that she didn't hear the argument with Martha reaching its exhausted conclusion, and she only realized that Mrs Thomson had returned when she saw the two shadows of her feet in the crack of light under the door. She was still rearranging the pages when the innkeeper came barging in.

Alyce stared guiltily into her broad, red face. It was difficult to tell whether she was angry or amused.

'You can read, can you, child?'

Alyce nodded.

'That's unusual. Never had a maid who could read. That Martha wouldn't know her own name if it was written in front of her.'

'My mother taught me.'

'And you can read what's written on those, can you?'

Alyce paused, unsure if she should tell the truth or feign ignorance. 'Well,' she said, picking her words slowly and carefully, 'I can read them, but I don't know what they all do. Goatweed will settle the humours. Not sure about the willow, I'd need to see what type it is. Feverfew is for fevers, obviously – but my mother always called it featherfew.'

Mrs Thomson's face split into a wide grin, revealing all six of her remaining teeth.

'Well! A proper young apothecary we have here!'

'I'm sorry for prying, Mrs Thomson, I just haven't seen these sorts of things since I left home.'

'No need to apologize, my poppet!' cried the innkeeper, sidling up alongside her in a strange, shuddering dance. 'I might have a job for you. An important one.' Suddenly the corners of her mouth sagged. 'If, that is, you can promise you won't break my poor old heart by running off the moment you get outside the inn.'

Alyce's chest suddenly felt hot and light. Maybe she would be able to get to Bankside after all.

She bit her lip. 'I promise,' she said solemnly.

'Very well then,' said Mrs Thomson, a conspiratorial smile returning to her face. 'As you know, I understand a little about herbs. And I do some small business with a mountebank. Foreign gentleman.'

'A mountebank?'

'A pedlar, of sorts. He sells remedies. Cure-alls. "Elixirs", he calls them. But he don't sell to me, he buys. Gets all his ingredients from me. He mixes them up and does his pretty shows and sells them on. Makes me a good few shillings, here and there. Nothing wrong with that, is there? Just making good use of what God's given us out of the earth.'

Alyce shook her head.

'Now – I need someone to deliver these herbs and roots and what have you. I been using Martha recently, but she don't know what it is she's handing over to him. She can't read the labels and she's always forgetting what I told her. You'd be just right for the job, though. And you could help me prepare the ingredients. *And –*' she held up a finger in Alyce's face to prevent her interrupting – 'come to think of it, the mountebank himself was saying he wanted a girl to help him with his shows. Reward you right handsomely, he would. What do you say?'

Alyce's thoughts ran and jumped too quickly for her to keep up. The dangers of going about the city in daylight, her anxieties about helping this foreign gentleman with his 'shows' – they were all overtaken by the hope of reaching John Dee, and deciphering the letter.

'Of course,' she blurted. 'I mean, if you think it's right for me.'

'You look well enough now, I think. And the *signor*, the mountebank, he'll look after you. He's a comely gentleman too,' she said, elbowing Alyce in the ribs, more painfully than she probably intended too. 'Better watch Solomon don't get jealous!'

To her surprise, Alyce felt the blood rise in her cheeks – and the more she blushed, the more foolish she felt, and the more fiercely her face burned. Mrs Thomson laughed.

'Don't you worry, your secret's safe.'

'We don't have a secret, Mrs Thomson.'

The innkeeper simply winked. 'Something about him

though, isn't there?'

'Yes, you can definitely say that much. I think he is . . . obscure.' She pictured him drinking alone in the common room outside. 'Did you say you were friends with his mother?'

'Friends. Associates. A right canny herbalist his mama was. Solomon used to come with her when she visited. But then – well, you know the rest. Her husband didn't take too kindly to her interests.'

'Because she was a witch?'

'*Alyce!* You know my thoughts on that word. Don't let me hear you say it out loud again.'

'I'm sorry, I just want to know a little more about her. About Solomon.'

'Well, that's for him to tell you, isn't it? Let's not go talking behind his back. Probably said too much already, haven't I.'

Alyce looked at her feet, chastened.

'Now,' said Mrs Thomson, 'Signor Vitali – that's his name, the mountebank. You go and talk to Martha, and she'll tell you where he lives. I'll send him a letter first thing tomorrow morning and let him know you're coming.'

'When will he want me to visit him?'

'Don't rightly know, my love. A week. Maybe a month. I made him a delivery in the New Year, so he might not need any ingredients for a little while.'

Another *month*? Alyce wasn't sure she could spend that long as Mrs Thomson's prisoner. Regardless of finding John Dee, what if those men and women who were looking for her traced her to The Swan? Even if they had to go door to door through the whole of London, it would probably take them less than a month to discover her new hiding place.

'Martha's out there doing her washing. Go ask her about him. I'll pen this letter to the *signor* now.'

Mrs Thomson shoved Alyce off the stool with her gigantic backside, nearly sending her sprawling on the floor. Alyce straightened up, checked that the letter to John Dee was unbent and unbroken in her pocket, and left the innkeeper scratching away with her quill.

The kitchen was quiet, and Solomon, drinking by himself somewhere out front, was nowhere to be seen. She stuck her head out into the yard at the rear of the inn. Martha had disappeared too, the bundle of grubby bedsheets abandoned next to her washing tub. The sky was a flat, featureless grey, the late afternoon still and dead.

It was strange. Martha had a habit of abandoning her chores after an argument with Mrs Thomson, but usually there was nothing quiet about her sulkiness. She would stomp around the bedrooms or the kitchen, sighing and snorting, noisily moving the pots and pans for no real reason, just so everybody knew how hard done by she felt. But after her most recent altercation, she seemed to have vanished into thin air.

'*Shoo! Get out of here!*'

The maid's voice suddenly echoed out of an alley that joined the inn yard to the main street. Alyce heard scuffling, punctuated every so often by a squawking that definitely wasn't human. There was something about the sound that clutched at her heart and made her feel inexplicably sad.

'*Go on! Get out of it! Bet you're the one that's been dirtying my washing and all!*'

Alyce came around the corner to see Martha armed with a broom handle, taking broad swipes at a huge black bird a few feet in front of her. Every time the wood cracked against the ground the bird croaked, sounding not so much aggressive as simply irritated. It flapped in the dust from one side of the alley to the other, and then up to the gables, where it perched and watched them both.

As Alyce approached Martha's shoulder, the bird cocked its head and flew back down to the ground. They stared at each other. It was a raven, the biggest and most dishevelled of its kind, feathers sticking out of its head and wings at all angles. As it pointed its beak at her, she saw that one of its eyes was black and the other milky white.

And that was when she knew that she had met the raven before. She had seen it a hundred times at her mother's cottage, and now it was here, a visitor from a life she no longer led. The odd, melancholy feeling tightened its grip on her chest.

In that same moment, Martha brought the broom down right on top of the black bundle of feathers.

'No! Martha!'

Alyce reached out to grab her arm, but it was too late. The raven cawed, hopped backwards in a daze, and then flew off over the roof of the inn.

'What was *that* for?' huffed the maid, wrestling her arm out of Alyce's grip and whirling round to face her. 'I should've broken its poxy neck! D'you know how much extra washing I've had to do because of that bird?'

But Alyce could barely hear her. The numbness in her heart had spread to her head, and now she felt a rushing, bottomless sadness. All she could think of was her mother, the dam broken by the sight of the raven, the memories flooding over her.

She stumbled out of the alleyway and back to the kitchen. The feeling that she was falling gave way to sickness, then to lightness, then to a strange vibrating sensation that rippled out from her belly to the ends of her fingers and toes. Her vision was going dark around the edges. Something was changing, inside and outside of her body.

Mrs Thomson heard her crash through the door and emerged from her study looking confused.

'Alyce? What is it? Lord, you look pale! Has that Martha been making sport of you again?'

Alyce ignored her and lurched though the kitchen to the stairs, desperate to get back to her room. She needed her mommet.

What's happening to me?

There was a roaring in her ears now, a distant, churning storm, like thousands of whispering voices. They were the sounds of the dead, she knew, sounds that she had last heard when she had been at home, her real home. But this was different. Everything she looked at seemed clothed in shadow now, and yet the shadows themselves had their own weird vividness. The darkness *glowed*.

She tripped on the first step, and suddenly Solomon was

beside her, trying and failing to get her upright again.

'Come on,' he said, fear showing plainly on his face, 'back to your room. They can't see you like this.'

Like what?

The staircase shook. Everywhere she looked, black luminescence burned her eyes. Somewhere in the back of her mind she heard the echo of Mrs Thomson's shouts, and the sounds of shattering glass and splintering wood. One of the maids screamed.

She wept for her dead mother, and it seemed that with every sob that escaped her, another piece of The Swan was torn to pieces.

HOPKINS

'You need to tidy this place up a bit,' said Hopkins, nudging a pile of books out of the way with his foot and watching it topple over.

The laboratory was a good deal smaller than he had been expecting, tucked into the attic of the Doctor's house at Mortlake. Every wall was lined with hundreds of books, the light from his oil lamp glittering on their waxy spines, their titles inlaid in Latin and Greek and other, stranger languages. In the centre of the room, scattered across several tables, were various scientific instruments – sextants, astrolabes, compasses, eye-glasses – and a range of surgical tools, now rusting, including forceps, scalpels and saws of several sizes.

The air was sour and vinegary, and underneath it was an ever-present smell of spoiled meat.

Hopkins picked up a bottle of yellowish liquid, containing something that might have been part of a body. Animal or human, he wasn't sure.

'Put that *down*,' said the Doctor, his great greying beard trembling. His robes billowed as he strode over, snatched the bottle from Hopkins' fingers and laid it gently back on the shelf with the others. 'Given the nature of our agreement, you might be a *little* more respectful.' He stacked the fallen books back on top of each other.

Hopkins bowed, and his wound ached when he did. 'A thousand apologies, Doctor,' he said, not even trying to sound sincere. 'I have nothing but the highest esteem for you and your work.'

'Ha!' the Doctor snorted. He returned to the far end of the laboratory, where there was a cage. He began feeding it's inhabitant something through the bars. 'There is no need to sound bitter, Hopkins. You are simply serving your punishment for the persecution you inflicted on our kind.'

'Of course. Perfectly fair.'

'Perhaps, now you are a little more enlightened, you are starting to see sense. Perhaps you can see how foolish you were in your mission to destroy us.' The cage shuddered, and for a moment the Doctor withdrew his fingers from between the bars, and looked up as though enraptured by some message from the heavens. 'You should consider it a very great honour to be working for us. Do you have any idea how profound a thing Her Majesty is trying to achieve? How *noble*?'

'I assure you I am quite humbled,' said Hopkins, eyeing up any number of sharp implements within arm's reach. He curled and uncurled his fingers. *Calm yourself, John Hopkins. Endure. Obey. All of this will end. The witch queen promised.*

'Of course, you don't understand,' said the Doctor, laughing to himself. 'You are a hired thug. Nothing more.'

Hopkins ground his teeth. There was a time when he would have executed the man on the spot. Perhaps given him the semblance of a trial, but it would always have ended in the stake and the roaring fire and the cheering crowds. But now...

He found himself staring at the bloodied workbench, trying to remember who he had once been. When he looked up, the Doctor was still fussing around the laboratory, muttering to himself. Hopkins watched him. Insufferable windbag. Sometimes he thought keeping company with this man was worse than anything the crones had inflicted upon him.

'This hired thug,' he said at last, 'is apparently the only person willing to get his hands dirty and actually look for the girl.'

'And who gave you all the information? Who gave you the leads?'

'You did. But would you be happy riding from one stinking village to the next in search of her? Would Mary?'

'Pah!'

'And you have us to thank for your new pet,' said Hopkins, nodding to the darkness.

The laboratory fell silent, except for the sounds of chewing coming from the corner of the room.

'Not new, actually,' said the Doctor. 'We have met before. This wretch is Anne Harper. She was one of *ours*, some years back. She'd had a vision – foresaw some misfortune regarding her son, I believe – and she wanted our help to try and save him. Wanted to learn our arts. Mary assumed you witchfinders had caught and killed her long ago, but here she is, her mind in pieces. It's no surprise she drove herself mad – she was a woman of little talent. Very mean intelligence.'

A whisper floated out of the cage.

'Black book . . . black book . . . black book . . .'

The Doctor laughed. 'Yes, Anne, *my* black book, and you never returned it, you little thief!'

'Has she been *useful*?' said Hopkins, growing increasingly impatient with the man. 'Can she see the girl?'

The Doctor smoothed his beard. 'We have made some progress,' he said grudgingly. 'Her visions are complicated. Past, present, future – all one hotchpotch. That's the thing that drives them mad. But as it happens, she saw Alyce in the flesh. She *claims* that the girl was under your very nose the whole time you were blundering around in Bedlam. I would like to think that this is simply more lunatic ravings, since it implies an incompetence quite beyond belief. But it seems to be true.'

Hopkins smiled thinly. 'Say it is true. It still doesn't help us.'

'Luckily for you, there is another extraordinary coincidence. The son she so desperately wanted to save is *with the girl*. Find the boy, and you'll find Alyce.'

'Very well. What do we know about him?'

'He is an actor, it would seem. She doesn't know, or won't say, which players' company he is with. But I'm sure a man of your remarkable talents will rise to that challenge. Find out where he lives, where he performs, where he goes drinking – he's harbouring her somewhere.'

'And do we have a name?'

The Doctor began to speak when suddenly there was a wild rattling of the cage, and gurgling from its occupant.

'My boy . . . my poor, poor boy . . .'

He went back into the darkness to calm the creature before he answered.

'The boy's name,' he said, 'is Solomon Harper.'

X

Alyce was awake before dawn, as usual. She hadn't slept properly for days. Whenever she managed to calm her racing mind long enough to drift off, she was plagued by hideous dreams — of Bedlam, of her mother, of the raven. Things that she would have rather forgotten were suddenly coming back to her with terrible clarity.

She sat upright in bed, staring into the darkness, tired and brittle from constant alertness. The last week had worn her down to a sliver.

Solomon had gone. He had not returned to The Swan since her delirium had struck. She knew he had helped her up to her room, and he had obviously done his best to explain away the damage she had caused, but then he had abandoned her. She missed him. And she wanted to talk to him, to ask him what had happened. He was the only one who might understand. There was no way she could talk to Mrs Thomson about it.

The innkeeper was in a permanently foul mood these days. It was understandable really, after what Alyce had done. Stools were broken, two barrels of ale had split, the inn's only glass decanter had shattered. For the time being, Alyce had come up with some unconvincing excuse that she had simply knocked them over, and Mrs Thomson had made equally unconvincing claims that she believed her. But there were other, stranger things too: food in the kitchen had spontaneously rotted, boughs of holly and ivy had withered and dried and dropped their leaves. There was no explaining that. Now there was an odd curtness in the way the innkeeper spoke to her. She looked at her differently too.

No such thing as witches.

The Other Side. She had been talking to Solomon about it just moments before it had all happened. The world of the dead, lying always just behind our own, was nothing new to Alyce – she had countless memories of she and her mother perching on a tomb or kneeling by the embers of the fire, listening for the voices of the departed. Sometimes her mother would ask them questions, and while Alyce tried hard to hear the answers, their whispering was no more intelligible than wind in the trees.

What happened in the Swan's kitchen was different, though. She hadn't just heard voices. That strange, tidal surge of darkness had overwhelmed her. More than that. She felt like she'd *let something in*, and had been powerless to stop it. And now, in the quiet of her bedroom, it lingered, a background hum that wouldn't go away.

Her mother could have explained it to her. Maybe even

Solomon. But they were both gone. She'd never felt so alone.

A cold, pale light began to bleed through the dirty window panes. Alyce willed the sunrise to go and bother other, happier souls who were ready to face the world. Today, of all days, she just wanted to stay in bed, preferably in a deep, dreamless sleep.

She was supposed to be meeting Signor Vitali this morning. He had replied quickly and effusively to Mrs Thomson's letter, saying he would be 'beyond delighted to meet Alyce', and that 'a beautiful young woman would be good for business, and good for him too'.

Alyce rolled over and buried her head in the pillow.

You need to get up now, Alyce.

The voice in her head sounded like it belonged to someone else. At any rate, her body wasn't listening to it.

Come on, you great lump. Is this what all your efforts have been leading to? Your mother's efforts? A nice long lie-in?

She opened one eye. The letter was still lying on the dresser, stained dubiously brown from its time at Bedlam. Perhaps she wasn't as alone as she thought. The mountebank's shop was on London Bridge, so a visit to Bankside would hardly be out of her way. She could find the hangman.

Even so, getting up felt like dragging several wet sandbags out of the bed. She stretched, and put on a smock with great effort. She pocketed the letter first, and then took her mommet from its hiding place under her pillow.

Mrs Thomson was already fussing over the stove when Alyce came down to the kitchen.

'Bowl of porridge on the end there for you, child,' she said, without looking up. 'And you'll get a boiled egg and a nice apple too. You'll be needing your energy today.'

Alyce drew up a chair and stared into the grey depths of her bowl. There must have been gallons of the stuff in there, and she suspected there was no way Mrs Thomson was letting her leave without finishing all of it. She dug out a few spoonfuls.

'I make it about seven o'clock. Which means you'll need to be on your way to the signor in an hour or so. Mustn't keep him waiting.'

With just Mrs Thomson for company, the inn seemed quiet and empty. Alyce swallowed and shivered. She wished Solomon were here.

'That bird got in the yard again this morning, no doubt you heard,' said Mrs Thomson, continuing to clatter around the kitchen. 'Got as far as the kitchen this time, helping itself to scraps, the little devil!'

The raven again. Alyce tried to ignore the very clear memory that rose before her eyes, and said nothing. She scooped up the dregs of the porridge, her belly feeling hot and strained, and sucked anxiously on the spoon. The innkeeper bustled over and took her bowl.

'How was that then?'

'Very nice, thank you.'

Mrs Thomson looked at her askance.

'You're very quiet this morning. You still feeling unwell?'

Alyce forced a smile. 'Quite well. It's just . . . I haven't been out into London for so long. I'm not really looking forward to it. The city hasn't treated me particularly kindly before now.'

'Didn't stop you running off with Solomon for the night, did it though?' Mrs Thomson glared at her for a moment, before her features softened. 'Don't you worry yourself. Signor Vitali is a gentleman, he'll take good care of you.'

If I make it there alive, thought Alyce. She hadn't forgotten that the witchfinders were almost certainly still looking for her.

'That reminds me . . .' Mrs Thomson waddled off into the study at the rear of the kitchen. When she emerged she was carrying four small leather pouches, and she dumped three of them in front of Alyce. They let off a queer smell.

'Now you listen. This is what he's asked for. They all got labels on them, so he knows what's what.' Alyce looked at one of the thin pieces of parchment, and read it aloud.

'*Crab's eyes.* I thought these were herbs?'

'Crab's eyes *is* a herb. Well, it's a plant. And a nasty one, withal. Thought you might know it.'

Alyce looked at the rest of the labels. 'Poppy seeds, ragwort...' she said aloud. Then she pointed to the fourth bag, which was small, black, and unmarked. 'What's this?'

'Ah,' said Mrs Thomson quietly. 'This ain't got no label on it because it's a bit . . . out of the ordinary. Just tell him . . . this one is for his *special* customers.'

Alyce looked confused, and gingerly took the leather pouch.

'Don't you go losing it, girl. And make sure he pays me in full. A crown for each of these three, and *two sovereigns* for that one you got there. You understand? Here.'

She handed Alyce a piece of parchment with the inventory and a list of prices scribbled across it. Alyce took it and slipped it into her front pocket along with the letter she had brought down from her bedroom.

'You're just about ready, I think. Wait a moment.' Again, Mrs Thomson disappeared into the study, and came back with a basket, a pair of floppy leather shoes and a bonnet, which she thrust over the top of Alyce's messy copper curls. She took a step back and cocked her head.

'There you are. A proper lady. Shoes might be a little big, but you need something sturdy. It'll be hard going after the snow we've had.' Then she placed the four pouches into the basket, and covered them with a cloth. 'You make sure no one tries to pinch those!'

Alyce pushed her feet into the shoes, and wiggled her toes. There was a good inch of empty space for them to rattle around in. The leather flapped absurdly at the ends.

'I feel like I should have a cockscomb to match these . . .'

Mrs Thomson laughed, for the first time in what felt like weeks. 'Nonsense! You look very fine. Now, you ready?'

'I suppose so,' said Alyce.

'You got the inventory?'

She nodded.

'You know where you're going?'

She nodded again. 'London Bridge, between the glass-makers and the silversmith.'

'Good. Never been there myself, but shouldn't be too hard to find.' The innkeeper patted her on the back with a warm, fleshy palm. That was what counted as affection from Mrs Thomson these days. 'Well then. God speed!'

And that was it. She had expected a bit more ceremony.

Alyce tramped out of the kitchen and across the dusty floorboards of the common room. Mrs Thomson had gone back to work by the time she had reached the front door.

No turning back now. She loitered on the inn's threshold for a moment, and noticed the broken stools and shattered barrels piled up in the yard. The memory of what had happened a week earlier flared in her imagination again, but she closed her eyes and forced it from her mind. Then she took three breaths of cold morning air, checked the contents of her front pocket again, and stepped out of the doorway.

The city and its shadows crouched in the mist, waiting to claim her.

XI

The snow from the previous week still lay in dirty, brown heaps around the alleyways, leaving a chill in the air that was damp rather than crisp. It soaked through Alyce's clothing, and she was shivering in her bones before she had even left the inn yard.

The townsfolk sailed silently past her in the mist as she trudged down Fish Street to the river. She jumped when a pair of caged geese came honking through the street behind her, but apart from that there was a reassuring calmness about the laymen setting up shop and going about their business.

At the bottom of the hill loomed the north gate of London Bridge, and the narrow archway was already spilling forth carts and bodies coming across from Southwark. Things were busier and more irritable here. Alyce found herself kicking and elbowing her way through the crush of bodies, knuckles white from clutching her basket of ingredients.

The bridge itself was a magnificent shambles – a hundred shops and houses clinging desperately to its sides as though fearful of falling into the brown, silty water below. Through the middle of these huddling buildings, the thoroughfare itself was little more than six feet wide. There was no place where two carts might pass each other, with coaches, carts, pedestrians and animals all crushing dangerously through the same narrow conduit. To make things more difficult for Alyce, almost everybody was going in the opposite direction to her.

Quickly, she checked that the pouches in her basket were all intact, and then dived back into the stream of people.

Once she was under the gate, the first set of shops formed a low tunnel over the bridge. Alyce clung to the walls and the shopfronts, ducking in and out of doorways so as not to be swept back the way she had come. Below her, underpinning the shouting and thumping of feet, she felt the slow rumble of the waterwheel in the northernmost arch. Most of the shops – haberdashers, milliners and the like, selling clothes and jewellery and rich fabrics – were still closed, since their wealthy clientele would not yet be out of bed. But even with the doors and windows shut, the elaborate shopfronts, and the expansive living quarters above them, spoke of the affluence inside.

Alyce skirted the crowds, glancing behind her periodically, and found herself in the middle of the bridge, where the tunnel of shops and houses opened up to the breeze. Out on the Thames, the masts of merchant vessels stretched almost as far east as the Tower, and on the north bank sailors were yelling and cursing as two galleons manoeuvred clumsily around the same quay. Alyce stopped and stared into the grey-brown flood, swirling around the islands of debris at the base of the arches. The torrents made her feel queasy, and she imagined herself sinking into the murk, weighed down by the pounds and pounds of heavy porridge still settling in her stomach. She turned her back on the river and steadied herself.

The glassmaker's premises was one of the first shops in the next grand arch on the bridge. For a moment, she wondered if she should keep going, forget about the mountebank, and head straight for Bankside, but she had no desire to further aggravate Mrs Thomson or any of her customers.

A boy no older than Alyce had opened the front door of the shop and was beating a dirty rug into the street. Within, the shop glittered with hundreds of glasses and bottles and phials. Alyce approached the boy, who seemed not to notice her and flung a faceful of dust in her direction. She tried to clear her throat politely, but found herself heaving a great phlegmy cough back at him. The boy regarded her distastefully. He was wearing an elaborately decorated silver doublet, and he had the stern, humourless face of a man five times his age.

'Excuse me, sir,' she said, wiping the grime from her eyes. 'I am looking for Signor Vitali. I am bringing him . . .' she paused, 'supplies. I was told his lodgings might be found here, but I can't see them.' Immediately next to the glass shop was the silversmith. There was no other shop or residency to be seen.

The boy twitched his head a little, so he was watching Alyce from the corner of his eye. Then he spat at her feet, disappeared into the shop, and slammed the door.

After a few baffled moments, the door reopened to reveal a fat, olive-skinned man with great pendulous jowls hanging under an unruly black moustache. His gut strained against the buttons of his undershirt.

'Who wishes to speak with Signor Vitali?'

'I do.' Alyce looked the man up and down. Her eyes roamed for several moments to take in his enormity. Mrs Thomson had called Vitali handsome . . . Then again, she wasn't a slight woman herself. 'My name is Alyce. Mrs Thomson sent me, from The Swan. I have the ingredients you asked for.'

The fat man spat on the floor too, more viciously than his boy. 'You think I am Vitali? Because I speak like this? I am from *Venezia*. Vitali?' He spat again. '*Cafone*. Vitali is from *Milano*. He is a dog. A child like you should not meet with him. Where is your mother? Why she send you here?'

That took Alyce a little by surprise. 'Oh, Mrs Thomson isn't my mother. I work at The Swan. I have something to give to Signor Vitali.' She held up her basket.

The glassmaker patted his belly. '*Bene*. Your mother is a fool—'

'I just told you, she isn't my—'

'But I will show you to this *cafone*. You give him your *something*, and then you leave. You do not talk to him. Is a waste of your breath.'

He barged past Alyce, and inside the shop she could see

the boy still watching her suspiciously.

'Forgive my son, Alessandro. He does not know how to talk to a beautiful girl.'

Alyce couldn't work out if he was joking or not. He didn't seem to be. With a solemn look upon his face, he went into the middle of the thoroughfare and pointed into a tiny gap between his own shop and the silversmith's next door. It didn't even look wide enough for Alyce to slip into, let alone this Venetian gentleman. It also seemed to lead nowhere, simply disappearing off the side of the bridge.

'You must go down below,' he said. 'He conducts his business underneath the rest of us. As he should.' He spat once more. '*Buona fortuna.*' Then he turned on his heel and marched briskly back to his shop.

Alyce looked around the bridge, confused, as though expecting someone else to give her more precise directions. Nobody did, so she poked her head in between the two towering residences and, sure enough, found herself looking over the sheer drop at the edge of the bridge. There was, however, a ladder that led down to the river, clinging to the side of one of the bridge's great stone bastions.

She grasped the highest rung, which rattled dangerously, and leant out over the abyss. Far beneath her, the violent currents of the Thames were rushing either side of a wooden pontoon that was built around the base of the arch. Every arch had one, she saw, accumulating silt and debris and turning the already swift streams of the river into narrow, raging torrents as they passed under the bridge.

With nowhere else to go, Alyce slung her basket over

one shoulder and began clambering down the ladder to the pier below. Once she was no longer sheltered by the overhanging buildings, gusts of wind tugged at the folds of her dress and threatened to snatch her bonnet from her head. Halfway down, the square of cloth that covered the basket's contents blew away and danced upstream on the breeze.

When she eventually reached the bottom, the pontoon itself was no more secure than the ladder. It creaked and rattled in the current, and felt like it might be swept completely clear of the bridge at any moment. She felt horribly exposed too, like everyone along both riverbanks was watching her. She hugged the base of one of the arches, and edged carefully around to the other side.

And there it was. Under the bridge, huddled like some vagrant escaping from the weather, was a tiny set of lodgings. They were constructed on top of the pontoon, and although the building itself looked sturdy enough, the timbers beneath it were black and slimy and seemed ready to dissolve into the relentless currents. The swells of the river ensured that both the pontoon and the lodgings were never totally still.

Alyce edged unsteadily to a little wooden door at the front of the house. In her haste to escape from the cold and the damp and the roaring threat of the river coursing either side of her, she didn't think to knock, and pushed straight in. It was at that point that somebody opened the door from the other side, and Alyce fell in a dishevelled heap on the floor.

XII

The bolt of the door *clunked* behind her, and the room filled with bright laughter. Alyce sat up, rubbing her elbow, and was struck by a heavy wave of perfume that smelt like roses on the verge of rotting. She wrinkled her nose.

'I thank God you are not Mrs Thomson. If she falls down . . . I fear she will never rise again!' Another peal of laughter. The voice was high for a man, and honey-sweet, with an Italian accent much thicker than the glassmaker she had met on the bridge.

Alyce pulled back the bonnet that had fallen over her eyes. The vision before her did not seem entirely real.

Signor Vitali was not handsome. He was *perfect*. And not in a pleasing way. He was an apparition so beautifully composed it was quite unsettling. Whereas most foreign merchants looked swarthy and weather-beaten, his skin was an unblemished white, and his beard and moustache were so precisely trimmed they looked like they'd been drawn on with a pencil. His jet-black hair fell in ringlets around his ears and glistened – along with the rest of him – as though he had bathed himself in oil or perfume.

'Lorenzo Vitali.' He bowed low and kissed Alyce's hand. 'I hope you had little trouble finding my lodgings.' His smile revealed two rows of perfectly straight, glittering white teeth.

'You are a very beautiful child,' Vitali continued, gently clasping her chin in his fingers to assess her. Alyce frowned. Was this the way all Italians spoke to girls? 'Very beautiful. And strong. This is good. Good for *you*, not for me. You will never need my potions, with such natural beauty!'

Alyce could not find the words. The man was ridiculous. She would have laughed out loud along with him, but the feeling of his gloved fingers on her skin was just unpleasant enough to stop her finding the whole situation funny.

'Do you speak?' He gave another chuckle. 'You will need to speak, if we are to be friends! I like to speak, maybe Mrs Thomson told you this.'

He pronounced 'Thomson' with two great booming syllables, and this time Alyce wasn't able to restrain herself from sniggering.

'Ah! You laugh! This is a good start. I like to laugh too.' He gestured to a pair of stools. 'Please, sit. You are Alyce, yes?' Again, his accent dragged out the vowels and put too much stress on the second half of her name.

'That's right, sir. I mean, signor. I have the ingredients you asked for from Mrs Thomson.' She went to pick up the basket that had skidded across the floor when she had fallen through the front door.

'No, no,' he said, grasping her wrist and leading her like a calf back to her seat. She shivered a little. 'We do not do business now. Now, we talk. There is no business without *amicizia*. We must get to know each other. Wait.'

Vitali turned with a flourish of his embroidered cloak and wandered into the back room. While he was clinking around, Alyce went over to his workbench and inspected the pots and bottles and phials of strangely coloured substances.

She was sniffing the contents of a pestle and mortar when Vitali returned with a flask of wine and two expensive-looking goblets.

'Careful, child!' he said, setting them down on his workbench. 'These are dangerous things. Only a physician of great skill can use them safely. Come, we drink.'

'Is this barberry?' She gestured to the mortar.

Vitali stopped, and smiled. 'Indeed, it is. You are a clever girl, as well as beautiful!'

'You need to remove the seeds.'

His smile faltered a little. 'Is that so?'

'Yes. If you crush the seeds along with the flesh, it causes problems with digestion.'

'Ah, you know a little of herbalism,' said Vitali, looking a little impatient now. 'Very good.'

'What do you use it for?' she asked.

'This I use to make a salve for the head. It makes your hair grow and shine like the sun!' He spread his arms dramatically.

Alyce frowned. 'How?'

'A very complex, very delicate process. You would not understand, I think.'

'I might.'

Vitali let out a short sigh. 'First we boil the berry in a solution with horsetail—'

'You can't boil horsetail! It makes it useless! And besides, you're meant to eat barberry. Horsetail is used on the skin, isn't it? Why put them together?'

The mountebank forced out an unamused laugh and clapped his hands. 'Please, Alyce, I thought we were not speaking of business? Drink with me.'

She returned to the stool, unsatisfied. Vitali followed, settled himself down opposite her and handed her a goblet of wine. She took a gulp.

'So. Alyce. Tell me about yourself. Who are you?'

Alyce laughed to herself. That question again. *I am Alyce Greenliefe*, she shouted inside her head, *and I am a witch*.

With the wine flowing through her veins, though, the lies came easily. In fact, she found the whole thing quite entertaining. Her father had been a soldier (she couldn't remember where he fought), her mother was disgraced for a liaison with another man while her husband was at war (she couldn't remember his name), Alyce had been forced to come to London after the family had been made destitute (she couldn't remember when) and had ended up working for Mrs Thomson to make ends meet.

At the end of her tale, feeling thoroughly pleased with herself, she turned the question on Vitali.

'What about you, signor?' she asked. She had drained her cup to the dregs, and her cheeks were flushed. 'What is your story?'

'Mine is not as interesting as yours,' he said, his eyes glinting. He waved his hand dismissively, wafting more sickly perfume in Alyce's direction. 'It is of no importance.'

'Why did you come to London?'

'Why, to sell my elixirs! The best in the world! Wherever there is sickness, Doctor Vitali will bring his cures and his salves. And London –' he shook his head, a comically pained expression on his face – 'is a very sick city.'

'But why did you leave Milan, I mean?'

Again, Vitali's mask began to slip a little. 'Many reasons, you—'

'Wouldn't understand?' Alyce finished for him, the wine loosening her tongue more than she had expected.

Vitali took a deep breath, and then leant in until his face was inches from Alyce's. 'Sometimes, child, it is unwise, and unfair, to judge a man by his past. Or to judge a girl by hers, for that matter.'

Alyce flinched.

'You don't ask me about how I came to be here, and I won't ask you how you could possibly know so much about barberry, and horsetail, and all the rest.' He grinned, wider than ever now. 'Mrs Thomson speaks freely with me, Alyce. We are very close. But there is one thing we have always disagreed upon. She does not think that women and girls like you really exist. But I know.' He tapped the side of his head. 'I know what you are, *strega*.'

Alyce looked at her feet, her head swimming. She was drunk, and confused, and a little angry, but with whom she could not say.

'Do not worry yourself!' said Vitali, sitting back and laughing just as easily as he had done when she first came through the door. 'I do not think ill of your kind. This is not a reason why we cannot work together. It will make you even more useful to me, I think.' He put a hand on her shoulder, and she smiled weakly.

'Now we know,' he continued, setting his empty goblet on the table, 'that we are both as sinister as each other. Yes? Yes. We shall work very well together.'

Alyce scrunched her eyes to try and clear her head. 'What kind of work do you have planned for me?'

'Many things,' said Vitali gleefully. 'In time, perhaps you can help me prepare my elixirs. But most of all I need you for my *spettacolo*!'

'Your what?'

'My show. My *spectacle*.' He took his time over the word. 'Some of your countrymen, they do not know what is good for them, and they need to see something wondrous, something miraculous, before they will think to buy my wares.'

'I don't see how I could persuade anyone to do business with you—'

'Lorenzo Vitali does not persuade,' he said, wagging his finger. 'He *amazes*. He *enchants*. I think you could help me in this, no? Maybe you could be a part of my little show?'

Alyce shrugged. 'Maybe.' She was prepared to agree to

anything if it meant she could escape his lodgings and get to Bankside.

'Enough of this for now. Let us see if you have succeeded in your first task. What has dear Mrs Thomson sent me today?'

She picked the basket up from the floor and handed it to Vitali, who took it over to his workbench. One by one he opened up the pouches and poked around inside, humming with satisfaction. When he came to the last bag, the one that Mrs Thomson had not labelled, he let out a long 'Ah', and immediately locked it in a small wooden strongbox.

'Very good!' he said, turning round to Alyce again. 'Please give Mrs Thomson my thanks.'

'I think she would prefer coin . . .'

'I think so too,' said Vitali, laughing. 'How much does she want from my coffers this time?'

'I have the prices here,' she said, reaching into the front pocket of her dress and retrieving the folded parchment. 'I hope they are what you were expecting.'

The mountebank took the crumpled document in between his thumb and forefinger and spread it out flat on the table. From the look on his face, Alyce knew immediately that something was wrong.

'Is it not correct?' she asked, getting up from the stool.

Vitali turned very slowly, eyes still scanning the words he held in front of him. His brow was more expressive than she had seen in the whole time she had been there.

'What is this?'

The letter. She'd given him the letter from her mother.

They must have got mixed up in her pocket, and somewhere between The Swan and here the seal that Solomon had reattached had fallen off. Her sweating fingers fumbled in the front of her dress again, and pulled out a second piece of parchment. Sure enough, it was covered in numbers scrawled by Mrs Thomson.

'I'm sorry, that's not for you . . . This is the . . . Can I please have that . . .?'

Alyce swallowed her heart back down to where it should have been. Vitali clapped in triumph.

'I knew it! I said it, did I not? *Strega!*' Alyce could only guess what that word meant, but she had a fairly good idea. 'But if I were you, I would keep something like this to myself, yes?'

'Yes I know. I didn't mean to give it to you—'

'You must be careful. Some people see this, they are not as kind as Vitali.'

'Can you . . . read it? Do you know what it says?'

Vitali shook his head. 'No. But I know the language of sorcery when I see it. The question is: which sorcerer do you give this to, hmmm?'

Alyce stared into his womanly, long-lashed eyes, and knew that the wine was making her far more trusting than she should have been, but decided to tell him anyway. He might even be able to help her.

'It's for John Dee. He's not a sorcerer. He's an executioner.'

'A what?'

'An executioner. A hangman.'

'Oh,' said Vitali. 'I see.' And then he began to roar with laughter so violently she thought he would bring all of London Bridge crumbling down on top of them.

'What?' Her skin prickled – she knew when she was being mocked. Still he rocked with glee. 'Tell me!'

'I am sorry,' he said when he'd finally caught his breath. 'Only . . . To imagine . . . John Dee, a hangman! I think he really *would* hang you if he heard you say these things!' He dabbed at the corner of his eye with a handkerchief.

'Well? Who is he?'

'You mean *Doctor* John Dee. The *great* Doctor John Dee – magician, astrologer, philosopher, alchemist, mathematician, and whatever else.' He rolled his eyes in feigned boredom. 'He is an advisor to Queen Elizabeth herself, and will tell you this whenever he has the chance. Hummm. Yes. Vitali and John Dee are not the greatest of friends.'

The certainty with which the mountebank was speaking made Alyce feel hopeful, in a way that she hadn't for a very long time. Advisor to the *Queen* . . . So Solomon and Mrs Thomson had been right all along.

'Then . . . What's this hangman business?'

'Ah,' said Vitali, obviously enjoying his new omniscience. 'The hangman is not a person, Alyce. The Hangman is a tavern. On Bankside. Although, it is not like most taverns. Its patrons are . . . well, people like you and me, Alyce. And Doctor Dee. Strange people. Different people.' He laughed once more. 'You plan to go there today?'

'Yes.'

'Alone?'

'Yes.'

He took a deep breath. 'No. I forbid it. Too dangerous.'

'You aren't my father, signor,' she said hotly, 'so I don't think you can forbid me anything.'

'Do you even know where to look for it?'

'You said. Bankside.'

'Ha! Then I wish you good luck. The Hangman, the Black Tavern which has remained hidden from the Church, from the state, from kings and queens for two hundred years; you, young Alyce, will find it like *that*, yes?' He snapped his fingers.

She thought for a moment. It was true, she had been rather optimistic – make that foolish – about finding her way there without any help.

'Then come with me,' she said eventually. 'If you won't let me go alone. I'll make you a deal. If you take me to The Hangman, I'll help you however I can with your spectacle. And I'll tell you everything I know about these herbs you are mixing.'

'Perhaps the first thing, yes.' Vitali's eyes narrowed. 'And if I don't take you?'

She shrugged. 'If you don't, you will have to find yourself another witch to be your apprentice.' Her face and chest warmed as the last words left her lips, and it wasn't because of the wine this time.

The mountebank regarded her carefully, and then held out his hand with a smile.

'Alyce,' he said, 'it would be my pleasure.'

HOPKINS

'Harper? Young lad?'

Hopkins nodded. The actor's voice had boomed when he was performing, but the audience had long since wandered away and now he was quiet and tense. He continued packing up the troupe's costumes in an attempt to avoid eye contact.

'He's with Sussex's Men. We don't have anything to do with them. We just do the inn yards.' He gestured around the muck-strewn square. 'They're performing at Court, for Queen Elizabeth herself. Got themselves a proper patron.'

'At Court?' said Hopkins.

'Whitehall Palace. Good luck getting in *there*.'

The Doctor could probably get him access to the palace, thought Hopkins, but it would be an unnecessary complication.

'What else do you know about him? Where does he live? Where does he go? Taverns? Brothels?'

The player straightened up, and was still no higher than Hopkins' chin. 'Master Blount!' he called. 'You played with Sussex's Men once upon a time. Gentleman here looking for the Harper boy.'

Another man left the wagon he was loading and approached warily. 'Ay, I was with Sussex's Men till that Adams knave threw me out. Solomon Harper joined a few weeks before I left. You'll have a job speaking to him now, they're—'

'At Whitehall, I know. Where else might we cross paths?'

The man gulped, and Hopkins knew he was looking at Caxton properly for the first time. 'He – he was always more of an errand boy back then. They'd send him to the market, send him to tailors and cobblers for the costumes.'

'You'll need to be more specific than that.'

'There was . . . there was an inn he used to visit a lot. Off Little East Cheap. It was a filthy place, but he knew the innkeeper. The Swan, it's called. When he wasn't with the company, he was there with her. Like his mother, she was.'

Hopkins laughed, and Master Blount looked confused. 'I can assure you,' he said, 'she was nothing like his mother.'

XIII

It was nearly midday by the time they'd crossed the bridge, and the sky was a clear, endless blue. Alyce very quickly realized that blending into a crowd was impossible with Vitali at her side, flouncing through the unwashed masses in his glittering cloak and bowing ostentatiously to virtually every woman who crossed his path. Still, she did her best to walk a few paces behind him, and kept scanning the crowds for anyone who might be following. The witchfinders forever hovered on the fringes of her imagination.

Bankside was just as busy as the centre of London, but felt different, more ramshackle, more desperate. Here the shopkeepers regarded them with suspicious eyes, and Alyce began to feel a little homesick for the warmth and safety of The Swan.

A few hundred yards further up, she suddenly heard the roar of a crowd, interspersed with unpleasant, vindictive laughter. That was followed by another, lower roar – that of an animal.

Vitali halted and made a sour face.

'Bear-baiting,' he said, when she had caught up. 'I do not know why you English take such delight in it.'

'That was a *bear*?'

'Fighting for its life, no doubt.'

'But . . . why?'

Vitali shrugged. 'For sport.'

Alyce had never seen a bear before. The most fearsome inhabitants of the woods around her house in Fordham had been foxes and badgers, but even those her mother had treated with the utmost respect. *Lots to be learned from animals*, she'd said. *They see things more clearly than we do.*

The beast moaned again. Up ahead, she could see the crowd pressed around the baiting ring, jeering and cackling. There were stray dogs too, probably drawn by the smell of the blood, weaving around between their legs. She felt an awful pain in her chest.

'I don't want to see it. Can we go another way?' she asked.

'You will not have to,' answered Vitali. 'We leave the street here.'

He took her hand and ushered her out of the thorough-fare. The bright midday sun disappeared, and Alyce found herself in a damp, murky alleyway that led down to the waterfront. Above her loomed a building whose timbers were so warped, whose facade was leaning at such an angle that she felt like the slightest breath of wind would cause the whole thing to collapse. The place was a wreck. It looked like it had been dredged up from the bottom of the river.

The door was a greying slab of oak that was beginning to rot around its edges, and the windows either side were blank and dusty. There was no sign of life inside. The only thing that suggested it might have been a tavern was a fraying hangman's noose, swaying ominously over the entrance and serving as its sign.

'Once we are inside,' Vitali said, 'I think it best if I talk. Yes?'

Alyce wasn't listening. She'd heard something else. A croaking. A ruffling of feathers. She looked up.

The raven was there again, perched on top of the tavern's crooked gables. She couldn't see its strange, mismatched eyes, but the silhouette was so bedraggled, it had to be the same one as from The Swan. She realized suddenly she was holding her breath. What if she lost control again?

Vitali gave the door a shove, and it groaned on its ancient hinges. Before Alyce could say anything, he pulled her inside. The raven watched her go, and its feathers shivered.

The room on the other side smelt of decay. It was dark and almost completely empty, apart from a table and chairs, on which were placed a fat, dribbling candle, a plate and some stale bread. A mouse was tentatively exploring some scattered crumbs.

Sitting in one of the chairs was a very old, very crumpled-looking woman. She looked like Mrs Thomson would thirty years in the future, Alyce thought.

The door closed behind them with a thud.

'Good afternoon, Grissel! Would you be so kind as to allow us safe passage to the tavern?'

The mouse froze, its nose twitching; then it abandoned the bread and disappeared up one of the old woman's sleeves. She stirred, and opened a pair of milky eyes.

Vitali gasped. 'My lady, you look so young, so radiant!'

She tottered over to them, peered at Alyce, sniffed, and then slapped Vitali across the face.

'Your poisons don't work, you painted fool,' she said, her voice much stronger than Alyce had expected it to be.

The mountebank looked like he was about to start weeping. 'My lady, you do me a disservice . . .'

'I expect your cure-alls to be a load of old swill, but I would've thought you could *at least* mix up something that can kill a man. Not that difficult, is it?' She directed this last remark at Alyce, as though looking for agreement.

'Please, your demands were not quite so simple . . .' Now Vitali looked at Alyce as well, embarrassment etched on his perfect oval face.

'Now all my son-in-law does is roll around in his bed all day, clutching his innards. He's worse than ever.'

Vitali splayed his hands helplessly. 'I don't know what to say.'

There was an uncomfortable moment when it became clear that the old woman was not going to budge.

Alyce cleared her throat. 'What did you give him?'

'It was a blend,' said Vitali, knowing he was on thin ice. 'Nightshade and wither root. My lady Grissel wished for the poison to do its work in the night, many hours after it had been imbibed.'

'I put it in his ale, like you said,' piped up the old woman.

'There's the problem, then,' said Alyce. 'The ale will have diluted the nightshade. And the wither root only delays the effects of a poison if it's a dry paste. Might make his hair fall out, though.'

'How d'you know all this, girl?' Her dull, pupil-less eyes still seemed to twinkle, somehow.

'My mother taught me.' A sober voice at the back of her head told her to keep her mouth shut. The woman was a stranger, and Alyce had already said too much.

'Well, my dear, seems I should be doing business with your mother instead of this great dullard.'

'My mother's dead.'

'Oh my.' The old woman pulled her old, tatty shawl around her a little tighter. 'Forgive me. And here I am, ninety years old and still taking up space in the world.'

'That's all right.'

Vitali seemed happy that he was no longer the focus of the conversation, and exhaled slowly.

'So, then, my young apothecary. What would you suggest?' The mouse who had crawled into her sleeve suddenly reappeared at the neckline of her dress, sniffed the air, and hid again. Alyce tried to ignore it.

'Well, some sort of mixture of hemlock and amanita, but—' She stopped, suddenly realizing that she might very well be consigning a total stranger to a very painful, protracted death. She wished she hadn't said anything – at this rate she was going to make quite a name for herself as a murderess.

'Do you have those?' snapped the old woman at Vitali.

'I think, perhaps, I do . . .'

'Good. Then get me some of that. And make sure she's around when you're making it up, she seems to know a hell of a lot more about killing people than you do.'

Alyce's skin crawled when she said that. The back of her skull began to itch guiltily. She'd always assumed her mother had taught her about such poisons purely as a warning, but now she wondered: had *she*, her mother, killed someone in the past? Alyce had never thought to ask her while she was alive.

Vitali bowed. 'As you wish, my lady. A thousand apologies. And of course, I will give you a very special price.'

'No,' said the old woman. 'You won't put a price on it at all.'

'Yes, yes, most fair.' Vitali's strange, fixed smile had been distorted into a grimace over the course of the conversation.

'Excellent. Well, then, I suppose I should let you in.'

From underneath her tatty old shawl, the crone produced a single, simple-looking key. She went and unlocked the plain wooden door behind her. There was a gust of warm air that smelt of wine and ale and incense and stranger, richer things.

'In you both go.' She looked at Alyce. 'Better pray there aren't any more of his customers down there waiting for him.' She frowned all of a sudden. '*You, stop wriggling or be out with you!*'

It was an alarming few seconds before Alyce realized she was talking to the mouse.

The stairs went down at least three storeys, the atmosphere getting warmer and damper the deeper they went, until it felt like they were under the Thames itself.

'Poisons, signor? Really?'

'They are only one small part of my work, I assure you. When I came to England I was very poor. I needed to use all of my skills to make enough coin to survive.'

'Skills? You're helping people kill each other.' Alyce thought back to the black pouch with the strange smell that Mrs Thomson had given her. 'For his *special* customers.' So *she'd* known too.

He shrugged.

'Death is the only business that a man like me can rely on in a city like this. There is always demand.' He turned to her at last. 'I am sorry if you feel I misled you. But we agreed that we both had secrets. Did we not?'

That was true. She'd killed someone too – had personally driven the dagger into his back. She couldn't work out whether that was better or worse than what Vitali did.

When they reached the bottom, Alyce was faced with a long, low-ceilinged common room that sprawled, warren-like, in all directions. The walls were illuminated by braziers that emitted a strange reddish glow, steadier and softer than firelight, but most of the patrons had tucked themselves away in dark corners. The whole place seemed to have been designed for people to disappear into.

'Welcome to The Hangman!' said Vitali, his voice

echoing more loudly than Alyce would have liked. 'Come, let us find somebody who might answer your questions. I have some more business to attend to, while we are here.'

While Vitali set off in search of a free table, Alyce skulked in a damp corner. Fragments of a muttered conversation drifted to her from the shadows, a man and a woman, and she couldn't help eavesdropping. One of them seemed tense. Alyce held her breath, to hear better.

'You're being hysterical,' said the woman.

'You mark my words. There'll be slaughter. I've never known the world so divided.'

'Witches have always been divided. *People* have always been divided. Everyone wants different things, and every-one thinks they know best. That's human nature. We'll all just rub along unhappily with each other, like we always have.'

'This is different.' The man slurped at his drink. 'Mary Stuart, the Queen of Scots. They love her. Her supporters are everywhere. And I don't just mean Catholics, or the Scots, or the French – I mean *our* kind of people.'

'You read too many pamphlets.'

'If she unseats Elizabeth, you know how she'll deal with her enemies.'

'That damned Scottish woman is in prison! Her cause is lost. Having a few witches on her side isn't going to help her.'

A pause.

'You haven't heard?'

'I'm not interested in your conspiracy theories,' said the woman wearily.

Alyce suddenly felt Vitali grab at her elbow and drag her over to his table. *What? What hasn't she heard?* She strained to catch the man's reply, but their conversation was lost in the hum of the other drinkers and Vitali's incessant babbling.

She sat at one of the stools, peering across the room, but the couple were sunk in a pool of darkness. A serving girl finally appeared in front of her and blocked her view entirely.

'Can I get you two something?'

With her pale marble face and a chaotic mass of black hair, the girl could have been Solomon's sister. Alyce felt loneliness creep back into her chest.

'Two cups of Rhenish,' Vitali said pleasantly, inclining his head. The maid gave a coy smile and swept away.

Alyce again tried to spy the pair who had been talking so seriously. They'd disappeared.

'Who are these people?' she asked, turning to Vitali at last.

'All sorts. What they have in common, though, is a desire to *know* things. To explore more than what is in front of their nose. Most people, out there –' he pointed above his head –'they are stupid, because they want to be stupid. Stupid is safe. Stupid is comfortable.'

'So there are witches here?' The couple had mentioned witches. *Our kind of people*, the man had said. Had *they* been witches? Maybe Alyce wasn't as alone as she thought.

'I think so, yes. Also astrologers, alchemists, apothecaries, sometimes – how do you say? – *magi* from far away. We come here to help each other learn, to share our knowledge. And to drink too much. Aha!'

The maid returned with two cups of wine, and some bread and cheese. Alyce was still feeling sick from what she had drunk at Vitali's lodgings, and she hadn't eaten anything since she had left The Swan.

'A thousand thanks, my dove,' said Vitali as the maid set them down on the table. Alyce fell upon the bread like an animal. 'So please you –' he laid a hand on the girl's arm as she turned to leave – 'could you tell us, is Doctor Dee still a patron of this place?'

'Oh yes, signor,' she said, nodding enthusiastically.

'Do you know when we might be able to make his acquaintance? We have some very important business to discuss.'

'Why, he's here now.' Alyce nearly choked on her crust, though whether it was from fear or excitement she wasn't sure. 'He's over in that corner, talking with the foreign gentleman.'

'My dear, you are as courteous as you are beautiful,' said Vitali. The maid laughed as though this was the hundredth time she had heard him say it, and returned to her duties.

Vitali turned to Alyce. 'Well, we have good fortune today! Are you ready?' He stood up abruptly, not waiting for an answer.

She looked over to where the maid had pointed, and saw the darkened outlines of two people, and something glittering being passed between them. One of these was the man her mother had told her to seek. The man she trusted above all others to keep Alyce safe. Why, then, did she feel such a cold sense of foreboding?

'You had better introduce yourself, Alyce. I must speak with one of my customers, but I will be close by. Let me know when you have finished your business.'

She stood up slowly, and felt Vitali place a hand on the small of her back, pushing her gently in the direction of the two other men. She took a few dazed paces, and suddenly she was there, at the table's edge, listening in on their conversation. Vitali had wandered somewhere else. Alyce was alone.

They were not talking in English. Alyce had encountered a few different languages on the streets of London, and Vitali's accent was so thick he may as well have been speaking in his mother tongue, but this was like nothing she had ever heard. It was guttural, and produced odd clicking noises.

The man whom she assumed was Doctor Dee was wearing a plain cloak of black sable that covered his whole body, as though he were a member of the clergy. A small white ruff poked out of the top of the cloak, but most of it was covered by a luxuriant beard that was just beginning to grey. In his hands he held a circular slab of black rock that sparkled beneath its perfectly smooth, polished surface. A mirror of some sort. He was turning it over and inspecting it, back and front.

His companion could not have looked more different. He was dressed rather like Vitali, Alyce thought, the golden threads of his doublet occasionally catching the light as he moved. His hair was like the mountebank's, too – jet-black and oily – but his skin was creased and tanned. He had scars on his face too, she noticed. Not scars from battle, though — these were regular, ordered, patterned even. They had been carved into his face deliberately.

Alyce fumbled nervously in her pocket, folding and unfolding the letter, while they continued to talk. Neither of them had noticed her. She gave a little cough.

The bearded man rounded on her, pinning her where she stood with small, sharp, black eyes under the most unruly pair of eyebrows she had ever seen.

'Yes, I know you are there, child, but you may have noticed that I am choosing not to speak to you.' His companion, the foreign gentleman, regarded her languidly.

'Forgive me—'

'What?'

Alyce's throat felt as though it was stuffed with damp wool. 'Forgive me, sir. I am looking for Doctor Dee.'

'Looking for him? And where do you think he is?'

'I think,' she said slowly, 'you are him.'

'You think? My child, if I were impudent enough to approach Doctor John Dee unbidden, I would at least be certain of his identity first.'

There was silence. This was not going well.

'Well . . . are you?'

The man heaved a great sigh of displeasure. His eyes did not move. His pupils were strangely small, she noticed. 'You are speaking to the man you seek. What could you possibly want of me?'

'I have a letter for you.' Her breath was fluttering as she withdrew the parchment from her dress. 'It is of great importance. To me, at least. And perhaps to you. I'm afraid the seal fell off, but I have it here . . .'

Doctor Dee's brows knotted even more than they already were, and he took the letter and the seal in his wrinkled, stained fingers. He muttered something in that odd, clicking language, and his companion nodded, got up, and left.

'My mother was Ellen Greenliefe. She's dead now. But she told me to come and find you. That you could help me.'

He spent a long time looking closely at the seal, before laying the parchment out flat on the table. Neither he nor Alyce moved. He must have read the message four or five times – the characters obviously made more sense to him than they had to her or Solomon or Vitali. Somewhere in another corner of the tavern, she heard the mountebank's tinkling laughter.

At last, without saying a word, Doctor Dee raised himself out of his chair, dropped the black mirror into a pocket inside his cloak, and laid his hands on Alyce's shoulders. His stern features suddenly broke into a grin.

'My dear girl,' he said. 'I'm so glad we've found you. Please, be seated. We have an awful lot to discuss.'

Alyce thought her heart would burst. She wondered who the man under the beard was. A friend of her mother's? A godparent? A relative? In the dimness of the tavern's light, his smile had suddenly transformed him into the kindly grandfather she'd never had.

She took her seat at his table, while John Dee went and spoke to the serving maid again. She turned her mommet over and over in her fingers while she waited, and when he returned she found yet another drink placed in front of her. She laughed.

'You are very kind, Doctor, but this will be my third cup of wine in as many hours. I don't think I have the constitution.'

'Oh, enough of that, child!' he said, dismissing the suggestion with a wave of his hand. 'Drink up. We must toast to your safe arrival.'

She relented and took a sip. The wine was very sour, and had a metallic aftertaste.

'So . . . Did you know my mother?'

'That is rather an understatement,' he said, and laughed.

'What do you mean?'

'You shall see.' He stared at her expectantly. 'Please, drink.'

Again she raised the cup to her lips. His eyes sparkled.

'Wait . . .' she either said, or thought, she couldn't be sure. Her thoughts became thick and sluggish.

Doctor Dee's face grew dark and distorted, although she could still see his expression was something like delight. She tried to speak again, but her lips and tongue were like lead. The room spun, and she thought she was going to be sick.

The wine . . .

The last thing she felt was her forehead hitting the hard table top.

XIV

The cage in Doctor Dee's lodgings was a lot smaller than Alyce's cell in Bedlam, and even more cramped because of her fellow prisoner. It also smelt worse – it was an unsettling odour, not strong or sewagey, but sinister somehow. She at least knew the source of Bedlam's stench, or could guess at it. This was a smell that didn't belong in the world.

Alyce watched the woman – she assumed it *was* a woman – in the opposite corner. She'd been sitting perfectly still for at least an hour, cross-legged, hands folded in her lap, her grey weed-like hair occasionally trembling in the draught. Runes and symbols and half-formed pictures had been scratched into the floorboards around her in an uneven hand. Alyce knew what she was, even if she didn't know her identity.

Dee's beard emerged from the gloom, followed by the rest of him.

'Not long now, child,' he said, and smiled. There was still something grandfatherly about him, until he licked his lips. 'I hope you will be on better behaviour when your Queen gets here.'

Alyce spat at him, and crawled away from the bars before he could strike her. He wiped the saliva from the hem of his cloak and disappeared among his piles of books, muttering.

She had spent the whole day in captivity, and her rage had nearly spent itself. Now she just felt empty, and desperately cold. Doctor Dee was answering none of her questions, perhaps understandably after she'd bitten him for a second time, and the letter had disappeared into the black folds of his robes. More confusing still was that the Queen was supposedly coming to speak with her. None of it made any sense. Half of her anger was pointed at her mother's ghost.

Why did you send me to this monster? What were you thinking?

Dee's muttering had become more persistent, and more rhythmic. He was now bustling around his workshop lighting a circle of squat, misshapen candles, and as each flame sputtered into life another dark corner of the laboratory was illuminated. Candlelight danced off the polished brass of scientific instruments, and pooled in strange colours around the racks of jars and bottles. A human skull cast grotesque shadows across the floor, almost reaching the bars of Alyce's cage. Different parts of the room shifted in and out of focus, and at no point was it bright enough to see everything at once.

Alyce glanced at the other woman. Still as stone.

Another light appeared, a cold, pale sun that hovered in mid-air and seemed to make the candle flames wilt. Doctor Dee withdrew, whispering, into the darkness. It was witch-craft, Alyce knew, but not like any that she had ever seen when she had lived with her mother. There was no roaring fire here. No scent of earth and foliage. No song. Just silence, and that sharp, vinegary tang in the air.

The light became a face, its hair pulled tightly back, its features icy and smooth and quite terrifying in their beauty. The face was followed by the tall figure of a woman, a phantom dressed in pearls and rich fabrics.

The candles were snuffed out.

'You are not much of a host, Doctor,' said the woman, in a voice that seemed to be summoned from hundreds of miles away. 'Why do you have the poor girl cooped up like a dog?'

Dee cleared his throat from the corner of the room. 'Forgive me, Your Majesty – I thought it safer to—'

'She is our guest, Doctor, not our prisoner.' The woman drifted forwards until she was in front of the cage. 'And even if she *were* a prisoner, lock and key are not necessarily going to keep a witch from running away, are they? They tried that with me.'

'Your Majesty,' said Doctor Dee, something like awe crossing his face. 'You are . . . at liberty?'

Her smile was like a sliver of broken glass. 'And sailing to London as we speak, Doctor.'

'But your gaoler, Shrewsbury . . . Does he not know?'

'Shrewsbury is still dutifully hosting a woman whom he believes to be Mary, Queen of Scots. In fact, she is one of my ladies-in-waiting, an apprentice who has served me well and deserves the luxuries of Shrewsbury's hospitality. The swap was made when I went to take the waters at Buxton. A simple enchantment was all that was required.'

The Doctor clapped his hands and fawned: 'Oh, marvellous cunning, Your Majesty!'

Alyce put all the pieces together. 'You're her,' she said, crawling forward and clasping the cold metal. 'You're Mary Stuart.'

The phantom inclined her head a fraction.

Then Alyce turned to Doctor Dee. 'You work for Queen Elizabeth, though.'

'The Doctor had a change of heart,' said Mary. 'Elizabeth proved something of an obstacle to his research.'

'So that's two women you've betrayed,' said Alyce, feeling some of the old heat return to her belly. 'Elizabeth and my mother.'

Mary Stuart laughed. 'Please, Doctor, unlock the cage. She'll break the bars if we don't let her out soon.'

The old man picked up a key on a chain from his workbench. He rattled it in the door of the tiny prison, and then stepped back quickly as though releasing a starved wild animal.

Alyce came out on cold hands and bruised knees, leaving her cellmate behind her. When she got to her feet she was still a head shorter than the phantom woman in front of her. She found herself staring through the transparent sinews of Mary Stuart's neck to the scientific apparatus behind. She shivered, all ideas of escape draining out of her.

'She's right about you, Doctor Dee. You're a born turn-coat. I wouldn't be surprised if you were plotting to betray me too.' The Doctor spluttered something through his beard. 'Yes. She's quite astute, this one. Quite canny. Considering how and where she was brought up.'

'You don't know anything about me.'

'On the contrary Alyce, I know more about you than you do. Your mother and I were firm friends,' she said. 'Once upon a time.'

The spectral face smiled again, and turned to look at Doctor Dee, as though there were some joke that Alyce was not party to. For a nauseating moment, Alyce considered the possibility that her mother really was in league with this witch queen, with Dee, that this was what she had intended all along.

'She's dead,' said Alyce.

'I know,' said Mary. 'Poor Ellen. It was not my intention, believe me, but these witchfinders do get carried away. They do a lot more than *finding*, don't they? Yes, poor woman. I would have them apologize to you in person, Alyce, but I'm told that even now they are out on the streets of London trying to hunt you down and make up for their previous failings.'

So the witchfinders, Doctor Dee, and now Mary were all part of the same merry band. She would have thrown herself at the Queen of Scots and Dee, clawed out their eyes, were she not so paralysed with rage and sorrow for her foolish, deceived mother. Ellen had sent her daughter straight to her murderers.

'Is it your *intention* to kill me?' she said at last, forcing the words through a cold, tight throat.

'Goodness, no, child,' said Mary, extending a translucent hand to smooth her hair, and bringing out Alyce's scalp in goose pimples. 'We are not barbarians. I just want to talk.'

'Talk?'

'Yes. That is all. A conversation between two like minds.'

'We aren't like-minded.'

'Not yet, perhaps, no. But I am hoping we will be when you have heard what I have to say. I am very much hoping you will choose to work with us, rather than against us.'

Alyce suddenly remembered the snatch of conversation she'd heard in The Hangman. *They love her. Her supporters are everywhere.* Was this Queen Mary's attempt at winning her allegiance? She had a strange way of going about it. Alyce laughed out loud: a sad, empty laugh.

'You killed my mother. And you hounded me out of Bedlam. You've kidnapped me and kept me in a cage all day. And now you would like us to be friends?'

'If that is possible, I would like it very much.' The black gaze of the woman's gaping eyes seemed to strip Alyce's flesh away from her.

'No,' was all she managed to say.

'No?' said Mary calmly. 'I see. Perhaps you already have enough friends? Or perhaps you are perfectly able to survive on your own?'

Alyce didn't reply.

'Witches have few allies, Alyce, and fewer friends. We should be wise enough to support each other.'

'You *killed* my mother. How was that supporting her?'

'A terrible mistake, and one that will not go unpunished.' She paused. 'And one which might yet be undone.'

'Undone?'

'How much did Ellen teach you of the Craft, Alyce?'

'The Craft?'

'Witchcraft. Sympathy. Prophecy.' She paused. 'Necromancy.'

'A little,' said Alyce slowly, sensing a trap, but not knowing where it lay. 'Some herblore. Some sympathetic magic. And I know about necromancy... about the Other Side.'

'Ah.' Mary's sigh ruffled some of the parchment behind her. 'The Other Side. And what did she say about that?'

'It's where the dead go. The other side of what we can see. She talked a lot about balance, keeping the balance between this world and the other. I never really understood what she meant.'

Mary nodded. 'No, you wouldn't have. You have only just come of age. A terrible shame to lose her at such a crucial time – you must have so many questions.'

Alyce thought of her fainting fit in The Swan. There was a great deal she didn't understand.

'Not just a shame,' Queen Mary continued. 'An irony too. If she had lived a little longer, she might have taught you how to bring her back from that place.'

Something lurched behind Alyce's ribs. 'You don't mean that.'

'I do, my dear child. It's all very well Ellen talking about balance, but the world doesn't *feel* very balanced, does it?

Feels like the odds are stacked rather heavily in Death's favour, does it not? All our loved ones passing over to the Other Side, and not one of them coming back. Ellen might have been happy to accept that state of affairs, as are many others. But some of us are less content. A true witch can not only commune with the dead, but also take control of Death *itself*. And if we wish someone to return to the land of the living, we can make it so.'

'But that's not . . . natural.' Alyce remembered the briefest glance that she had given the stake as she had escaped Fordham, the charred figure still tied to it, barely recognizable as a person. What on earth would it look like to revive her?

Mary's face darkened a little. 'Natural? According to whom? It is we who define what is natural. We *are* nature, Alyce.'

Something about those words resonated. Despite the whispers in the village, from her and her mother's point of view it was the villagers themselves who were the outsiders, the odd ones, the unnatural ones.

'Why are you telling me all this? What do you want with me?'

'Because, like I said, we need to be of one mind. I would like us to be friends. And I would like to count upon your support.'

Mary's phantom seemed to grow brighter as she spoke. Alyce could see the pale blue light reflecting in Doctor Dee's eyes.

'Go on,' said Alyce.

'The time is coming when I will replace Elizabeth as Queen of England,' she said. 'I will be restored to the Scottish throne. I will be Queen of Spain or France, or both, once I am free of my halfwit husband and able to marry again. Think upon what it means, Alyce. The greatest union in Europe, with a *witch queen* at its head. A queen who will conquer not just the nation's living enemies, but who will *conquer Death* for her subjects. My claim to the throne is not a matter of petty, personal ambition, as the pamphlets and the gossip-mongers would have you believe. It is for the good of all mankind.'

'And what about *our* kind? Is it for the good of witches too? So far I haven't felt the benefits of your mission. My mother certainly didn't.'

Mary smiled.

'I shall lead our kind out of the shadows. Out of the dirt and the shame we have lived in for millennia. Listen: when I was Queen of Scotland, I spent years concealing my true nature. I hid myself. Denied myself. For fear of a backlash, not just against me, but against witchfolk. A lot of good that did. And now my ingrate of a son has supplanted me. My father, my father-in-law, my uncle, two husbands: they all died around me, while I was forbidden to practise the arts that would have saved them.' She gazed through Alyce. '*En ma fin est mon commencement.* Do you know what that means?'

She shook her head.

'*In my end is my beginning.* A family motto. I have just decided to take it more seriously than most. I am offering people hope, Alyce. When I take the throne, I will banish

Death from the world of men, and they will worship me for it. Worship *us*.'

Alyce considered this before she replied. The woman's arrogance was staggering. But to live in a world where she wasn't under constant suspicion, where she was exalted even – that would be something.

'You may have a job convincing your subjects of that, Your Majesty,' she said in the end. 'You've yet to convince me.'

'You will be persuaded, Alyce, I assure you. If you'll allow me a demonstration.'

'What do you mean?'

'A demonstration of what I can perform. What *we* can perform, together. Join us, and I will bring your mother back for you.'

In that moment's pause, the crooked timbers of Doctor Dee's house sighed as the wind passed through them. Somewhere in the back of the laboratory, a pile of papers stirred and fell to the floor. Alyce could hear Dee's breathing too, strained and nasal.

It was nonsense, surely. You couldn't bring people back from the dead. The world didn't work like that. She was fairly sure. But then . . . what if it were true? She'd give anything, absolutely anything, to see her mother again.

There was something else bothering her too.

'You still haven't explained *why*,' she said.

'Because when I am Queen I shall need allies.'

'No. Stop talking about yourself. I don't mean that. I mean, why *me*? Why go to so much trouble to get *my* support? Why am I so special?'

'I simply care for your well-being Alyce—'

She stopped. The face of infinite sympathy that Queen Mary was wearing suddenly drifted and changed, like ink clouding water. Then it hardened, and her frown was a terrible thing to behold.

There was a groan. The wind was not whistling outside the laboratory, but inside. From behind Alyce, the woman in the cage was drawing one long, rattling breath.

'She lies she lies she lies she lies she lies . . .' came the chant, broken and manic, and only then did Alyce realize this was the same inmate of Bedlam who had spoken to her when she was looking for the letter. How on earth had she ended up here?

'Shut her mouth, Doctor,' Mary commanded. Dee leapt from his stool and fumbled with the key.

'Vile thing. I have seen what you are. Seen what you would do.' The madwoman's fingernails scratched the floor-boards as she crawled out of the cage. 'Be gone, Alyce. This one is an outcast. She brings only pestilence. She would see the world devoured.'

The instruments and vessels on the Doctor's workbench began to totter and roll and smash, and the man himself froze, torn between stopping the woman and saving his work.

'*Silence her!*' screamed Mary, and her luminous skin seemed to evaporate and reveal the lines of her bones underneath.

'She would have us all as her slaves,' said the woman.

'The living and the dead. The Other Side, bent to her will. To the will of the black book.' A storm issued from her mouth. The great curtains of her hair were suddenly blown back, and Alyce was able to see her face clearly for the first time. It looked so young, so gentle. Tired too – purple rings around her eyes, like Solomon's.

Just like Solomon's.

'But the dead see you, false witch. Just as I see you.' There was a moment of almost perfect stillness, of held breath. And then, in a small, human voice: 'They're here.'

Her words cleaved the air. The spectre of Mary, Queen of Scots seemed to be rent into shreds in the gale, and Doctor Dee was thrown backwards into a bookcase, whose leather tomes tumbled heavily on to his head. Beams were wrenched from the ceiling and crashed into the workbench; sections of the roof collapsed, revealing the purple light of dusk overhead.

The woman slumped on to the floorboards in the pool of her hair, her body emptied of breath and life.

Alyce saw the Doctor getting unsteadily to his feet, rubbing his head and picking splinters out of his beard. Somewhere in the clouds of dust, the faintest outline of Mary's gown was floating among the timbers. Alyce had already started down the stairs into the shadows of the house when she heard Mary's voice, like a surgeon's blade:

'*Get her.*'

Alyce bounded down the steps two or three at a time, stumbling on the last few and tripping head-first into a wrought-iron strongbox on the ground floor. Pain blossomed above her right eye.

Don't stop, stupid!

She hauled herself upright, steadying herself on the passage wall. The throb in her head was nauseating. A stream of blood stung her eye and then pattered on to the floor as she staggered to the front door.

The air felt freezing, and painfully clean, when she exploded out into the road. She spun around, panting. She didn't recognize anything. *Mortlake*, she remembered faintly. Vitali had told her Doctor Dee lived upstream from London. She looked around for somewhere to hide, her head still whirling in the opposite direction to her body, making her twice as sick as she was already. The village was just marshland and few drab houses, with none of the crowds and alleyways and hidden corners that would have helped her inside the city walls.

She tried to think.

The river.

Alyce ran unsteadily, hearing thunderous footsteps inside the house behind her. A little further down the road, beyond Doctor Dee's carriage, was a jetty where a tilt boat had been moored. The rowers were nowhere to be seen – night was fast descending, their day's work was probably done. She reached the riverbank, glancing over her shoulder just as Doctor Dee himself stumbled out of the entrance hall after her. He was slow and still dazed from the collision with his books.

Come on Alyce, don't tell me you can't outrun somebody's grandfather.

The mooring rope was thick and tightly knotted to the stake that rose out of the river. More than that — it was so old and so weathered that the fibres had started to fuse with each other, to melt into the wood itself. When she picked at it, she just came away with damp, foul-smelling hemp under her fingernails. Her hands were numb too, and wouldn't do what she told them to.

She could hear Doctor Dee's heavy tread. The rope wasn't loosening at all.

Alyce turned, squinting through the blood that covered her right eye, and saw his grave, implacable face. His beard raged around him like a snowstorm.

There was no other option. She climbed into the tilt boat and scrambled under the canvas covering to the bows, which pitched violently in the cold waters. Then she clutched her mommet, held her breath, and jumped.

HOPKINS

The Swan's common room fell completely silent when Hopkins and Caxton stepped through the door. That always pleased him. He took a moment to taste the air and savour the patrons' fear.

'Good afternoon, gentlemen,' said the innkeeper, standing stout and red-faced next to the fireplace. 'Or is it good evening? Neither one nor t'other right now, is it? Can I get you something to eat and drink?' There was a false, forced jolliness in her voice that Hopkins despised. It wasn't working, either – all of her customers were still silently watching Caxton, who hovered ghostlike at the door, as though forbidden from entering the homes of the living.

'Neither, thank you. But we would like to speak with one of your patrons. A Solomon Harper.'

The woman frowned and scratched her head, a worse actor than those he'd questioned in the inn yard of The Popinjay. 'Never heard that name before, I don't think.'

'Are you quite sure?' said Hopkins pleasantly. 'He may have come here in the company of a girl who we would very much like to speak to.'

The innkeeper shrugged. 'Don't get many girls around here, neither. Unless you mean Martha. *Martha!*'

Her bellowing was enough to break the spell cast over the common room, although the conversations that were struck up now lacked ease and laughter.

The girl emerged sullenly from the kitchen, her dark, fine hair stuck with sweat to her forehead. She wiped her nose on her sleeve.

'What?' she said.

'That isn't her,' interrupted Hopkins. 'We are looking for an Alyce Greenliefe. Very short red hair. Shaven-headed. From her time in Bedlam.'

The innkeeper threw a glance at the serving girl, which he noted, and then bustled over, wiping her hands on her apron.

'Bedlam? Well, I'm sure I don't know who it is you're talking about. Not seen Solomon round here for weeks, and if I'd served a lunatic I'm sure I'd remember it.'

'I see,' said Hopkins, his eyes still on Martha. 'This is a shame. Well, since we've had a wasted journey, I suppose I should stay for an ale after all.'

'I am sorry, sir. Was the girl a relative of yours?'

Hopkins smiled. 'A relative, no. Her mother and I were very close friends, though.'

The innkeeper looked at him oddly, at least three different expressions fighting for control of her face.

'Well,' she said at last, 'like you say, things won't seem quite so bad after an ale or two. Would your friend like something too?'

Hopkins shrugged. 'Possibly. He can't say one way or the other. I think he'll be happy to stay outside.'

'Very well.' The innkeeper smiled unconvincingly and went back to the kitchen, and Martha followed her, muttering something.

Hopkins surveyed the other patrons. Everyone was taking stiff, tentative sips at their drinks, snatching glances at him over the rims of their tankards. Their eyes darted away again as soon as they met his. He smiled back at them and straightened the pearl buttons on his doublet.

While he was getting the measure of every man in the inn, Martha came over and threw his mug of ale heavily down on to the table. The frothy stuff sloshed over the brim and nearly soaked his lap.

She said nothing. He rather liked how unapologetic she was. Just as she turned to go, he took her gently by the arm.

'Careful, sir,' she said, 'it's not that kind of place.' She didn't try to move away, though.

'What does she pay you?'

'Eh?'

'The innkeeper? What does she pay you?'

'Mrs Thomson? Not enough, by half.'

'How much? Tell me.'

'Sixpence. A day. And she feeds me.'

'Sixpence,' said Hopkins, digging into the purse that hung off his belt. 'Then how about I keep things competitive, and offer you a gold sovereign for your services.'

'Services?'

'Tell us where the girl is. We both know your employer is lying.'

Martha's eyes widened, the bright, yellow coin reflected in them. Then she blinked.

'Double it,' she said.

Hopkins laughed. 'I beg your pardon?'

'Double it. Two sovereigns, and I'll take you straight to her.'

'Look in her pockets!'
'Don't feel right about this Jack . . .'

'Leave her then. More for me.'

'She's still breathing, look.'

A pair of hands rolled Alyce on to her back, and groped around the sodden folds of her dress. The fingers closed around something and withdrew.

'Well, *there's* a pretty thing . . .'

'*Look*, Jack, she ain't *dead*.'

'What are you talking about? That's the deadest face I ever seen.'

Alyce forced her eyes open. Two faces, dirty, unshaven, were peering down at her. The man closest to her, Jack, she assumed, was counting the coins he'd stolen in his palm – the payment from Vitali to Mrs Thomson. He stopped when she started to move.

'By God, you're right! This fish is still wriggling!' He

showed her a mouthful of brown teeth. 'We'll have to throw it back in then, won't we?'

Grinning, he knelt down to haul Alyce up from under her shoulders.

No, she thought, *not now. Not like this.* She squirmed clumsily in his arms. A dizziness overtook her – she was cold, she was tired, the wound on her head still felt raw – but there was something else too. The world throbbed and rippled. Figures crowded around her, hundreds, thousands, darkly luminous. She heard their voices. Urgent, whispering, dead voices.

She struggled free of the man's grasp and lurched to her feet, fearing the enclosing shadows more than she feared him. Then, as though her movements weren't her own, she seized him by the wrists. He gasped as though he had been branded with a hot iron. His face was a mask of horror, but he didn't pull away. Or couldn't.

The other man was backing away down the pier. 'Let her go, she ain't right, this one.'

Alyce felt herself drawn upright, taller than she thought she was. Her attacker's limbs collapsed like dry stalks until he was kneeling in front of her, eyes bulging, mouth agape, his arms still caught in Alyce's fingers.

'Give it to me,' she said. Her voice sounded distant, deeper, slower.

'Do what she says, Jack, she got the Devil in her!'

Jack moaned and swayed on his knees, sounding like a terrified infant.

'Give it to me,' Alyce said again. She released one of

his arms.

The man named Jack opened his fist and dropped the coins on to the boards of the pier.

'No. The other thing.'

He frowned, reached into his leather jerkin and withdrew her mommet, soaked and bedraggled and not looking much like a person any more. He threw it at her feet.

As soon as Alyce let go of his other wrist, he crossed himself and ran like a man hunted into the darkness of the storehouses. His accomplice followed, and the pair of them disappeared.

Her heart slowed, her blood cooled. The sounds and the shapes of the dead were carried away on the breeze, and the pier fell silent. She stared at her hands. What was that feeling, that lightness in her head and chest? It wasn't fear any more – that had passed, leaving this other feeling in its wake. Pride? Power? There was something else mixed in, though – shame? But why should she feel ashamed?

She bent down and picked up the mommet, which was soaked and fraying and missing the lock of hair from its head. The currents of the Thames had done their work. She was suddenly very weak. All of the weight of the day now seemed to fall upon her at once, and she could no longer bear it. She sank on to the wooden walkway and began to cough and shiver violently, a pool of stinking water slowly spreading around her.

It was nearly completely dark now. The lights on London Bridge were reflected prettily in the river, and the docks, while not completely empty, were much more subdued. London seemed almost peaceful.

Alyce's teeth were chattering so uncontrollably that she bit her tongue. She cursed, but the pain and the hot taste of blood woke her up a little. She prodded gingerly at the cut on her eyebrow. What a wreck she was. It seemed the currents had carried her all the way from Mortlake to the Legal Quays – she'd gone under the waves just before London Bridge, and been spat out on the bank with a mouth full of river water and no immediate memory of how she had got there.

Visions of Mary Stuart and Doctor Dee rose to the surface of her swimming head, but she forced them back down. She didn't want to think about them now. She didn't want to think about them ever. She hoped they would simply fade and disappear with time, like an unpleasant dream. All she wanted was dry clothes, something to eat, and maybe a couple of stitches. The Swan couldn't be too far away, if she retraced her steps from the bridge. With any luck – and she must be due some by now – she might still be back in time for supper.

She wondered what sort of mood Mrs Thomson would be in.

Soaked, frozen and barefooted, she trudged in the vague direction of the inn, quietly thankful that she still had the hard callouses on her feet from her time in Bedlam.

After a few minutes' wandering, she emerged on to a broad street that she thought she recognized as Little East Cheap. But every building looked familiar in the half-light.

As she tried to get her bearings, she heard someone coming towards her. Their steps were slow, deliberate, a bit flat-footed.

She peered through the gloom. She would recognize that stride anywhere.

'God's breeches . . .' said Solomon, grabbing her freezing hand. 'What happened to you?'

Alyce looked into his dark, tired eyes and immediately thought of the wretched woman in Doctor Dee's cage. There was no doubt about who she had been. How on earth could she begin to tell him? She should have tried to help her. But she'd left her behind – left her body behind – at the mercy of Dee and Mary. The guilt made her sick and silent.

'Hello?' said Solomon, waving a hand in front of her face. 'What happened? What's the matter?'

'Do you care?' she said at last. It wasn't the answer she had been expecting to come from her mouth, but there it was. 'I haven't seen your face in more than a week.'

'I know. I'm sorry. I'll explain later. Right now, you've got to turn around and walk away.' He pulled her into an alley.

'What?' Alyce's lips were numb from cold, and could barely form the words. 'What are you doing?'

'Saving your life again. What is this,' he said, counting on his fingers, 'the third time? Fourth?'

'Saving my life? I'll die of fever if I don't get back to The Swan before nightfall. In case you hadn't noticed, Solomon, I've had rather an *eventful* day.' She stopped and splayed her sopping wet dress.

He surveyed her. 'Your face . . .'

'My face? What about my face?'

'You're bleeding.'

'*Am* I? I didn't know you were a physician, Solomon.' Oh yes, she was angrier than she'd anticipated.

Solomon shook his head. 'Listen, there'll be plenty of time to make fun of me later. Just come with me. You can't go back to The Swan.'

'Why not?'

'*They* are there. The witchfinders. I was coming to find you when I saw them going into the inn. They're talking to Mrs Thomson right now. Looking for you *and* me.'

The cold on Alyce's skin now burrowed into her heart. A memory flickered into life – Queen Mary had said the witchfinders were still at large on the streets of London, looking for her.

'What did Mrs Thomson say?'

'From what I could hear she did her best to mislead them. But I couldn't get too close, in case they recognized me. It's definitely the same two men. That strange man in the mask. I went round the back, checked the kitchen, checked your bedchamber. I noticed your letter was gone, so I thought maybe you'd gone to Bankside. It was the only thing I could think of.' He pinched at her wet sleeve and frowned. 'You know there's a bridge across the river don't you? It's easier than swimming.'

Alyce couldn't begrudge him trying to lighten the mood. She made an unimpressed half-smile. 'Like you said – making fun can come later.'

'I'll hold you to that. Come on. If we don't get to Ludgate before it closes, I'm not sure we'll have anywhere to sleep tonight. It might even be closed already . . .' He removed his cloak and wrapped it around her shoulders.

'Ludgate?' said Alyce as he set off again through the alleyway. 'We're leaving the city?'

'Yes. I've been thinking. You should stay in my lodgings.'

Alyce suddenly realized she had never thought to ask Solomon where he lived. She tried to picture his home, but based on the evidence of his tatty doublet and moth-eaten hose she could only envisage some poor, damp hovel outside the city walls. But a roof over her head, even a leaking one, would be welcome enough after the day she had endured.

When they reached Thames Street, they turned right and walked westwards across the city without speaking. Alyce occasionally tried to find the words to explain the day she'd had, to talk about Vitali, about Doctor Dee and Mary Stuart. About his mother, kept in a cage like an animal. She'd been *right there*, in Bedlam, with Solomon a matter of yards away in the gatehouse. It was too awful. She thought of her own mother, and of Solomon's, and she wanted to cry, more from frustration than from sorrow. It wasn't a feeling she would wish upon anyone.

I can't tell him, she thought. *I won't tell him. It will ruin him. And he'll hate me for it.*

She stayed quiet, at least for the time being, furiously blinking away the tears before they could appear. Besides, she needed time to digest everything herself, to separate truth from imagination. On top of all of this, her head still felt like it was full of silt from the Thames, and she was putting most of her energy and concentration into simply staying conscious and upright.

London Bridge quickly came and went on their left-hand side, and they continued past the various guildhalls of vintners, joiners and blacksmiths until the spire of St Paul's was just visible over the tops of the houses, silhouetted against the purple sky.

They turned towards it and quickened their pace past the cathedral and the beggars congregating outside. Alyce's heart sank when they saw the great iron portcullis barring their exit from Ludgate, but as they approached they noticed that a handful of the city's watchmen were still clustered around a postern gate, which was still open.

After a little negotiation, and a number of suspicious sideways glances at the barefooted Alyce, they were let through.

'They're probably glad to have a vagabond like me out-side the walls,' said Alyce once they were the other side of the gatehouse, and the air was fresher. 'I must look terrible.'

'Hmmm . . .' Solomon nodded, apparently lost in thought. 'I hadn't really thought of that. You're going to have to dress in something different once we've arrived, or they won't let you in.'

'Let me in? Where? Who are *they*?'

'You'll see when you get there,' he said. Alyce began to sense he was rather enjoying all this secrecy. 'I'll probably need to go inside and fetch you some clothes, you should keep out of sight.' He suddenly stopped, and looked Alyce up and down. 'Yes . . . you're nearly as tall as me. That's good.'

The clouds above them had turned dark and velvety, and it was difficult to see where they were going. The road followed the river, turning sharply south. The houses began to thin out, but up ahead Alyce could see a huge building looming over the water, its monumental towers more sensed than seen in the darkness. There was something threatening about it.

The building grew larger, its elaborate, skeletal stonework emerging from the gloom in greater and greater detail, until they found themselves at the entrance of a broad promenade, with a great complex of halls and towers and arches on their left-hand side. From the other side of the road drifted the hot musk of straw and horse manure, which Alyce assumed was coming from a block of stables.

Up ahead, the road met a gatehouse, guarded by two wardens with halberds. Solomon stopped.

'Well, here we are.' He grinned.

Alyce looked at him blankly. 'Where are we?'

'The Palace of Whitehall.'

'Why?'

'Because this is where I live.'

She shook her head dumbly. 'Solomon, I'm not in the mood . . .'

Solomon laughed. 'Wait here. You can hide in the stables. It'll be warm and nobody will see you. I'll return with some clothes for you in a moment.'

Alyce watched, open-mouthed, as he disappeared

through the gate and loped across the courtyard as confidently as if he owned the place.

Suddenly she felt very exposed and very alone, standing in the deserted road, her dress still damp and clinging to her limbs. Strains of music and raucous laughter drifted over the palace walls, but they didn't sound at all inviting to her ears. She crept into the shadows alongside the stable wall, and found an open doorway to the deeper blackness within.

The snort and thud of the horses in their stalls was something Alyce found reassuring. Their long faces and sparkling black eyes regarded her calmly and without judgement as she crawled into the corner and curled up in the old, dirty straw, rubbing her feet.

While she waited, she started to convince herself again that this was all part of an elaborate joke that Solomon had conceived. Or perhaps worse than a joke. A *trap*. Perhaps he had gone to fetch the palace guards. Or Doctor Dee. Or the Queen herself. Or at least *one* of the queens. She was soon feverish with worry.

But return he did, and alone, after all. She heard him going from stable to stable whispering her name, and she quietly crept from her hiding place. He saw her and waved with the torch he was carrying, which made the horses a little skittish. Alyce came out into the light. Under the other arm he was holding a bundle of clothes.

'Come around the back so you can see what you're putting on,' he said. 'They should fit you.' She saw him bite his lip.

They went around the side of the stable block, out of

sight, where a stony path led from the road to a broad expanse of parkland.

'Whose clothes are these?' asked Alyce.

Solomon let them drop to the ground, and held up a pair of coarse woollen breeches. 'Mine.'

Alyce folded her arms. 'I am *not* wearing those.' She looked at the pile on the floor. 'A leather *jerkin*?'

'You'll have to. If you're going to stay in the palace, you'll have to join our company. And our company, if you hadn't noticed, is called Sussex's *Men*.'

'You want me to be a boy?'

'And besides,' he continued, ignoring her protests, 'if there are people looking for you, a disguise is no bad thing.'

Alyce puffed indignantly through her nose.

'What do you say?' said Solomon, trying to sound upbeat. 'How would you like to be an Alex instead of an Alyce?'

XVI

Alyce was doing her third lap of Solomon's bedchamber, running her fingers over a silver candelabra in front of a crackling fireplace. She had thrown off his giant, buckled shoes, and her feet were finally beginning to thaw, but his breeches were impossibly itchy. Even the smock she had worn in Bedlam was more comfortable than these instruments of torture.

'Why didn't you tell me?'

Solomon frowned. 'I did tell you.' Now they were alone together with the door closed, he was starting to behave a little awkwardly. He stood in the centre of the room, shifting his weight from one foot to the other.

'You said you were performing at the palace, not *living* here.'

'It's the same thing. All of the company have their lodgings here. Our patron is the Earl of Sussex; he has to accommodate us as part of our deal. We have two more weeks here, and then we have to leave London to visit other towns. We'll be playing at the Theatre on Bishopsgate Street next. The Queen wants us around here at least until February, though.'

Alyce put down the candelabra and stared at Solomon.

'The Queen?' she said. 'You mean Queen Elizabeth?'

Solomon laughed. 'That's the one. Is there another Queen of England I should be aware of?'

Sort of, Alyce thought to herself. She went back to looking at the tapestry that hung on the wall opposite Solomon's bed, preoccupied now. Stupidly, she felt like she was some sort of traitor – just hours beforehand she had been talking face to face with the woman who was planning to remove Elizabeth from the throne, and with Doctor Dee, the man who had betrayed Elizabeth in the first place.

'What's she like?'

'Elizabeth? I don't know. I don't really see her. I certainly don't get to talk to her.'

'Is she . . . nice?'

He shrugged. 'Think it depends on her mood. I don't think she's disposed towards being merciful at the moment, if that's what you mean.'

Alyce sighed. 'Solly, I need to tell you about what happened today. I'm getting the feeling that . . . Ow!' She stubbed her toe on his chamber pot – empty, she was relieved to see – and looked up at him and raised an eyebrow.

'Don't worry, I can use the servants' latrines while you're here. You'll just have to tell me . . . when . . .'

'Right.'

There was an uncomfortable pause.

'You were saying.'

'I was saying: I'm getting the feeling that everything is more complicated than we first thought. That I'm part of something much bigger than me. Than us.'

'What makes you say that?'

Alyce went and sat on the bed, and looked at her fingers. 'Remember back at The Swan, that time when you said Queen Elizabeth was in a bad mood all the time? Because of Mary Stuart?'

'Yes . . .' Solomon's face had stiffened, as though he were preparing himself for some very bad news.

'Well. I think she has every reason to be angry.'

Solomon came and sat next to her, and she told him of Vitali, and The Hangman, and her run-in with Doctor Dee and Mary, Queen of Scots. She stopped short of speaking about the woman in the cage, but it was becoming impossible to avoid.

While she spoke, Solomon's brow became so knotted Alyce was worried it might never untie itself.

'But why would your mother send you to Doctor Dee in the first place?'

'I don't know.'

'What do you think the letter said?'

'I don't know that either.'

'Do you think Elizabeth has any idea that Mary is coming to London? Is plotting to overthrow her?'

'*I don't know, Solomon.*'

He got up and paced around the room. 'I mean . . . this is unbelievable. It's *treason*. And Mary is . . .'

'A witch.'

'I heard she was charming to her gaolers, but I didn't think she was literally casting spells on them.'

'What I still don't understand,' said Alyce, 'is why *me*, in particular? Why would she be so desperate to get my support? Surely there are plenty of others like me out there.'

Solomon scratched his chin. 'From where I'm standing, the *why* doesn't seem so important right now. The most pressing thing, Alyce, is that you, for whatever reason, are now at the centre of a conspiracy that will throw the whole country into chaos. The whole world, even.'

'We,' she corrected. '*We* are at the centre of it.'

Solomon gulped.

'Bet you wish you'd stayed well away now, don't you?' said Alyce. 'You should have stuck with your plan of abandoning me.' She laced the comment with a bitterness she didn't really feel, or at least had stopped feeling on the walk to the palace.

'I didn't abandon you. I just needed time to think about things, after what happened at The Swan.'

'Think? About what?'

'About you. About my mother. I've done everything I can to put her out of my mind since she disappeared, but being around you, seeing what you did . . . I can't just pretend she didn't exist.'

Now? Alyce thought. *Shall I tell him now?* The words had

started leaving her lips before she'd actually made up her mind.

'Solomon, there's something else,' she said. 'I'm not sure you want to hear it. But I think you should.'

His face went strangely blank as he waited for her to go on.

'I saw her. I think it was her.' She paused. 'I know it was her.'

'Her?'

'She was in Bedlam all along, Solly. I didn't know who she was at the time. But then I saw her again, properly, at Doctor Dee's house. They'd captured her. Imprisoned her. She was the one who helped me escape.'

Only the flicker of one eyelid showed Alyce that Solomon had understood the truth of what she was saying.

'Are you sure?'

'You two look very alike.'

'People always said that. They said I had none of my father in me at all. Did she say anything? Did she mention me?'

'Nothing about you. She spoke against Mary. Said she could foresee what would happen if she became Queen.'

'Imprisoned,' he said flatly. 'How was she?'

'Honestly?'

He nodded.

Alyce groped for the words. They all seemed so callous, however she put it. 'She was . . . a ruin. Wild. Distracted. I'm not sure . . . I don't think she would even know you if she saw you.'

'And you left her there?'

The flush of guilt spread from her navel to her face. 'I couldn't have helped her. There was no breath left in her when she finished speaking.'

'She was dead.' It was a statement rather than a question.

'I'm sorry, Solomon.'

'No need to be. This doesn't change anything, does it? At least I know what happened to her.' He sat up unnaturally straight. Alyce could see he was hurting, and trying very hard to pretend he wasn't.

'Maybe,' she suggested, 'we could go back for her . . .'

'What good would that do?' he said. 'I wonder why they took her from Bedlam. She must have done something wrong.'

'I don't know. They had little love for each other, she and Mary. Perhaps she'd done something to anger her.'

They both stared into the fireplace in silence for a minute or two. When Alyce tried to put a reassuring hand on Solomon's arm, he suddenly stood up and went to the foot of his bed, where there was a large, iron-bound chest, and began fiddling with the clasps.

'What are you doing?' Alyce asked. Fatigue was starting to claim every inch of her now.

The lid of the chest groaned as he opened it. He threw a couple of armfuls of clothes on to the floor, and then, one by one, began to produce a collection of books, their leather bindings cracked and ancient. He piled them into a wobbling tower at Alyce's feet.

'They're hers,' he said. 'I found them locked in one of

her cupboards, and I took them with me when I left home.'

She picked up three tomes from the top of the pile and read their spines: *De Operatione Daemonum*, *De Potestate Hieroglyphica*, and one simply called *Arcana*.

'Maybe you can understand them better than I can? We could read them together, I thought. Teach each other. Or something like that.' Again, he unstraightened and straightened his ruff. 'That's why I came back to see you at The Swan. Eventually. She never taught me very much, my mother. Kept things to herself a bit more than yours, sounds like. Maybe because I'm a boy, I don't know. But I want to learn. I feel like I owe it to her, more than ever now.' He took a deep breath. 'Witchcraft wasn't something she *did*. It was who she *was*. So if I can learn from these, it'll be like I'm keeping her alive in some way.'

Looking over the covers, all Alyce could think of were the hundreds and hundreds of books in Doctor Dee's study. Conversely, her mother had owned very few – a handful of storybooks and compendiums of flora and fauna, which she had used to teach Alyce everything she knew.

These books looked severe, forbidding.

'You say your mother kept these locked away?'

'Yes. To stop my father finding them.'

Alyce wasn't sure that was the whole story. She felt like she was fumbling towards some sort of conclusion, but she was too tired to get there. Everything had taken on a fuzzy, detached quality. Even the business with Queen Mary now seemed distant and unimportant.

'Can we read them tomorrow?' she said. 'I can barely keep my eyes open.'

'Of course. I'm sorry. You must be tired after the day you've had.'

'Well, yours hasn't been much better. I'm sorry too. About your mother. I wish I wasn't the one to tell you.'

'Look at us,' said Solomon, smiling sadly. 'What a wretched pair of orphans we are. I've performed plays about people like me and you. If this were a comedy, our story would only last for five acts, and we'd endure all sorts of hardship and confusion, but then at the end of it we would discover that our parents were still alive all along, that we were separated from them at birth, and everything would work out happily. But this isn't a story, is it?'

'No,' said Alyce. 'I'm starting to realize that too. In my mother's books, the clever witch always got the better of her enemies. Overcame the mischievous spirit, banished the evil demon, returned order to the world. But it's more complicated than that.'

Solomon started gathering the books up again and stacking them on the writing desk. Alyce yawned with her whole body, stretched and curled up on the bed. Already the sounds of Solomon talking and pattering around the chamber seemed distant and muffled. Her leaden eyelids closed once, twice. On the third time, just as she was about to fall asleep, she saw something in Solomon's hands that made her suddenly rigid and alert. Two vague memories, one from Bedlam, one from Doctor Dee's house, connected with each other, and as she stared at the volume he was carrying, all she could hear was the voice of his doomed mother:

Black book. Black book. Black book.

XVII

When she woke the following morning, Alyce was certain that the previous day had been one long, vivid, exhausting dream. As the grey light of dawn crept over her face, she knew that when she opened her eyes she would see the interior of her tiny garret in The Swan, Solomon would still be an estranged memory, and in a few moments Mrs Thomson would come thundering in and shout at her for spending too long in bed.

There was a snuffle from behind her. She rolled over, squinted, and saw Solomon curled up around the hearth like a dog, breathing heavily. So he hadn't thought to share the bed with her. Quite the gentleman. She smiled and rolled back to the wall again.

Suddenly her legs prickled, and she remembered she was still wearing the breeches and hose Solomon had given her. The more she scratched and wriggled under the blanket, the more her skin felt like it was on fire, until she leapt out of bed, cursing.

'How do you *wear* these things?'

Solomon woke up with a jolt and looked around, confused.

'Hmmm?' He rubbed his eyes and propped himself up on his elbows. 'Oh, sorry,' he mumbled. 'They're not very comfortable, are they. But they're smaller than my other clothes, so they're a better fit.'

Alyce stuck a thumb down her waistband and pulled it away from her hips. There was at least two inches of room for her to fill.

'A better fit?'

Solomon made a strange grunting noise that sounded vaguely sympathetic, and then closed his eyes again, trying to snatch the last vestiges of his night's sleep.

'Can't I be Alyce while I'm in here,' she said, 'and Alex when I'm walking around the palace?'

'I suppose so,' said Solomon, rocking slowly forward on to his haunches, and then getting to his feet. 'Although, I think, for the time being, you shouldn't just go wandering around Whitehall. Remember, the guards we met last night might think you're a member of Sussex's Men, but Sussex's Men themselves don't know anything about you. I'm going to talk to them today, see if you can join the company. Although the Earl is Lord Chamberlain now, I don't know how easy it will be to get his consent . . .'

So I'm a prisoner again. Wonderful.

'Very well,' she said, trying hard to sound bright about it.

'It's not for long,' Solomon tried to reassure her. 'And like I said, it's probably not a bad thing for Alyce to stay out of sight. You don't want to bump into Doctor Dee.'

She hadn't thought of that. 'Does he come to the palace?'

'All the time. I told you, he's the person Elizabeth trusts most in the world.'

Alyce gave a hollow laugh. 'Well, she made a bad choice there. Do you think—'

'No. Don't say it.'

'What?'

'I *knew it*. I knew you'd suggest this. We are *not* going to go to Queen Elizabeth and tell her about the plot. You're already in way over your head.'

'But maybe she'll reward us! And she'll put Doctor Dee in prison, and then we can get the letter back and *make* him answer all our questions.'

'The very fact that Mary tried to convince you to join her shows that you have something in common with her. I don't think Elizabeth is a huge fan of *any* witches. She'll probably put you in prison too. Or worse.'

'But she employed Doctor Dee. He's sort of a witch.'

'*Please*, Alyce,' said Solomon, coming over and grasping her hands. 'Just stay put. Until we figure out a plan.'

Alyce sighed. 'Fine. I'll bide my time. I've things to do here, I suppose.'

'Will you make a start on the books?'

'I'll try. First, though . . .' She got up and went to the pile of damp, stinking clothes that she'd been wearing when she dragged herself out of the Thames. She rummaged in the pockets and produced the ruined mommet. 'I need to repair this old thing.'

She took it over to the writing desk, which was pushed up against the wall under the chamber's single, narrow window. She held it in the shaft of white morning light and began to tidy and tighten the wet straw.

Solomon watched her. 'I'll be rehearsing with the rest of the company for most of the day, but I can bring you something to eat from the Great Hall,' he said. 'It'll be third-hand leftovers, I'm afraid – players and servants get whatever the gentlemen and ladies don't want to eat.'

'How disappointing. I thought I'd be sitting at High Table with Her Majesty.'

Solomon laughed. 'I'll put in a good word for you.' He preened himself in a very dull, cloudy mirror at the far end of the bedchamber. 'Right, I need to go and show my face. I'll be back soon. Don't worry about being interrupted, we're not good enough to have servants, and no respectable courtier would be seen dead in the company of an actor.'

He waved and shut the chamber door behind him, leaving Alyce alone with the books.

The mommet didn't take long to fix, but adding her hair to the finished product was a painful business – there was no knife or pair of shears in Solomon's room, so she was forced to pluck them from her head one by one until her eyes watered. When she had half a dozen strands she wove them tightly around the doll's bulbous head, and set the whole thing down next to the embers of last night's fire. As she did, her chest and fingers and toes all seemed to warm at once.

Her tiredness melted away, and with it her inhibitions. She looked over the pile of books, inspecting and discarding them one by one until she had the big black one in front of her. She looked over her shoulder, feeling, for some reason, like someone was watching her through the keyhole.

As she opened the book, the spine creaked in her hands, and the vellum of the pages let off a queer, poisonous smell. It reminded her of the dampness inside Doctor Dee's laboratory. Plainly printed, with no illustration or decoration, the frontispiece read:

NECRONOMICON

The pages were so dirty they looked as black as the leather binding. In places the vellum was discoloured a dubious shade of red. The text itself seemed to be in several different languages, much of it in runes like the letter her mother had written. It was broken up with pictures of men and animals, and stranger things that seemed neither one nor the other; diagrams too, complex and anatomical, explorations of the flesh that made Alyce's stomach churn.

It was like no witchcraft she had ever seen – certainly nothing like the charms and spells her mother had taught her. She had listened to the dead, had spoken with them. 'Kept them company,' was how she had put it. 'The Other Side is the loneliest place there is.' But the spells here – some of them didn't even look like spells, more like surgical operations – weren't about keeping the dead company.

Their aim seemed to be nothing less than bringing them back from the grave. And Alyce couldn't look away.

Solomon had barely been gone half an hour before he returned to the bedchamber, smuggling two bread rolls in his pockets. Alyce threw another book on top of the *Necronomicon*, and kept her face down to hide her guilty flush. He threw one of the rolls on to the desk at her elbow, the heavy thud suggesting it was well past being stale.

'Rehearsal's cancelled,' he said. 'Change of plan. We've got to go back into London. Sorry.'

'We? Why *we*?' she said, opening the *Arcana* to a page that seemed to be about constipation remedies.

'Well, I've got to go and get some supplies from the butcher at Newgate. And I can't exactly leave you here.'

'Why not?'

'What if somebody finds you?'

'I thought you said I wouldn't get any visitors.'

'I'd just be happier . . .' Solomon groped for words. 'I'd be happier if you were with me. I don't like the idea of you being alone in the palace.'

'That's very chivalrous of you.'

'It's just safer. Even being down there in the Great Hall didn't feel right. I need to look out for you.'

Alyce frowned. 'You're making me out to be some help-less maiden. You can stop that right away.'

He glanced down at what she was reading. 'Bowel remedies? I was hoping you'd teach me something a bit more advanced.' He tugged at the corner of the book, revealing the open *Necronomicon* underneath. 'What's this one?'

His mouth twisted into a grimace.

'Oh,' he said. 'The black one. I don't think you should start with that.'

'Why not?'

'I've looked through a few pages. It's . . . strange.'

'It's necromancy, I think.'

'It's not right, that's what it is.'

'You did say your mother locked them away. Maybe we weren't supposed to have them.' She paused. 'Maybe *she* wasn't supposed to have them.'

'Why don't you read one of these instead . . .' said Solomon, perusing the covers of the other books. 'Alchemy . . . Sympathy . . . Demonology? Maybe not the last one.'

'You know,' said Alyce, ignoring him, 'Mary Stuart tried to make a deal with me. She claimed she could bring my mother back from the dead. She said she'd do it if I joined her.'

Solomon looked up and made a pained face, but didn't reply.

'Do you think she could?' Alyce pressed.

'It's not a question of *could*, it's a question of *should*.'

'Tempting though, isn't it . . .?' she said, tracing her finger over one of the dry, dusty pages.

'No!' He whipped the book out from under her nose. 'It's not *right*, Alyce. It's not natural.'

Ah yes, she thought, *but we* are *nature.*

Solomon threw the *Necronomicon* in the chest at the foot

of the bed and closed the lid. 'Let's at least be practical about it: whatever is in that book is advanced stuff. We should start from first principles, shouldn't we? You *are* meant to be teaching me, after all.'

'I suppose so.'

'Good,' said Solomon, smiling for the first time that morning and obviously feeling like he'd won. 'Come on, you need to get your shoes on and pack all that hair into a hat. We need to get to the market early, before things start to smell.'

Alyce got out of the chair and went to the fireplace, checking, on the way, that the chest wasn't locked.

'To smell? What are we buying?'

'Offal. Liver, kidneys, intestines. Special effects for tonight's performance.'

'Delightful,' said Alyce, standing up and rearranging her tights. 'Well, you're carrying them, not me.'

Together, they slipped out of the chamber and down the passageway. The guards, with their eyelids hanging heavy from the night shift, seemed unconcerned as Solomon and his fellow actor trotted across the courtyard to the palace gate.

'Going to Newgate Market,' said Solomon cheerily to one of them. 'Can't have a good revenge tragedy without some blood and guts!'

The guard just looked at him, and grunted. He might as well have been asleep.

'Good to know Her Majesty is in safe hands,' Solomon muttered to Alyce, as they emerged on to the road to Ludgate.

Just as they were leaving, Alyce heard the tramp of feet in the courtyard behind them. A detachment of palace guards were making their way past the Great Hall towards the walled garden, accompanied by a riotously colourful train of cloaks and breeches and feathered hats. And at the front of them all was a woman in a silver and white gown that almost doubled her width – and she was already as tall as the guards and the courtiers – her red hair bound in pearls.

'Ah,' said Solomon. 'There she is. You still want to tell her all about the plot? You go ahead and stroll right up to her.'

'Queen Elizabeth,' said Alyce, staring open-mouthed.

'Good old Bess. That's her.'

'She looks so . . . familiar.' She couldn't make out the Queen's face properly from this distance, but even so . . . Why did it feel like this wasn't the first time she'd seen her?

'Of course she's familiar, she's the *Queen*. You've probably seen her on coins, or posters, or pamphlets or something. Her picture gets everywhere.'

But it wasn't just the way she looked. It was the way she *moved* too.

'You were right,' she said to Solomon. 'She does look like she's in a bad mood.'

'More so than usual, seems like. She's really storming across that courtyard!'

It was true – the guards and her attendants periodically had to break into a run to keep up with her. It was quite funny to watch.

Elizabeth disappeared through the arch in the garden's high wall, and Solomon turned to go. Alyce lingered for a little longer, though, and she was glad she did. Just as the last of the guards followed her out of the courtyard, a winged shape descended from one of the palace's towers.

The raven. She knew it was the same one from its size and shabby silhouette. Only this time it wasn't watching Alyce. It was watching the Queen.

XVIII

The market was immediately on the other side of New-gate. Even at this early hour, it was a riot compared to the tranquillity of the palace and its grounds – butchers for the most part, but also fishmongers, grocers and flower-sellers, all hawking their produce in voices to split the ears. Now they were inside the city walls the air was warm and close, and everything smelt of meat and vegetables just on the cusp of rotting.

They had barely gone as far as the first row of stalls when somebody grabbed Alyce's arm and spun her around. She didn't even have time to look at her assailant's face before she was being smothered in plush velvet. Pearls or jewels of some kind pressed into her gums and her cheekbones.

For a moment she thought it was Doctor Dee, but the doublet her face was crushed against didn't seem the sort of thing he wore. Then she thought it was the men from Bedlam. But she heard laughter. And she smelt perfume so strong and sickly sweet she wanted to throw up.

'Alyce!' said a voice, the pronunciation and stress on each syllable completely wrong. 'You are here! You are alive!'

She extricated herself from the embrace, and looked up to see Signor Vitali's painted face beaming back at her.

'You came back!' he exclaimed in a voice that was far too loud. 'To help your friend!'

Alyce felt her heart race. 'Um. No, that's not actually why—'

'You kept your promise!'

'I didn't—'

'My child, you are as faithful as you are beautiful.'

'Thank you . . .'

Vitali looked at her askance.

'Although, today, you are not as comely as I remember. What is this apparel you wear? You dress so strangely!'

Solomon, who had been standing a little to one side watching the whole bizarre exchange unfold, snorted. The mountebank himself was wearing a gold doublet, gold hose, gold shoes (smeared with dung), and a delicate ruff so broad that it almost covered his shoulders completely. His fingers and wrists were covered with jewelled rings and bracelets, and he clinked whenever he moved.

Alyce saw Vitali register Solomon's laugh, without actually acknowledging his presence.

'I am afraid today I cannot be Alyce,' she said. 'Today I must be somebody else. That's why I'm dressed like this. Please don't ask why, it's . . .'

'A secret?'

'Yes.'

'Very well. I shall ask no more. I fear we already know too many of each other's secrets. Wouldn't you say?' He gave her a knowing smile, and then suddenly affected an expression of comically exaggerated disappointment. 'But I am sad! You did not say farewell to your Vitali yesterday. I was so worried. I thought maybe I would never see you again – that this Doctor Dee had snatched you away from me!'

Alyce didn't reply.

'Was he able to help you with the meaning of your letter?'

'Not as such,' she said, glancing at Solomon, who looked away.

Vitali tutted. 'I confess, I looked for you all day yesterday, after you disappeared. I paid a visit to Mrs Thomson in the evening, she did not know where you were either.' His face softened, as much as it could under the layers of make-up. 'She looked very worried. Very worried indeed. She even looked *thin*, and I never thought I could say such a thing.'

Alyce wondered whether she would ever go back to The Swan again. She had assumed that Mrs Thomson was glad to see the back of her, but apparently not.

'You need not tell me your secrets,' the mountebank continued, 'but maybe you should tell her? She is nearly ill with worry.'

'I shall, signor. But not yet.'

He nodded. 'And who is this?' he said, turning at last to

Solomon. 'A friend? A rival for my affections?' He obviously meant this as a joke, but there was a coldness in his voice.

'Just that,' said Solomon. 'A friend. Alyce is staying with me and the company while she is out from under Mrs Thomson's roof.'

Vitali eyed him suspiciously. 'The company?'

'Sussex's Men. Are you a player yourself? That's quite a spectacle you're constructing.' He pointed over Vitali's shoulder. 'I've never seen such a marvel of stagecraft.'

Propped up against Newgate itself, Vitali had erected a complex timber scaffold that looked more suited to siege warfare than to the selling of potions and lotions. It had three separate stages on different levels, all as rickety as each other, the highest tottering eight or nine feet above the ground. The whole structure was draped with heavy sail-cloth, dyed purple and blue, and hung above it was a back-drop of the same colour, decorated with stars and crescent moons.

Vitali kept smiling, but spoke through slightly gritted teeth. 'I am not a player, no. I am a doctor. A physician.'

'Oh, I see,' said Solomon in a mock-apologetic tone. 'I've just never seen a physician dressed like this.'

'I am not any normal physician.'

'Yes. I can see that.'

'Ah, a cynic. Perhaps I can prove the efficacy of my wares when the spectacle is over?'

His words had taken on a hard edge. Alyce remembered Vitali's sideline in poisons, and quickly tried to change the subject.

'Forgive us, signor – I'm afraid we won't be able to stay and watch the show. We have errands to run.'

He looked at her for a moment, like she was speaking a different language. 'I do not understand. My dear, *you* are the spectacle. That is why you are here, is it not?'

Alyce was disconcerted by the fact that his usual fixed smile had not returned to his face. She started to feel hot and agitated under her borrowed clothes.

'I am sorry –' she lightly touched his arm – 'but this is coincidence. We're here for the market.'

'We had a deal, child. You swore an oath. I took you to the tavern, I introduced you to a very important man. The kind of man you *never* would have found without my help.'

She turned to Solomon for reassurance, but he looked as guilty as she did. As much as she wanted to get away from Vitali, he had a point. She did have her end of the bargain to uphold.

'I am *sorry*, signor – but I would rather nobody saw me. Not like this.' She waved her hands around. 'Not in public.'

'You promised, Alyce,' he said, not moving an inch.

'But—'

'It would mean very much to me, if you kept your promise.'

'I—'

'It would mean very much to *you*, if you kept your promise.'

Was that a threat? Alyce thought. Then Vitali's broad smile returned, unannounced.

'Besides, why do you worry about being *seen*?' he said.

'You do not even look like Alyce. This is a perfect disguise.'

That was true too. Her nerve failed her, just as she'd known it would from the moment she had seen him. She nodded.

'Very well,' she said, sick with anxiety the moment the words left her lips. 'Only, I don't know what it is you would like me to do.'

'*Ottimo!*' Vitali exclaimed, and clapped his hands. 'It is nothing. You are a talented girl. You learn quickly. Come!'

Alyce followed, but spoke to the baffled Solomon before she did. 'Just wait here,' she said. 'Keep your eyes open for anything unusual.'

The crowds were beginning to swell now. Passers-by were already stopping to stare at the construction, at Vitali, at Alyce.

Around the back of the stage, Vitali beckoned Alyce over to an enormous strongbox resting on the ground. The inside was mostly piled with the glass bottles, bowls and phials that Alyce had seen in Vitali's lodgings, but it also contained other, stranger things: a ram's skull; a sword in an ornate scabbard; a dead, stuffed dove in a cage; several coloured leather bags of something that looked suspiciously like gunpowder; and a lute. Alyce looked warily at this last item and hoped that she was not expected to give some form of musical accompaniment.

'All of these, they must go up there.' He pointed to the stage. 'Then we begin.'

She watched him arranging the items across the stages of the scaffold, and followed his lead. The last things to be unpacked were the coloured bags of powder.

'What are these?' said Alyce, poking her finger into one of them.

'Careful, child!' said Vitali, gently pulling her away and sealing the bag. 'This is a little sorcery of my own. You shall see. Perhaps, with a real witch here, we will not need it in future?'

He winked, and Alyce felt her blood boil beneath her cheeks. *How could he mention it so openly?* She turned her head away, pretending she had seen something in the crowd, and she hadn't heard what he'd said.

With everything set out, the mountebank stood back a few paces and surveyed his stage. He humphed with satisfaction. 'Good. Very good. Alyce, let us show these men and women something they have never seen before!'

'Us?' She turned back to him, aghast. She had hoped, vainly, that Vitali had simply wanted an extra pair of hands to unload his wares. 'What else do you want me for?'

'Do not worry yourself! Simply watch the spectacle with everybody else, and when I call upon you, you do as I say, yes?'

He didn't wait for an answer, but just patted her patronizingly on the head and disappeared around the back of the scaffold.

Alyce scanned the crowd for Solomon, and found him besieged on all sides by dirty, sickly, gormless townsfolk, all jostling for the best view of the platform. Even in his shabby apparel, he looked almost regal by comparison. He had gathered his slender limbs into the sides of his body, trying not to make contact with the men and women around him, and his face showed a look of such distaste Alyce wanted to burst out laughing. She weaved in between the bodies, took his hand, and pulled him to safety at the side of the stage.

'Can we call it even now?' she said as he dusted himself down.

'What do you mean?'

'Saved your life.'

Before he could reply, she turned back to the scaffold and waited for the show to start.

HOPKINS

'I don't see her,' said Hopkins, loitering by the edge of one of the market stalls.

The crowd had cleared around him, which was really the opposite of what he wanted. Even the stall's owner had abandoned her table of root vegetables and was having an urgent conversation with the shopkeeper opposite. The only company Hopkins kept in that strange, empty circle of fear was Caxton and the girl, whose shoulders he clutched like an over-protective father.

'But,' said Martha, 'she should be here. She was sent to work with him. She was going to deliver his ingredients, and then help him with his spectacle.' Her voice was quiet and scared now. All of her usual cockiness had left her the previous night, after they'd arrived at London Bridge, and found Vitali's home dark and abandoned.

'I am an honest man, Martha, so I shall speak honestly – things are not looking good for you at this moment in time. First you show us an empty set of lodgings in the middle of the river; then you drag us to this lice-ridden pit, first thing in the morning. And no sign of her all night. Where next? Back to Bedlam? If I didn't know better, child, I'd say you had us chasing our own tails in the hope of making a couple of quick sovereigns. Or maybe you're in league with Mrs Thomson after all, and you're giving the girl time to escape?'

'I'm not! I promise!' He could see she was deliberately trying not to look at Caxton, her neck twisted unnaturally. 'Signor Vitali is there, that's him. That's his stage.'

'But no Alyce.'

'Please, I was trying to help. Just wait a moment. Maybe she's late . . . or . . .'

Hopkins could feel her shoulders were now shaking with sobs. He watched the mountebank fussing around the scaffold and exchanging words with his manservant, and gripped a little harder.

XIX

A great *BANG* shook the crowd.

There were gasps from some, screams from others, and, after a moment, a smattering of uncertain applause. A plume of dense, blue-black smoke filled the highest stage where the firework had exploded, and out of it, as though descended from heaven on a thunderbolt, stepped the glittering Vitali. He already had the lute in his hands, and he began to pluck and sing. Alyce and Solomon looked at each other, completely bemused. The rest of the audience were transfixed – young women in particular.

Absurd as he looked, Vitali's voice was strong and rich. He was not a particularly proficient lute player, and his tune was a simple one, but the crowd found something exotic and intriguing in his Italian ditty – even if they didn't understand a word of it. He strutted from one stage to the other, singing of *salute eterna* and his *doni divini*, and every few paces another firework would *boom*, releasing more

coloured clouds of smoke and setting a few more dogs
barking in terror.

He finished his song with a flourish and made several
bows to different corners of his audience. Some clapped,
others simply began shouting their ailments and their
symptoms at him. He smiled serenely and quieted their din
with a raised hand.

'Gentlefolk of London,' he called to the crowd. 'Most
worthy patrons. A thousand thanks.' He paused to survey
the sea of faces, beaming. '*Salute*. Health! O, health! This is
what you clamour for, is it not? With not only your mouths,
but with your very souls, I think. Nourishment corporeal
and spiritual! I, Doctor Vitali, with rarest Aesculapian skill,
can grant you both of these. Give me leave, honourable
gentlemen and ladies, to amaze and delight you with this
humble scene –' he gestured around the grand, tottering
scaffold – 'and, by virtue of extraordinary chemical art,
dispel all of your ailments and ill vapours. No cheap salves
these, no dust of dried caterpillars and beetle wings, nor
greasy unguents of sheep's eyes, but true *elixirs* that may
grant new life even in the very throes of death.'

He took the stuffed dove from the cage on the highest
platform and displayed it to the onlookers. Then he turned
his back, and suddenly, with a flourish, the bird was flapping noisily into the air, very much alive. The crowd
whooped and clapped.

While Vitali launched into a tirade against the scheming,
duplicitous nature of virtually every physician in London,
Solomon whispered in Alyce's ear.

'He's the one who should be performing at Court. Our plays are nothing like as impressive as this.'

Alyce turned to reply, but suddenly realized that everyone in the crowd was staring at her. So was Vitali. He was extending his hand to her.

'Behold, my beautiful daughter, Maria!' he cried.

He's forgotten, Alyce cursed silently. *I'm supposed to be a boy. Look at what I'm wearing, you fool.*

He hauled her up on to the stage.

'A poor, sickly, wretched thing when she was born. She killed her mother as she fought from the womb.' That jarred with Alyce's nerves. 'But from this tragedy I learnt my arts. And look at her now, hale and healthy, and kissed with fire!' He took off the hat that Solomon had lent to her, and let her red and gold ringlets fall around her ears.

Perfect, she thought. *There goes my disguise. Thank you, signor.*

At the release of her hair, several of the balder members of the audience suddenly began to pay more attention. Others were losing interest and were beginning to mutter or wander away. Vitali sensed their waning attention and puffed himself up a little more.

'Maria will aid me in a demonstration of a new creation of mine.' He picked up the sword that had been left on the highest stage and handed it hilt-first to Alyce. She took it, frowning. 'I intend to show you, honourable patrons, a salve so wondrous as to be beyond belief – a gift from God, no less.' The crowd began to shout, some of them goading Alyce for her strange choice of clothing. She looked down at Solomon. He was fidgeting with his ruff.

'Well. To be a drunken knave, this is an incurable disease, beyond even the powers of Vitali. But with this *salve* you may heal any wound dealt by a man who wishes you ill.'

A housewife at the front of the crowd snorted. 'Ha! Is this a jest? I seen physicians try and stitch up me husband, an' even they make a bloody mess of it more often than not. What good's a bit of oil going to do?'

'You are as wise as you are beautiful, my lady.' Vitali winked. Alyce rolled her eyes. 'But you shall see anon. This divine liquid need only touch the offender's lips, and the flesh will heal with not even the *slightest* scar.'

The same woman cried out. 'The *offender*? So you got to find the man who did it, and get him to drink your potion? I don't think murderers are such an agreeable sort!' Others began to murmur in agreement.

Vitali's fixed smile was beginning to twitch into a grimace as the crowd grew restless. Alyce wasn't helping matters – she had lowered the sword, and was looking at him sceptically.

'*Cut me,*' he hissed.

'What do you mean?'

'*Cut my arm.* It is not a *real* sword.'

Still she hesitated. The mood among the onlookers was beginning to turn hostile. Some of the murmuring had turned to booing.

Vitali's face looked panic-stricken. It was perhaps the first time Alyce had ever seen him express a genuine feeling.

'*Please.*'

Alyce opened her mouth to reply, but no words came out. Something was wrong. The roaring and booing of the crowd had stopped. The press of bodies had parted, and walking towards the stage were two men dressed in black.

At least, she assumed they were both men. The figure who caught her eye first moved spectrally, more floating than walking, and wore a nightmarish, bird-like mask under a broad-brimmed hat.

The second man frightened her even more. He was the most handsome, healthy-looking corpse she'd ever seen. He was dead, and she knew it, because she had been the one who had killed him – a knife in the stomach while he'd stood triumphantly over the entrance to her mother's cellar.

The townsfolk watched in bewildered silence as the pair mounted the stage. Out of the corner of her eye, Alyce could see Solomon desperately trying to shoulder his way forwards. And behind everyone, her stooped posture unmistakeable, she glimpsed Martha skulking away between the market stalls.

The little snake . . .

'Gentlemen and ladies,' said the dead man, his voice every bit as commanding as Vitali's, but with none of the warmth. 'I beg you, put away your purses. Avert your eyes. Stop your ears. Turn away and never come back. For this foul pair – I swear it by Almighty God – desire payment not with your coin, but with your souls.'

The audience's faces were blank, unsure of what to think or to say, waiting to find out whether this was a genuine interruption or just another contrived piece of Vitali's theatre. Vitali himself, oddly, was still smiling; but it was a vacant smile now, as though something had broken in his brain.

'My lord,' he said, 'if you are not convinced by my craft—'

The dead man laughed. 'Your *craft*? You flatter yourself, signor. You are a trickster, a charlatan like every other man of your kind. Your only skill is deception – though I'll admit, you are most talented in your practice of it.'

Vitali spluttered with indignation. The crowd murmured. Somebody shouted in agreement, and others began to join in. For Alyce it was horribly familiar – she was back in Fordham, crouched in her mother's cellar, listening to the witchfinder work his audience in exactly the same way. Her fear was as cold now as it was then.

How is he still alive?

'No, your tricks are the least of our worries. This girl, however . . .' He finally turned to look directly at her, although his words were directed at the townspeople. She stared back, and saw nothing behind his black eyes. 'She really does have a Craft. One that is strange and terrible. Try as she might to conceal it under this boyish apparel, this creature who comes before you is a foul—'

A black blur suddenly flew into the pair of them, and the scaffold shook with the weight of a body falling upon it. Somebody screamed. Alyce shut her eyes. It was a few seconds before she opened them again and realized what had happened.

The dead man was no longer standing in front of her, but

lying on the stage, his feathered hat rolling away into the dirt. The raven was on top of him, savaging his neck and face.

The masked man tried to step over his companion's body to grab Alyce, but the bird flew up at him, and for a moment their black, beaked heads were a bizarre mirror image of each other. Then it sank its talons into the leather mask, and they both tumbled into the crowd. The onlookers scattered, shrieking, and Alyce saw Solomon's face disappear and reappear and disappear again, swallowed up by the stampede.

She struck the dead man on the arm with the sword as he rolled himself over, but Vitali had been quite right. It was a prop, about as sharp as a table leg. It made a satisfying *thud* when it hit flesh, but it wasn't enough to stop the man getting to his feet and lunging for her. She backed away and clambered up on to the next level of the scaffold. Behind her, Vitali simply ran and jumped headlong into the street, landing awkwardly and twisting his ankle. Then he crawled, whimpering, under the stage.

On the second level, among the pots and bottles, sat one of Vitali's homemade fireworks, and next to it a still-smouldering taper. Alyce stuck one inside the other and hurled it at her pursuer. It made a pathetic *thump* as it hit him on his embroidered chest, then sat uselessly at his feet for a moment before exploding with a burst of pretty pink flames and knocking him backwards. The decorative backdrop of the scaffold caught fire, and began to disintegrate.

The dead man howled, clutching at his face. As he stumbled blindly towards her, Alyce climbed higher still, and from her vantage point saw the raven and the masked man still struggling in the dirt.

Then, above the roar of the flames, she heard the voices again. The world seemed to slow like she'd been plunged underwater, and the red and orange turned to silver. There was a kind of patience in the way she looked at everything. Among the rushing crowds were other, indistinct figures, drifting and swaying like seaweed. They were made of an intense, radiant blackness, as opposed to the living bodies, which looked grey and dull. The Other Side.

Her pursuer looked different too. His body had the same definite edges as the living, but he seemed to have a second, darker figure inside him, one that twisted and writhed. Like it was trapped in there against its will.

Even as she stood, she could feel the floorboards rotting beneath her. She knew that *she* was the one doing it. Again, that feeling she'd had at The Swan, of the veil being torn. Of something crossing from the Other Side to this one. And of her being powerless to stop it.

'Jump down Alyce! I'll catch you!'

Solomon's words came to her suddenly, as though through a mist.

She wiped the soot from her eyes, took hold of the waist of her breeches, and leapt down from the charred, disintegrating scaffold. Solomon didn't so much catch her as break her fall, and he collapsed underneath her, arms splayed.

The air was blissfully cool away from the fire, and Alyce took a deep breath as they got to their feet. The visions disappeared. Solomon was massaging the small of his back.

'I think Mrs Thomson fed you a little too well – you're a lot heavier than when I carried you to The Swan.'

'It's not my fault you're such a waif—'

'Look out!'

The scaffold was now totally engulfed in flames, and blackened timbers were crashing to the ground around them. They saw Vitali scurry out from his hiding place, his golden cloak turning to ash as he disappeared into the crowd.

Terrified onlookers huddled under the arch of Newgate. In front of the conflagration, the dead man was still spitting and coughing. The other man had lost his beaked mask to the raven, who had wrenched it free with its talons. The ravaged face beneath it was too horrifying to look at. Beneath the bridge of his nose, there *was* no face. Just a blackened, blistered, skeletal grin.

'Come on!' said Alyce, seizing Solomon by the arm. 'Back to the palace! They won't be able to get in there, will they?'

He was paralysed, though, and it took a couple of tugs on his elbow before he started to move again. He looked at her as though he'd never seen her before in his life, then blinked, and nodded. They forced themselves through the crowd, ducking and weaving through the crush until they were outside Newgate. They could hear the clatter of the scaffold finally collapsing from over the city walls.

From there they ran up Holborn Hill, and once they were back on the road to Whitehall they slowed to a walk, so as not to appear suspicious.

It was only then that Alyce realized the raven had kept pace with them the whole way, and was gliding patiently through the ash-flecked air.

XX

Alyce stared into the cold, soot-stained hearth in Solomon's bedchamber. He had offered to light the fire, but that was the last thing she wanted. The skin on her face was still pink and tender, and now and again she would catch a whiff of her own burnt hair.

'Well, that's proof, then. That witchfinder was dead. Now he's alive. Mary Stuart really can do what she promised.'

'Are you *sure* you killed him? People can survive a knife wound, you know.'

'I'm sure. I waited. Right until the end.' The memory of it was a weight she felt like she always carried. More than a weight. A stain too, a black stain.

'Tip of the cap to your feathered friend, though. He did a good job.'

Alyce smiled despite herself. 'Yes.' She thought for a moment. 'Did your mother ever have a familiar?'

'A familiar?' said Solomon, sitting at the desk and

thumbing through the pages of the *Arcana*. 'No. I never thought they existed, to be honest. Having an animal companion that just follows you around, doing your bidding. Sounds a bit fanciful, doesn't it?'

'You've picked the wrong time to start being a sceptic, Solly.'

He turned a few more pages.

'Well. There are lots of nice pictures of animals in here, but nothing about familiars,' he said without looking up.

'He was trying to find me all along,' said Alyce distantly. 'Even on the night I escaped from Bedlam, he found me. He's been watching over me ever since. In fact . . .'

She paused.

'What?' he said.

'I think he's been watching over me since even before that.'

Solomon's puzzled expression turned suddenly to dismay as there was a tapping at the door.

'Hide!' hissed Solomon. He looked around frantically. 'In the chest? Can you fit?'

But Alyce was not in the least concerned. The tapping and scratching continued, and small clusters of shadows shuttled back and forth across the gap at the bottom.

'What if it's *them*?' Solomon was throwing the remaining contents of the trunk on to the floor. 'What if it's Doctor Dee?'

'It isn't,' said Alyce, rising from her stool next to the dead fireplace to investigate the source of the noise. 'Unless he's shrunk a lot since I last saw him.'

'What are you *doing*?'

'It's him. I know it.'

She slowly drew back the bolt and opened the door a fraction.

Solomon grabbed her shoulder. '*Alyce* . . .'

A polished black beak appeared through the crack, and two mismatched eyes. The raven bristled, and then forced its bedraggled body into the room, where it flapped in a couple of frantic circles and settled on the candelabra. Its plumage was more of a mess than ever, and Alyce couldn't help laughing. It was a wonder the animal could even fly, given how disordered its feathers were.

Solomon looked pained. 'It can't stay in here! I've already taken in one too many guests!'

'I thought I told you to wait outside?' said Alyce, speaking to the raven. She tentatively patted its head, and it croaked back at her.

'How did it even know we were here?'

'*He*, Solomon. It's a *he*.'

That afternoon, when they had reached the palace, Alyce had tried to tell the raven to stay around the park and the stables, so as not to get them into trouble, and had felt more than a little foolish as she did so. But the bird seemed to understand, and had perched above the palace gate and watched them go with his clever little eyes.

But he obviously hadn't been able to keep away. And regardless of the mischief he might cause, Alyce was glad he was here. Only now did she admit what she'd suspected all along, ever since she had seen him battling Martha in the alleyway. How many ravens could there be with one black and one white eye? And of such monstrous size?

'So you know him?' said Solomon.

Alyce blinked, forgetful of where she was. 'I'm sorry?'

'You were saying something, before we were interrupted. Something about seeing him before you got to London.'

'Yes. No. I don't know. Maybe it's just coincidence.' But she knew it wasn't.

'Go on . . .'

'When I lived with my mother, there was a raven that used to come to the cottage. She used to feed it scraps. Sometimes it would come with us when we went walking in the woods. It was exactly like this one.' She pointed at the bird, who flew down to investigate the pile of Alyce's old clothes, nipping them with his beak. 'Pecke. That was what my mother used to call him. Master Pecke.'

The raven suddenly cocked his head and croaked. He grew perfectly still and stared at her with his one white eye.

'Well, that settles it then,' said Solomon. 'It is him.'

Alyce continued to look back at the bird. His gaze pinned her to the spot.

'Maybe he's my mother's familiar, then, not mine.'

'Perhaps she told him to protect you if she was killed. Perhaps that makes him yours now.'

The ghost of Ellen Greenliefe flitted briefly before her. She remembered her sitting outside their cottage at dusk, waiting for the raven to appear, a spirit from the woods come to receive her offerings. Alyce had actually been frightened by the sight of him gliding out of the darkness –

she used to go and hide inside the cottage while her mother chatted with him. She never considered that they were *actually* having a conversation, though.

In the familiar's tiny marble eyes, she felt as though it were really her mother looking at her. Judging her, even. Her mother had died for her, been burnt alive, and never called out for mercy or offered the witchfinders anything about her daughter. She had allowed her to escape. And what was Alyce doing in return? There was a *reason* she was in London. Was she really going to give up, go into hiding? Pretend the whole thing wasn't happening?

'I don't know what I'm doing here, Solly,' she said morosely. 'What's our plan?'

'Well, I was thinking, maybe you could try and join the Sussex's Men. I can talk with Master Adams. Then you can come touring with us. It'll at least ensure that you're clothed and fed.'

'Um. Solomon. You know I'm not *actually* an actor? Or a man, for that matter? Have you been fooled by your own disguise?'

'I know, but there are other things you could do besides acting. Making costumes, scenery, that sort of thing.'

She smiled at him sadly. Going on the road with a company of players was the last thing she wanted to do, and it was hardly a solution. Yes, it would get her away from the witchfinders – possibly – but it wouldn't answer any of her questions. That damned letter. Why couldn't her mother have just written it in plain English? Why couldn't she have just told her everything when she had the chance?

'Alyce?'

She hadn't even realized she was crying.

'Sorry,' she said, wiping her eyes. 'I just wish she were here.'

She glanced at the chest. It was only the briefest of glances, but she knew Solomon had seen it.

'I know,' he said.

'Very well then,' said Alyce, trying to change the subject. 'You may as well ask if I can join the company. At least then I won't have to stay locked up in here all the time. And I can watch you working your magic on the stage.'

She curled up on the bed, and Pecke flapped across the room and settled on one of the bedposts

'I'll see what I can do in the morning,' said Solomon. 'But now you should rest.'

As Alyce closed her eyes, she saw him open the chest, take out the *Necronomicon*, and hide it under a pile of his clothes.

XXI

The following morning, Solomon left the bedchamber while Alyce was still fuzzy with sleep.

When she at last hauled herself out of bed, still stiff from the previous day's exertions, she went straight back to the books. Pecke watched the pages as she idly thumbed through them, hopping from the table to her shoulder and back again. At times he seemed to get bored, and would patter over to the door on his claws, staring at it as though expecting visitors.

Alyce spent a frustrating hour skimming the books that she didn't have the any inclination of reading. It was only the *Necronomicon* she wanted. Even though she couldn't understand a word of it, it called to her, demanded her attention. Alyce was just on the verge of reaching for the pile of clothes where it was hidden when Solomon burst through the door.

'He wants to see you,' he said.

'What?' she said, sitting back in the chair and brushing a stray curl away from her eyes. She looked guilty as sin. 'Who?'

'Master Adams. This afternoon, during rehearsals. I told him I had to go and fetch you from town, because you were doing some work with Worcester's Men. You'd better get your story straight.'

'My story?'

'Well, not your story. Alex's story. If that's who you're going to be.'

'Ah. Yes.' She got up to get a drink. Her mouth was unusually dry. Solomon had brought back some water in a pewter jug the previous night, but had forgotten cups, so she had to slurp straight from the spout. 'Sorry,' she said, wiping her lips. 'It's just those books are making me feel . . . strange.'

Solomon gave her the same penetrating look as the bird sitting on the candelabra.

'Any book in particular?'

'No,' she said, feeling her cheeks burn.

'Listen,' he said, picking up the *Arcana* from the table. 'If you're going to meet the company, you need to put this stuff from your mind. Actors are a superstitious bunch. Master Adams won't let us play *Murderous Michael* any more because he thought he saw the Devil standing next to him in the final act. Master Gavell has a pair of lucky breeches that he hasn't washed in a year. He stinks.'

'What's your point?'

'My point is that the slightest *hint* of anything that isn't natural is not going to go down well. So keep the sorcery under wraps, yes?'

Pecke squawked.

'Well, I can try,' said Alyce. 'But it's not all that simple.'

'Yes it is. Just don't go casting any spells or whatnot.'

'But I don't always have a *choice*. When I had my . . . moment . . . back at The Swan, I wasn't doing that on purpose. The same thing happened yesterday, on Vitali's stage. And when those mudlarks tried to rob me on the riverbank. When I get scared, something happens. I don't speak to the dead. The dead speak to me. It's like . . .'

'Like what?'

'It's like they *seek me out*. Like they're *using* me for something.'

The chamber fell very quiet. Solomon looked more worried than ever.

'In that case,' he said at last, 'you'll just have to make sure you don't get scared.'

The Great Hall was dark and cavernous, and it took Alyce's eyes a moment to adjust after the dazzling sunshine of the courtyard. A fire had been lit in the enormous hearth. The last of the diners had left, the long tables had been cleared of the midday meal, and now the only sound was the echo of three men shifting boxes and props at the end furthest from the door. Two of them were trying to move an angular wooden replica of a tree – painted leaves nailed to its straight branches – while the third was pulling costumes out of a chest and inspecting their condition. They stamped around heavily on a small stage, raised about four feet from the hall's flagstones.

'That's Master Adams in the middle, grey-haired fellow. I'll introduce you. Just be warned, though – he isn't always very friendly.'

'I wouldn't expect anything less,' said Alyce dryly.

'Remember what we said. Compliments will go down well.'

When they approached, John Adams was inspecting a red velvet cloak. It was badly stained, and it had a large hole near the hem. He stuck a finger through it and cursed under his breath.

'Master Adams,' said Solomon. 'This is the man I was telling you about. The craftsman. Master –' he missed a beat – 'Greenliefe. Alexander Greenliefe.'

Adams spun around and stared at Alyce, his mouth a slack grimace. His face had the loose, leathery look of an empty wineskin.

'Crafts*man?*' he said, stressing the second half of the word.

He knows, thought Alyce, heart sinking. *He knows I'm a girl. He's seen through me already.*

'He doesn't look like he's seen ten summers,' he continued. Alyce relaxed, trying not to sigh too audibly.

Adams took a step forward. 'Harper here tells me you worked with Worcester's Men.'

'I did, sir. And before that I was apprentice to the great Lorenzo Vitali of Milan.'

He scrunched up his face. 'Vitali? Where have I heard that name?'

'If you'll forgive me, sir, all the world has heard his name. He is the greatest engineer the stage has ever seen.'

'And why are you leaving Worcester's company?'

She spoke just as they'd rehearsed it. 'Because they are unenlightened peasants who don't know genius when they see it. You, I am told by Master Harper, are rather more of a visionary. More open-minded. I feel that under your direction, my art will be more able to fulfil its potential. If, that is, you'll have me.' She bowed slowly. Out of the corner of her eye, she saw Solomon smiling.

At the mention of the word 'visionary', Adams' face seemed to have plumped out a little, and his lips were straining upwards into something approaching a smile.

'So you are an engineer. Not an actor.'

'The most talented in London.'

'You have a lot of confidence for a boy so young.'

'I am older than perhaps I look,' she said. 'There is more to me than meets the eye.'

'Usually men with such a high opinion of themselves think they should be rewarded more than their due. The Earl of Sussex is not a man who recklessly throws away money.'

'I do not ask for a wage. Just food and lodgings.'

'You don't want to be paid?' Adams scoffed.

'The opportunity to practise my craft is payment enough, sir.'

He looked her over with sharp, grey eyes that matched the hair on his temples. He had probably been handsome as a young man, before time had undone the firmness of his skin. There was silence. Nobody moved. The other two players were looking at her too.

'I will make you a deal, boy,' he said at last. 'Let me see what you can do. Not tonight, of course – I won't risk our reputation at Court, in front of Her Majesty – but when we play the Theatre, on Bishopsgate, you can show me your craft. You shall eat with us, and you shall stay here in the palace, but only in Master Harper's lodgings. And you shall receive no pay until I deem you deserving of it.'

'You are most gracious, sir,' said Alyce, giving him another measured, stately bow, despite wanting to collapse from relief.

'Harper can show you the plays in our repertoire – rather more sophisticated than that dross Worcester's Men put on – and you should watch tonight's performance.'

'I would be honoured.'

'Right. Very well. Good.' His gaze lingered on her a little longer, and then he briskly turned back to the box of costumes.

Alyce was about to speak to Solomon, when suddenly Master Adams called to her again over his shoulder.

'You're a craftsman, Master Greenliefe. Can you sew?'

Alyce shrugged. 'Of course.'

'Then you can start by mending these clothes. Women's work, I know, but I'm sure you'll manage.'

Alyce and Solomon looked at each other, and saw that they were both straining to keep a straight face.

HOPKINS

'So you lost her again then,' said Doctor Dee, picking through the debris covering his laboratory. He picked up his astrolabe, its interlocking brass discs now warped and misshapen, and threw it to the floor.

Hopkins stared at him for a moment, laughed, then coughed violently, the soot from the fire at Newgate still clinging to his lungs.

'*I* lost her? *You* had her imprisoned, Doctor. In a cage. In your own house. And she still managed to destroy the place and escape. You're in no position to be casting blame around.'

The Doctor huffed. He tried to shift one of the fallen beams, but cursed and recoiled, sucking at a splinter in his finger.

'It wasn't the girl who did this. It was *that*.' He pointed at the body of the Bedlam woman, propped up like a withered doll against the bars of the cage. 'She summoned . . . something.'

'By God! A piece of sorcery that the Great Doctor Dee doesn't understand. We are in new territory here.'

Dee stormed over to him, and thrust a bony finger into his face. 'Need I remind you that I have the ear of Queen Mary? You would do well to keep your mockery to yourself, you knave. A word from me and she will introduce you to agonies you have never dreamt of. Who knows? Perhaps she will return you to the crones.'

Hopkins felt his dead heart thump. *I won't go back*, he thought. *Can't go back*. And then, in panic, he realized that the decision wasn't his to make.

'Where's that swagger now? You don't mean to say that the fearless, fearsome John Hopkins is afraid of a handful of old women?' Doctor Dee laughed. 'You should be thankful we intervened. We *saved* you. Mary could have left you to endure their hospitality, but she saw a better use for you. She *bartered* for ownership of your life, in a most undignified fashion. But now it is hers. You're a dog on a leash, nothing more. Both of you are.'

Hopkins drew his sword. He heard Caxton flex his fingers behind him. This two-penny apothecary wouldn't make it out of his house alive. Hopkins felt like his brain was boiling inside his skull.

'Careful now,' said the Doctor, taking a couple of paces backwards. 'The Queen arrives in London imminently. If you ever want to be free of your cursed, wretched life, killing me would be the wrong way to go about it.'

They faced each other across the ruined laboratory in silence. Hopkins took several breaths, nose and throat still burning from yesterday's fire. A dove flapped lazily in and out of the broken rafters.

Later, he told himself. *You can deal with him later*. He let his anger simmer down before he spoke. Was it anger?

No – it was grief. Grief for himself. Grief for his own death that had happened months ago.

'You need us as much as we need you, Doctor,' he said, straightening himself. 'You may have Mary's ear, but she'll have your head if she comes to London and you still haven't recaptured the girl.' He waved the sword point around Dee's neck. 'And your seer is proving less than useful these days. So you need us more than ever.'

'I have other arts—'

'Save your bluster, old man. We know where she's been taken. Let us forgive each other any offence given –' *for now*, he added in his head – 'and complete the business we have been assigned.'

Doctor Dee's eyes narrowed, in a way that suggested he was as happy about cooperating as Hopkins was. 'Very well. Enlighten me.'

Hopkins sheathed the sword. 'We had a little talk with the Italian gentleman she worked for. It seems she is still with that creature's son, and has joined Sussex's Men disguised as a boy.'

Hopkins saw Doctor Dee's face suddenly tense. 'She has joined the company?'

'Yes.'

'Then the need to act is even more urgent.'

'Why?'

'Sussex's Men are currently at Court. Performing at Whitehall. In front of Elizabeth.'

'And when exactly does Queen Mary arrive?'

'Her Majesty will be with us in person at midnight tonight,' said Doctor Dee. 'All being well.'

'Then get us in there as soon as possible. She can have the girl as a welcoming gift.'

XXII

It took the best part of an hour to stitch up the hole in the cloak, and all the while Sussex's Men bellowed their way through various scenes of what seemed to be a rather bombastic revenge play. Two more of the troupe arrived halfway through, although, from what Master Adams was saying, there were still others missing.

Alyce watched the rest of the players as she sewed, and had to admit that she preferred Solomon's performance to all of the others' – there was something sensitive and softly spoken about his character that was pleasing to watch and listen to amidst the thrusting and booming of the older men. Since none of the actors was in costume, it was some time before she understood the reason: Solomon was playing a female role. She thought that he might overstate the woman's femininity for comic effect – all blushing and swooning – but on the whole his portrayal was very measured.

When Alyce was finished, Master Adams halted the scene and came over to inspect her work.

'Very impressive,' he said, holding the stitching on the cloak up to his eye and sniffing. 'And the others?'

'The others?' said Alyce.

'The other costumes! Zounds, we have three chests full of them, boy!' He gestured to two more boxes at the corner of the stage. 'They all need some attention. And when you've finished with them, you can have a look at the trap-door. Something keeps sticking when we open the gates of Hell.'

Alyce began sorting through the piles of cloaks, hats, shirts, breeches and underclothes. Each box released the sweet and savoury smell of old sweat, making her wonder quite how long it had been since any of the costumes had been washed.

The repairs were going to take hours. Days, even. She hadn't really considered the implications of being accepted into the troupe, beyond being able to stay longer at the palace. Of course she would be expected to work.

But then, as her fingers found their rhythm with needle and thread, she wondered if she would be quite happy if she really *did* join Sussex's Men. Permanently. Perhaps she should just escape all of this intrigue. She could get away from London, and she could lose the witchfinders, lose Mary; she would have more time to learn her Craft; and she would be able to spend more time with Solomon.

She pricked her thumb with the needle, and cursed. A tiny, round jewel of blood appeared on her skin. How had that last thought sneaked in there? Not only that – it had sneaked in and outshone the others.

She glanced at Solomon, his brow furrowed, silently mouthing his lines, then shook her head and went back to darning his tights.

Alyce worked until her joints were sore and her eyes ached. She had been concentrating so hard, she barely recognized the transformation that the Great Hall had undergone as the daylight had faded.

While the actors rehearsed, the dining tables had been removed by servants, and rows of benches placed around three sides of the hall. In the middle of the floor, directly in front of the stage, was a set of perhaps a dozen larger chairs, surrounding a single, ornately decorated throne.

The prop tree had been manoeuvred into the corner of the stage, and a noose had been hung from one of its branches – obviously a key feature of the play that was about to be performed. Two painted gilt screens had been brought in too, to cover the entrances to the buttery, and the three enormous candle wheels that hung from the ceiling now flooded the boards with light. Lanterns had also been placed around the edges of the stage, leaving the rest of the hall in shadow. The space seemed to hum with an uncanny energy that felt a lot like sorcery.

When the black windows of the Great Hall showed only the reflection of the lights within, Master Adams summoned the company to the area behind the screens. Their number had grown by another six men – four players and two musicians – but from listening to his agitated muttering, it seemed one man, Master Gasper, was still missing.

'Then we choose another play . . .' The suggestion came from Master Gavell, he of the unwashed breeches.

'We *cannot*,' hissed Master Adams. 'Her Majesty *specifically* requested *The Shameful Kiss*.'

Alyce's ears pricked up. The Queen was definitely going to be in the audience, then. And if *she* was there, perhaps Doctor Dee would come with her.

For a moment, she again had the idea of approaching Elizabeth, informing her of Doctor Dee's treachery and of Mary's plot. Then, once the Doctor was imprisoned, she could ask him whatever she wanted.

Under torture, maybe.

She shivered, suddenly aware of how black her thoughts had become.

Servants brought the players bread, cheese and cold meats from the kitchens, and Adams continued to argue with Gavell. From beyond the screens, Alyce could hear the hall filling with courtiers returning from their own suppers, and from the sounds of things they were all very well lubricated with wine.

'When I find that jackanape . . .' Adams' fists had turned white; the script he held was on the verge of disintegrating. 'No doubt he is lying drunk in a ditch somewhere.'

Another actor, Master Lyons, who had been sitting in a corner of the buttery studying his dinner with great concentration, suddenly threw his arms in the air and rocked back on his stool. Alyce had been watching him all afternoon. When he was off stage, he twitched and muttered constantly. He seemed quite mad.

'I shall take Gasper's parts! I can play Furio, and the servants. I know the lines. I know all your lines. In fact, you can all go home!' He laughed and clapped.

'You cannot play the servants, Master Lyons,' said Adams desperately, 'because then we have nobody to play the Devil.'

'Ah, exactly, no *body*,' said Lyons, wagging his finger. 'But that is all you need. A body. The Devil has no lines to speak, I'm sure we can simply find a man to stand in for him on stage.'

Adams thought for a moment.

'He is right,' Gavell intoned, nodding furiously and causing his several chins to bulge.

The company leader took a deep breath, and looked around the players assembled backstage, many of whom were now beginning to put on their attire.

Alyce froze when his gaze came to rest on her.

'You, boy,' he barked. '*The Shameful Kiss*, do you know it?'

'Worcester's Men never performed it.'

'No matter.' Adams waved his hand dismissively. 'You will do. You certainly have an impish look about you. I think you will make a very fine Devil.'

'But Master Adams,' Alyce began to protest, 'I am no player at all . . .' She had proven that much in Vitali's performance, and was happy never to set foot on a stage again in her life.

'You won't have to do any playing,' he said. That was what Vitali had said too. 'You wear the costume, we see you come out of the trapdoor, Master Harper will make his speech, we have the kiss, you disappear again. You have until Act Two to look at the script, anyway.'

This didn't feel right. Suppose Doctor Dee was in the audience? The blood in Alyce's veins began to crawl like warm treacle.

'I really don't—'

There was a chorus of approval from the other players. Some even came over and slapped her on the back by way of encouragement. Everyone agreed with Master Adams. Everyone, that was, apart from Solomon, who was twisting his ruff in his fingers and pretending he hadn't heard any part of the discussion.

'Well, if you really think I won't ruin the whole play . . .' Alyce said.

But the matter was settled. The players went back to eating and preparing their costumes. When Master Lyons presented her with her own, she suddenly realized that there was no way she could get down to her small clothes in front of the company. She took herself off to the pantry to get changed, which in itself looked slightly suspicious.

The costume consisted of the same cloak that she had spent much of the afternoon mending, a blood-red doublet and breeches, and a bizarre, tight-fitting cap fringed with crimson and black feathers. It smelt bad when it was in her arms, but even worse when she was actually wearing it, the warmth and movement of her body releasing all of its hidden vapours. The material also felt slightly damp, as though it had never properly dried out after Master Lyons had finished exerting himself on the stage.

When she finally put on the ridiculous curly slippers and waddled back through to the buttery, the rest of the company crossed themselves. Somebody muttered a prayer. They really *were* superstitious. As far as Alyce was concerned the Devil was just a story that was told among the villagers in Fordham. It seemed so strange that Alyce, her mother, and their way of life had been woven into that story, without even knowing or believing it. Strange, and unfair too.

But even here in the city, at Court, the Devil was something all men feared. Even when he was as stupidly dressed as Alyce was. All men apart from Solomon, of course, who was the only one smiling. He was trying not to look at her as he straightened the sleeves on his gown, his face now caked in a woman's make-up, his lips heavily rouged.

Master Adams eventually came over and tutted. 'You are very slight, even for a boy. Find him a belt, somebody!' One of the other players obliged. Alyce looped it around her waist, but even at its tightest, the breeches still felt as though they slipped with every step.

'You'll have to do,' said Adams with a sigh. Then he turned, composed himself, and went out in front of the screens.

The crowd in the Great Hall suddenly fell eerily quiet. There was a great deal of rustling, before the silence was finally punctuated by a woman's voice. Master Adams was speaking too, but Alyce could not hear what either of them were saying.

The players were all listening intently too. Alyce shuffled over to where Solomon was standing.

'It's the Queen,' he whispered, noticing her at his elbow. 'Adams is asking for her indulgence before the play begins.'

'Indulgence? Forgiveness, you mean,' said Alyce. 'Look at me. This isn't going to work.'

'You'll be all right. Just stand in the middle of the stage and look devilish. You can do that.' He squeezed her shoulder.

When the exchange out front seemed to have ended, the company's two musicians began playing recorders, accompanied by one of the actors on a drum. Adams then gave a speech of introduction, and before Alyce could gather her thoughts, Master Lyons had leapt on to the stage, his words trilling and ringing bright and clear from his lips. The play had begun.

'When are you on?' Alyce hissed in Solomon's ear. He didn't reply. He seemed to be lost in a moment of intense concentration. When she jabbed him in the ribs with a finger, he simply handed her his script, and then with strange, slow grace, proceeded out in front of the audience in his woman's weeds.

He stayed out there for what seemed like hours. Alyce listened to the first act feeling a little ill-at-ease. Not frightened or nervous, exactly, but wobbly, not quite together.

As far as she could make out, *The Shameful Kiss* centred around a wicked stepmother (Solomon's part), who had married a wealthy widower and was intent on getting her hands on his fortune. She was also trying to do away with his children, and had resolved to go to grisly lengths to remove anyone who stood in the way of her inheritance. It wasn't until just before the end of Act One that Alyce suddenly realized exactly what was implied: Solomon was playing a witch. A *witch*. It was too ridiculous for words.

As Act Two opened, Master Lyons popped up in front of her with a pot of greasepaint, and before Alyce could protest, he had smeared a pair of thick black eyebrows and a pointed beard and moustache on her face to complete her transformation.

'Not long now,' he said under his breath, pointing to a line in the script on the following page: *Devil intrat*. 'Good luck!' His grin seemed too big for his face; unsettling rather than reassuring.

Immediately in front of the buttery's doorway was a very small flight of wooden steps that led backstage. Master Lyons beckoned her over, but instead of ascending to the stage, he pointed at the floor, where there was just enough space for a grown man to crawl beneath the floorboards. Alyce took one more look at the script to memorize her cue, then squatted down on her haunches, and inched her way awkwardly into the darkness.

The trapdoor could be seen as a thin square of light up ahead. The other actors' feet thundered overhead, dislodging small clouds of dust from between the boards and sending them down on to her nose. The thumping of her heart seemed to match them beat for beat.

Solomon's words rang through the Great Hall, a spell, in Latin: *Nunc, per vota nostra, diabolus ipse surgat!*

That was her cue.

Alyce pushed on the trapdoor. It didn't budge. Master Adams' words floated back to her, too late: *Something keeps sticking when we open the gates of Hell.*

There was silence from the hall. She could hear Solomon's feet shuffling with embarrassment. She tried again. Nothing. It was as though it were nailed shut.

Then, gradually, a low swell of coughing and muttering began to arise from the audience. Alyce thought of the Queen, shifting restlessly in her throne, thought of the shame she was bringing upon the whole company, upon Solomon, standing alone on the stage bearing the brunt of the Court's displeasure.

Straining with her whole back against the trapdoor, something finally gave way. It fell noisily, clumsily open. Somebody out in the hall sniggered. Alyce began to panic, the hot prickle of humiliation running up and down her backbone. Poor Solomon didn't deserve this.

She heaved herself out of the hole in the stage with as much dignity as she could muster, which wasn't much in the circumstances, and stood looking out at the fidgeting audience. Set back from the lights of the stage, she could hardly see any of their faces – what she *could* see, though, was the dark shape of the raised dais in the centre of the hall, and the shimmer of silks and jewels where the Queen sat on her throne, watching the debacle unfold. Alyce's heart felt like a clenched fist.

Solomon was standing to her left, perfectly still. She turned to face him. At first she thought he wasn't going to say anything, that her entrance had brought the play to a grinding halt.

His Adam's apple bobbed up and down in his throat. Then he opened his bright red lips and in his falsetto woman's voice he began his speech.

'*O fiend, conjured by black, forbidden arts,*

Look thou upon my work with baleful eye . . .'

And she did. Her gaze never left him as he stalked the stage, verses pouring from his chest, bewitching her where she stood. She was aware of the spectators settling abruptly. They were just as transfixed as she was, apparently. All of the Great Hall seemed to hold its breath, tensed like the air moments before a thunderstorm.

'*. . .and twixt our lips the dev'lish pact is sealed.*'

Before she knew it, his speech was ended, his warm breath was upon her skin, and he was kissing her.

She wanted to laugh — half from fear, half elation. Solomon, a young man, dressed as a witch, kissing her, a witch, dressed as a young man (dressed as the Devil). But even if there had not been an audience watching, she would not have laughed, because then she would have had to pull away from him, and that was the last thing she wanted to do. Instead she laughed inside, a laugh that rang through her whole body and made her glow.

Solomon took a step backwards. The spell over the pair of them broke, and Alyce suddenly felt very exposed. There was silence, an oppressive stillness. It felt like no one in the audience had so much as blinked since she had appeared clumsily through the trapdoor.

When she looked out at them, she saw why. It was nothing to do with her, or her entrance, or Solomon, or the kiss.

Queen Elizabeth had left her throne and proceeded to the edge of the stage. Behind her, attendants wrung their hands and glanced nervously at each other. From this distance, Alyce was able to see the Queen's face properly for the first time: thin, angular, unnaturally white. Sad too. Her melancholy eyes studied Alyce's face in return, and, locked in that stare, she suddenly knew where she had seen the Queen before.

Bedlam. It was the witchfinder who had come to take her from Bedlam on that freezing midwinter night, the night of her escape. Those cheeks had felt the sharpness of Alyce's fingernails, once upon a time. Alyce took two steps backwards, all of her fears coming together in the form of this one woman. Solomon cleared his throat. The orange light of the lamps and the candles became colder.

No. Not now, thought Alyce. *Not in front of all these people . . .*

That same luminous veil descended over her eyes and the voices returned, louder than ever. Formless black wisps crept through the hall, drifted over the stage, causing the screens and the lanterns to sway and rattle. One of the prop tree's branches cracked and fell, and the spectators gasped in terror – all apart from the Queen, who calmly watched Alyce as the dead flocked to her.

Alyce gritted her teeth and willed it all to stop, but the voices became deafening. Then she looked around the audience, at the men and women to whom she would never belong, and realized, with the feeling of some great burden being lifted from her chest, she didn't need it to stop. Didn't *want* it to stop. Perhaps it was because this had already happened three times before, or perhaps it was because she had been reading the *Necronomicon*, but the presence of the dead no longer frightened her. Intentionally or not, she had summoned them. And if they were here, they may as well make themselves useful.

She exhaled, and her breath broke the storm. The candles and the lanterns went out, and the Great Hall was plunged into complete darkness.

XXIII

The Devil and her lover leapt through the chaos of the hall, shoved this way and that by panicking courtiers. Alyce pulled Solomon along by the sleeve of his dress, able to find her way through the rushing bodies and the over-turned chairs thanks to the eerie luminescence that hadn't yet drained from her vision.

They slipped out of the crack in the hall's great double doors and fell into the starlit courtyard.

When they were at the entrance to the passageway, Solomon tugged his arm free and refused to go further.

'Come *on*, Solly . . .'

'Why did you just do that?'

'I tried to tell you, I can't control it!'

That wasn't entirely true any more, though.

Solomon looked behind him. 'But you can't just run away from the *Queen*, Alyce. She's going to kill us. Or Master Adams will, if she doesn't.'

'It was *her*, Solomon.' She started off towards their chamber, and he reluctantly followed. 'I *knew* I'd seen her before.'

'You *have* seen her before – we saw her in the courtyard just the other day . . .'

'No, before that.' They'd reached the chamber door, and she whirled around. 'She was the woman from Bedlam. The one who tried to kidnap me the first time.'

Solomon looked at her and blinked. Faintly they could hear the sounds of the audience again, babbling as they finally found their way outside.

'That *is* madness,' he said at last.

'I swear. It was her. And another man.'

'No,' said Solomon firmly. 'That's ridiculous. What does she want with you? It wouldn't make any sense anyway. You said they were witchfinders. She's not working for Mary Stuart, is she?'

'Well, exactly.' Alyce's brain furiously tried to sort and connect the information. 'That can't be true. So let's say they weren't who I thought they were. That points us in the other direction: perhaps she was trying to *stop* Mary and the real witchfinders from getting their hands on me.'

She pushed into the room and started throwing off the various pieces of her costume.

'But why?' said Solomon distantly.

'I still don't know that,' Alyce said, peeling off her tights. She watched Solomon wandering aimlessly around, his woman's gown rustling in agitation. 'Come on, get changed!

We've got to *leave*, Solly. Go. Now. Far away. This is all too much.'

The clothes that Solomon had lent her were still backstage in the Great Hall, so she had to throw on the tatty old smock that she'd been wearing when Solomon found her in the street. It was still cold and damp, and reeked of stagnant river water.

She fought her way out of the smock as though she were trapped in a bedsheet, and saw that the boy still hadn't moved.

'Solomon . . .'

'I'm just thinking . . .'

'Think later, Solly.'

'No, listen.' His serious expression was slightly undermined by his giant red lips. 'Maybe Elizabeth is the one your mother wanted you to find. If she thought Doctor Dee was her closest advisor – and there's no reason why she would have thought him a traitor – he would be the best way of putting you in touch with the Queen. I mean, it's not like you can just turn up at the palace and demand an audience.'

'But my mother didn't know Elizabeth . . .'

'Did you ever ask?'

Alyce didn't say anything. Now, it seemed, Solomon was the one talking nonsense. But then, there was a logic to his theory.

'How would Queen Elizabeth have known I was in Bedlam in the first place? My mother didn't have time to write her a letter too.' She suddenly stopped. 'Hold on, where's Pecke?'

They'd left the raven in the room when they went to the Great Hall, but now he was gone.

As if to answer the question, the chamber door crashed open, and the great black bird flapped to Alyce's shoulder. Behind him, standing on the threshold, was a lean, athletic man, with a close-cropped beard and moustache, and a pearl earring in his left ear. His dark brown curls were starting to recede a little in the lamplight, but his face was youthful, his eyes bright. He looked as though he spent most of his life being amused by other people.

'Good evening Alyce,' he said. That voice sounded familiar too. 'Time to pack.'

He produced a sack from under his travelling cloak, and as it parted it revealed a dazzling white doublet and ornate sword hilt underneath.

'Who are you?'

'Not now. I'm taking you to the Tower. Alone. By order of the Queen.' Then he grinned, and handed her a handkerchief. 'You might want to wipe your moustache off, first.'

The only things that Alyce's could call her own were her mommet and the clothes she was wearing, but Solomon insisted on giving her an undershirt, a pair of breeches and all of his mother's books.

'Those aren't mine,' she said, as he threw them into the bag.

'Take them. I can't use them. And they might help you, wherever you're going.'

She wanted to protest, but the man was watching them closely.

'Solly...' she began, but then found herself with nothing to say. There *wasn't* anything to say, because she had no idea what was actually happening. It didn't make sense. If she was heading to the Tower as Queen Elizabeth's prisoner, why was she being allowed to pack her possessions? Why wasn't she being dragged off in chains?

While she ruminated, Solomon came forward and embraced her in his long, spidery arms.

'It'll be all right,' he said.

Alyce didn't reply, couldn't reply. She held him just as tightly.

The man in the doorway sighed. 'Come on,' he said, fingering his moustache with impatience. 'No time for romantic farewells.'

They parted and Alyce picked up the bag. The man ushered her out of the room, followed by Pecke, who flew ahead of them.

'Don't try to follow us,' the man said as they left, resting a hand meaningfully on his sword hilt. 'I suggest you return to Sussex's Men. There's a fair bit of tidying to be done.'

Alyce got one last glimpse of Solomon standing alone in the bedchamber, looking all the more sad and absurd in his women's clothes. Still she couldn't think of anything to say. 'Sorry,' perhaps, but that hardly seemed to cover it. Then the door closed, and her heart convulsed. *I'm never going to see him again,* she thought.

The man directed her to the left, in the opposite direction to the Great Hall, down the passageway towards the servants' quarters. The raven was already out of sight.

'You probably don't remember me, do you?' he said brightly.

'No,' Alyce said.

'Last time I saw you, you were doing your best to ensure that I never father any children.'

It took her a moment to work out what he meant. And then she remembered who he was. She pictured him doubled over and clutching his groin in pain as she bolted for the open door. Here he was, then, the Queen's accomplice.

'Still feels a bit bruised, sometimes,' he continued, shifting his weight as he walked. 'But I think my lineage is safe. I don't blame you. Should have expected you to be a bit spirited, given your—'

He coughed and abruptly stopped speaking. Alyce was still totally confused. For someone who was supposedly her captor, this gentleman was being remarkably friendly. Friendlier than Doctor Dee, at least.

Past the servants' lodgings, the passageway opened up into a courtyard, this one smaller than the one in front of the Great Hall. The cobbles had turned white and glassy in the light of the moon. They crossed into a corner and entered a narrow alley, which ended in a set of slick, black stairs descending into the waters of the Thames. Tied to a post at the bottom was a battered rowing boat, bobbing like a dry leaf on every ripple that reached the riverbank.

'So you're in this together, are you?' Alyce said at last.

'Hmmm?'

She'd stopped at the top of the stairs, and the man didn't

seem particularly concerned about forcing her down them.

'You and Elizabeth. You're working together?'

'Yes. Incidentally, she sends her apologies that she can't be with us at this very moment, as much as she would like to be. Now that we have you, she wants to keep an eye on Doctor Dee.'

'You know about him? You know he is—'

'A craven, dog-hearted villain? A vain, fawning, two-faced, milk-livered miscreant?' He took a couple of breaths to compose himself. 'Yes. We know. And we know about Mary.'

'But—'

'Later, Alyce,' he said. 'We can't spend all night chatting.' He extended a hand to her. 'Careful now, we don't want you cracking your head open when we've nearly got you safe.'

'Safe? I thought we were going to the Tower.'

'We are. You're going to the Queen's private quarters. And I mean *private* private. Safest place in England.'

Alyce was totally confused. Maybe Solomon's theory had been right. Maybe her mother did want to send her to Elizabeth.

She looked at the black waters lapping the bottom of the staircase.

'Um . . . Is *this* even safe?'

'Don't worry yourself, girl. Tide's nearly out, it'll be a millpond, you'll see. And I do have a little experience in sailing.'

He winked at her again, as though there was some joke

she was expected to get, but she didn't know what he meant. He threw her bag of possessions into the stern, and then stepped down into the boat, the hull ringing hollow under his boots. He obviously hadn't been joking about his sailing prowess, because he had impressive sea legs – as much as the vessel rocked and spun, he never lost his balance, and stayed standing with his arms outstretched to catch her when she came off the stairs.

Alyce then wobbled her way into a seated position next to her bag. The man sat opposite her, grinned, and untied the rope that moored them to the side of the palace.

'Oars, please,' he said, nodding to the side of the bench.

Alyce picked up one by its handle, and accidentally thrust the blunt paddle between the man's legs. She only looked up when he cried out, slapping a hand over his mouth to prevent it echoing over down the whole river.

'Stop *doing* that! What argument do you have with my manhood?'

'I'm sorry,' she said, but couldn't resist a snigger. 'I didn't do it on purpose, honestly.'

'I don't think I believe you.'

She carefully handed him the second oar, and he fixed them both into the boat's rowlocks. Then he rowed them a little way out into the river, the plop and splash of his strokes beating a slow, peaceful rhythm against the silence of the night.

'So you're a sailor, are you?'

He laughed in between straining on the oars. 'A sailor? I am Walter Raleigh.' He waited expectantly for her reaction.

Alyce shrugged. 'I've never heard of you.'

'Really?' He paused again. 'Oh. Right. Yes, I am a sailor, among other things. A captain, actually. I have sailed to the New World more often than . . . Well, lots of times.'

'My mother told me about the New World. I always thought she was making it up. It sounded like a faerie story. Some untouched country at the ends of the earth.'

'I can assure you, it's quite real. You might even get to go there, one day. But believe me, the Atlantic Ocean is a little choppier than this.'

'Why do you go there?'

'Mostly because Bess asks me to. In secret sometimes, which is no mean feat given the size of the ship and the crew I have to take.'

'What are you, her servant or something?'

Raleigh's moustache twitched with amusement. 'Feels like it most of the time. But no. What am I? Difficult to say. I'm too young to be her advisor, or her lover. She doesn't trust me enough to make me her confidante. I don't know what that leaves. Her plaything, perhaps? I suppose the important thing is that we share certain . . . interests. Pursuits of a specific nature. But, yes, let's just leave it at servant. My orders tonight are to get you out of the palace in secret and then somewhere safe as quickly as possible.'

'Why?'

'That's for her to tell you, I'm afraid, but—'

'Let me guess: later?'

He nodded.

Before Alyce could press him, there was rush of feathers

overhead, and Pecke descended out of the night to perch on the prow of their rowing boat.

'Aha!' exclaimed Raleigh. 'You've decided to join us after all, Master Pecke?'

Alyce gaped. 'You know him?'

'Of course. He's the reason we know about Dee. And all about you, of course.'

'I don't understand . . .'

Raleigh suddenly looked uncomfortable. 'It doesn't matter. I shouldn't be saying all of this so soon.'

'So *soon*?' said Alyce incredulously. 'I think I've waited long enough for answers, actually.'

'I'm sorry, Alyce, I shouldn't have said anything. Bess wanted to explain herself . . .'

'Does Pecke belong to the *Queen*?'

Raleigh's silence was the only answer she needed.

She felt like the waters of her brain began to clear, after months of being muddied and dark and swirling. Pecke, that tatty heap of feathers who had perched on the thatch of her old home so many times, belonged to Queen Elizabeth. So, she and her mother must have known each other. *That* was what the letter had been about. Her mother had been trying to get her to Elizabeth, via Doctor Dee.

Why hadn't she *said* so?

Alyce watched the lights of the city blinking lazily among the waves, and let her imagination run away with itself. She indulged every fancy. Maybe, she thought, she was going to be brought up by the Queen. In a palace. In several palaces, probably. And Elizabeth had no children of her own, so what would that make Alyce? Desperate hopes and wild fears tumbled into a colourless blur, until she thought she was going to keel over in the bottom of the boat.

She only returned to the present when she saw Raleigh had stopped rowing, and was looking over his shoulder.

London Bridge was fast approaching in the darkness. She could even make out Vitali's strange house under the arch on the opposite side of the river, its windows blank.

'Hold on tight, now,' said Raleigh. 'Things can get a bit exciting here, even at low tide.'

The current began to sweep them towards the wooden pontoons that jutted from the base of the bridge. The little boat yawed and spun, and Raleigh occasionally dipped an oar on either side to control the rotations. If he misjudged it, Alyce realized as she gripped her bench, they would be smashed to splinters on the bridge itself, or, worse still, crushed under the waterwheels near the bank.

Pecke abandoned ship. The moon disappeared behind the roofs of the shops overhead, and Alyce shut her eyes tightly. The rush of water was deafening; it echoed around the colossal arch as it swallowed them whole.

They slammed into the slimy timbers and leant violently over to one side. Alyce opened her eyes to the green darkness and gripped the edge of the boat as they were levered into the air. One of the oars was stuck under the water, and as Raleigh tried to yank it out, all he succeeded in doing was dragging that side further down towards the waves. Alyce saw her bag of possessions sliding away from her, and flung out an arm to save it.

She shouldn't have tried. She only managed to snatch a corner – and in attempting to pull it to safety, she simply emptied its contents over the edge of the boat.

She yelped. Most of the books, Solomon's clothes, and her trusty mommet disappeared without trace. As soon as the doll hit the water her flesh seemed to freeze and shatter.

Their vessel finally righted itself – nearly catapulting Alyce overboard – and spun out from under the arch into a calmer stream. They were through. Alyce looked over her shoulder miserably, hoping the mommet might bob to the surface, but the currents were so strong and the waters so dark it may as well have been sunk in tar. Up ahead were the lines of galleons and other ships tied to the Legal Quays, their masts and rigging criss-crossing the moonlit sky.

All the excitement of the revelations only moments ago seemed to have gone cold, doused by the merciless waters of the Thames. Her mommet. She needed it. It had been her faithful companion for so long. Without it she felt weak, slow, as though she herself was beneath the cold fathoms of river water.

Raleigh set to rowing again.

'Sorry,' he said. 'About your books. Although, if I'm honest, Bess has always been suspicious of them, so maybe you're better off without. Your lot know it all intuitively, anyway. It's only dullards like me and Dee who have to learn the Craft from books.'

Alyce fished the limp bag out from under her seat and was surprised to find it was still heavy. There was something at the bottom. She carefully placed it on her lap and peered inside to see what had survived.

It was square and black. She knew what it was before she'd opened it, or even read the spine.

She shivered. It was the *Necronomicon*.

HOPKINS

Hopkins was too late. He knew it would be that way. Doctor Dee had wasted too much time trying to contact Queen Mary, then part of the road from Mortlake to London had been flooded, and when they'd finally reached the palace the guards had stubbornly refused them entry. And now the play was over.

The servants were still clearing the Great Hall when he and Caxton entered through the double doors. They stopped their sweeping and stared with frozen, frightened eyes as the pair of them strode up to the remains of the stage, Caxton's mask – repaired lovingly by Doctor Dee – casting monstrous, rippling shadows across the flagstones.

Hopkins hated the theatre. The playhouses had always been full of stinking, rowdy peasants, and it seemed that even at Court the audiences weren't much better. The Great Hall was a complete shambles. It looked like there had been a riot.

He not only hated the theatre – he hated actors too, as a breed. He could already hear them braying to each other as they packed away their props and costumes. There seemed to be an argument going on, an argument so forceful it was impossible to tell whether they were still acting or not. Several of the players had turned on one of their own: a thin, crow-haired young man who wasn't putting up much of a fight.

There was no sign of the girl.

'Gentlemen,' he called. *Animals*, he thought. 'Forgive me for interrupting.' They all fell silent at the sight of Caxton. One of the players dropped his armful of wooden swords.

'Can I help you?' asked one of the older members of the group – the company leader, Hopkins suspected.

'I very much hope so,' he said, hopping up on to the stage and perusing the costumes half-stuffed into boxes. There were women's clothes here, but that didn't necessarily mean there was a girl in the troupe.

Men cavorting in public in *women's* apparel. Obscene.

'Strange as it might seem,' he continued, 'we were wondering if you had a young woman in your company. Name of Alyce Greenliefe.'

'You mean *Alex* Greenliefe. And yes, he *was* in our company until he lost us our patronage.'

Hopkins laughed to himself. 'Of course. *Alex* Greenliefe. Do you know where I might find him?'

'Ha!' One of the other actors barked. 'If we knew where he was, we'd be throttling him right now. Everyone's looking for him. Even Her Majesty.'

Hopkins listened to him without turning. He was looking at the slender boy in the centre of the group, with his tufted black hair, purple rings around his eyes, and an odd red smear around his lips. He knew who this was. He'd even seen him before, in the flesh, in the gatehouse at Bedlam.

Hopkins smiled at him.

The boy jerked and ducked behind one of the other men, then leapt over one of the boxes of costumes, down from the stage, and began sprinting to the entrance of the Great Hall.

'*Solomon!*' cried the company leader, and the rest of the actors spat in disgust.

'He's the one you want!' said another. 'He brought the Devil among us!'

Hopkins didn't have to speak, didn't even have to move. Caxton somehow managed to catch the boy without even breaking into a run. The length of his strides was enormous, unnaturally so. He snatched the back of his ruff and hauled him to the floor.

'Would you mind,' said Hopkins, addressing the company leader, 'if we asked your fellow actor a few questions?'

'You would be most welcome,' said the older man, the fear plain to read in his watery eyes.

'My thanks,' said Hopkins. 'We shall do our best to return him in one piece.'

Doctor Dee's carriage was waiting outside. His horses snorted and pawed at the dirt, looking just as impatient as the man himself. When Hopkins approached the carriage door, the Doctor was peering into his black scrying mirror, anxiety etched across his old face. He looked up.

'Where is the girl, Hopkins?'

'We don't have the girl,' he said, stepping up into the opposite seat while Caxton took the reins, 'because she's been taken to the Tower.'

Dee seemed to look at him from every angle, searching his face for some sign that this was a joke. Then he laughed, long and loudly.

'The Tower?' he said. 'Well. There *is* a happy coincidence.'

They heard the clink of the horses' bridles, then the carriage shuddered, and rattled into the night.

XXIV

Raleigh paddled them slowly past the floating hulks, past the spot where Alyce had been washed ashore and robbed a few days earlier, past the sounds of revellers drinking themselves into oblivion in the dockside taverns.

Then she saw it. It wasn't just one tower, as the name suggested, but countless towers, squat and immovable, connected by walls and walkways on which the guards' torches bobbed and flickered. At its centre, she could just make out the crenellations of the great White Tower, standing ghostly sentinel over the whole fortress.

She heard it too. From somewhere within, a bell tolled the hour. Ten? Eleven? The wind snatched some of the peals from her and carried them downstream.

Their boat drifted along the Tower's wharf. Some of the guards had spotted them, and yellow torchlit faces peered over the edge with their halberds hovering next to them. Raleigh manoeuvred them out of the current and under the wharf itself, until they were stationary in front of a large, semi-circular gate in the fortress's wall. Here the river water swept through a closed portcullis into the moat within.

Pecke had briefly rejoined them, but now flew high over the battlements and disappeared inside.

'Who goes there?' called one of the warders from above.

'Ho there, warder!' Walter shouted back. 'It is Walter Raleigh. With an enemy of the Queen. Open the traitors' gate.'

'Raleigh?' The guard did not pronounce the name with any fondness. The face disappeared, there was the sound of footsteps from above, and then it reappeared from a lower window. 'It *is* you. Why can't you just use the front gate like everybody else, you dog? Have to make your entrance as dramatic as possible, don't you? Well, no one important's going to see it, because they're all in bed.'

He spat something, which plopped into the water next to Alyce's elbow.

'An old friend,' Raleigh said to her, as the waves nudged the boat backwards and forwards. He fetched a loop of sodden rope from underneath his bench. 'Here, put this round your wrists. You're going to have to be my prisoner for a while.'

Just how she was meant to tie up her own hands, Alyce wasn't sure. She made a loose loop and slipped it over her fingers, but it didn't look very convincing.

After a moment, there was the creak of a wheel being turned somewhere behind the wall and the portcullis began to rise, dredging up all kinds of filth from the riverbed with it. It dripped on to Alyce's head as Raleigh rowed them under the arch and into the Tower's outer ward.

At the top of the steps leading out of the moat, two guards fell about laughing.

'Quite a catch, Walter!'

'Thank God you caught her, she looks dangerous that one!'

'You'll get your knighthood for this, no doubt!'

They slapped each other on the back, and Alyce started to get hot with anger, more for her own sake than for Walter's. But as soon as the boat was tied up, the joke had passed and they'd returned to their duties.

'They can laugh all they like,' muttered Walter, helping Alyce out of her seat. There was at least an inch of water in the hull now. 'Chances are I *will* get a knighthood after all this.'

Once they were on dry land, he led her through a gate in another, inner wall, where two more warders regarded her suspiciously, and across the lawn to the gigantic White Tower. In the grass, she saw half a dozen ravens, among them Pecke, conspicuous for his size and odd-coloured eyes.

Some wooden steps led them into a room not unlike the Great Hall at Whitehall, although it seemed sparser and more functional. More guards, more nods, more tipped hats, and then they were climbing a spiral staircase that wound up inside the far corner of the tower. At the top, they emerged into a gallery that ran along one side of the keep, and in front of them was a large oak door studded with iron. Raleigh fumbled under his cloak, and again Alyce saw the blinding white of the man's expensive clothes beneath. He produced a ring of keys, and tried a few before the lock clicked and he was able to heave the door open. Then he lit a taper from one of the torches on the stairs, and led her inside.

The room beyond was like nothing Alyce had seen before. There was so much gilding it hurt the eyes, brighter and more garish as Raleigh went around lighting the candles. At the centre was a four-poster bed, a vast sea of blue velvet, and opposite that a dressing table that looked as complex and impenetrable as the Tower of London itself. Intricately detailed and richly coloured tapestries hung from every wall. It made Solomon's room look like a stable.

'Is this where I'll be staying?' In all honesty, she wasn't sure she would be able to sleep, the room glittered so much.

'No, no,' said Raleigh. 'This isn't Bess's private chamber.' He went and checked outside in the passageway, and then closed the door. 'Follow me,' he said.

Behind one of the tapestries was a gap in the wall, only wide enough for one person to fit into at once, and a slender person at that.

'Breathe in,' he said, and disappeared into the passage. She followed him, shoulders grazing the damp stone on either side. 'This is actually the safest way to make sure nobody finds it,' he said as they shuffled along. 'You should see the size of the breeches that courtiers wear these days. And the ruffs. And the peasecod bellies. They wouldn't stand a chance of fitting through here.'

An incredibly tight set of stairs went up further still, this time seemingly *within* the thick walls of the White Tower, until they reached a small, unimpressive wooden door. Raleigh retrieved another key from under his cloak – enormous, this one, its head an intricate labyrinth of wrought iron the size of her palm.

The strangest thought arose in her head when the door swung open.

I'm home.

Something about the low orange light mixed with the musty smell of earth and roots and the spice of incense, put her right back in her mother's cellar. And the more she saw, the more comforted she felt. Here were all the things she had grown up with, so normal, so familiar: bowls of dried herbs and fungi, skulls and bones of animals, countless figures of men and beasts woven from straw and hair. Candles the size of her thigh, some even larger. A great iron brazier smoking steadily in the corner.

'Queen Elizabeth is a witch,' said Alyce.

Raleigh didn't reply. There was no need.

How on earth had she concealed it so completely, and for so long? Did other people know, besides Raleigh? What if her subjects were to find out? It was too much to take in: Her Majesty, Good Queen Bess, a sorceress, a crone, a handmaiden to the Devil Himself. She couldn't help smiling at the thought of it; but then, at the same time, her heart broke a little to think that even the Queen of England was forced to hide herself away in her own palace.

Alyce wandered from one end of the chamber to the

other, examining the kinds of charms and trinkets and artefacts she hadn't seen for months. Elizabeth and her mother: they *must* have known each other. Not only were they fellow witches, but their tastes seemed completely identical, at least as far as their lodgings were concerned.

'Make yourself comfortable,' Raleigh said at last, dropping the bag containing her book on the floor. 'I need to return to Whitehall to find Elizabeth. And to find Doctor Dee.' If there had been anywhere to spit, he would have done. 'I'll return tomorrow, with Bess, I hope. Until then, lock this door, and don't open it to anyone.' He handed her the gigantic key, and turned to go. The last thing she saw was the flash of his scabbard as he slipped back through the door.

Alyce looked around the chamber, alone but not lonely. Under the room's single arched window was a table covered with candles. She picked up her bag from the floor and carried it over with her, and opened the *Necronomicon* in the pool of their light. She sat and gazed at the symbols and pictures, and thought nothing of the key's weight in her pocket.

XXV

It was still dark outside when Alyce woke, and she had no idea what time it was. She had a vague memory of a bell sounding, a single, clear ring, which would mean it was well after one o'clock in the morning. If the bell had been at all real. Chances were, she wouldn't have heard it, sealed into this warm, comfortable tomb.

She had fallen asleep at the book, and she had to peel her face off the damp pages before she could sit upright. She rubbed her eyes and looked around. Still alone. The embers in the brazier were almost dead. Something was bothering her – a feeling that someone had been speaking to her in her dreams, trying to tell her something important, something she had to remember, and Alyce had promptly forgotten it as soon as she had opened her eyes.

On the shelves that lined the room's curved walls there were various bottles and jars, but she was fairly certain none of them contained anything that would quench her thirst.

She got up and peered at the dark glass, seeing only her reflection. It was intolerably hot, and she hadn't had anything to drink since before the play, which seemed years ago now.

Alyce. Open the door.

She nearly dropped the flask she was examining. The voice sounded no louder than a draught from outside. Maybe she was still dreaming after all.

Alyce. Please.

Her blood rushed to her head so ferociously she thought she was going to faint. She knew the voice, but wouldn't admit it to herself. This *had* to be a dream.

There followed a scratching noise on the other side of the door, as if someone were trying to knock, but were too weak to do so.

Alyce.

She rushed over and pulled on the circular iron handle, its weight and coldness proving that she was awake. She suddenly remembered she hadn't locked the door as Raleigh had instructed her.

It opened on to nothingness.

Below her, on the narrow staircase, she heard the patter of bare feet on stone.

Alyce ran down after the sound, leaving the door to Elizabeth's private chamber wide open. She slipped on the damp steps a couple of times, feeling her way along the walls while her eyes got accustomed to the darkness. At the bottom, already out of breath, her heart surging through her ribs, she emerged from behind the tapestry to find the great bedchamber door also open. The candles had long since burnt out, or perhaps Raleigh had extinguished them when he had left, but in the gloom she saw a white heel and a flutter of fabric disappear out of the room.

This was stupid, she decided. She should stay put. Lock herself up in the attic, as she had been told.

Don't stop. Follow me. We can escape, together.

That voice again. Sometimes it sounded as though it were drifting to her from outside in the passageway, sometimes it echoed behind her. Sometimes it seemed to come from within her own head.

Alyce? Don't you want to see me again? Don't you want to go back?

It brought tears to her eyes. Of course she wanted to go back. It was all she had ever wanted, since she had heard that voice last. Since it had been brutally silenced.

Quickly now.

She ran into the gallery outside. The footsteps were echoing down the spiral staircase that she and Raleigh had used when they had arrived. Round and down she went, two floors, then three, lower even than the entrance to the Tower, following the warm, familiar scent that was always just ahead of her.

The basement was poorly lit, and cruel angular shapes lurked in the shadows. Imagined or not, Alyce smelt old blood. And at the far end, among the racks and cages and other pieces of machinery, she finally saw her. Her face was obscured, but there was no doubting the figure and the way it moved. It was her mother.

Alyce's tears were scalding. It made no sense. It was madness. Agonizing, blinding, joyful madness.

The figure was crouching down to open a trapdoor in the corner of the room. Even that movement reminded Alyce of being at home, despite her current grisly surroundings. Her mother pulled on the handle just like she used to before entering the cellar in their old cottage, the same cellar where Alyce had hidden herself.

Down here, Alyce!

Again, the voice didn't seem to come from the right direction.

The figure dropped herself into the square black hole in the ground. Alyce wiped her eyes to clear her vision, snatched a torch from a sconce, and hurried to catch up.

Yet more spiralling stairs, but now slimy and moss-covered, burrowing deep into the earth. Pale, maggot-coloured fungus forced its way between the stones and brushed her cheeks and hands as she tiptoed past. It was much colder down here, a profound cold that reached the marrow of her bones.

Her hands and feet were numb by the time she reached the bottom. There she found herself in a maze of low-ceilinged chambers and passages that had not so much been built as hollowed out of the ground. The walls themselves had spaces roughly hewn into them – long, shallow, body-sized spaces. Catacombs of some kind. The air was foul with decay, overlaid with a sharp smell of pickling that reminded her of Doctor Dee's house.

The walls of the passage glowed with something too

steady, too eerie to be firelight. Her mother was waiting for her at the end, facing her now.

So close Alyce. Follow me.

She spoke the words without moving her lips. The cold now clutched at Alyce's heart.

Alyce came forward very slowly. Each step seemed to take hours to complete. In the alcoves on either side of her, she saw the source of the weird half-light: alchemical globes. In their glow, she glimpsed things far more horrifying than any of the instruments of torture in the Tower. They seemed, in fact, to be the end products of those instruments. People. And parts of people.

The nearer she got to her mother, the more it felt like her blood was draining out of her, as though she were physically shrivelling in the darkness. The apparition grew taller, broader around the shoulders. Its face became longer, too, its features stern and imperious. Her mother's wild curls disappeared, bound tight and straight behind the figure's high forehead. Instead of her mother's plain, loose smock, this woman wore an elaborate and voluminous dress that clutched stiffly at her neck and waist.

Mary Stuart stood before her, but not as a phantom this time. The woman herself. In the light of the globes she cast a blunt, definite shadow on the floor of the catacombs. Her breathing was loud and a little strained, emerging in hot, irregular clouds. She looked old.

Before Alyce could take a backward step, two leather-clad hands pinned her arms to her sides, and when she tried to pull herself free she saw that long, awful beak over her shoulder and the glassy, lifeless eyes at the other end. Her torch fell to the ground. The other witchfinder melted out of the darkness at her side, and then, completing the party, she saw Doctor Dee hovering at Mary's shoulder.

She was trapped. All of her bile surged out of her at once.

'You heartless coward,' she spat.

Mary Stuart laughed. 'Yes, a cheap trick. Forgive me. But you will see your real mother soon enough. I will uphold my end of the deal.'

'There *was* no deal.'

'Yes, I am aware of that. A great shame, because we will have to kill you as a result. But even so, I will keep my promise: I will bring your mother to you.'

'No! I don't *want* . . .' Alyce strained against the crow-man's grasp, grinding dirt into the soles of her feet. She looked wildly from one alcove to the next, at what she assumed were the remains of Doctor Dee's experiments. Each one looked like a butcher's stall. Collected around the benches were same kinds of tools and instruments and books that she'd seen at his house in Mortlake.

The thought of her mother being brought back like this – a creature, a monster like the man in the mask – terrified her more than anything.

'Hush, Alyce,' said Mary. 'It's not what you think.' As the Queen of Scots came closer, Alyce saw more of the lines and fissures in her greying skin. She looked more than just old. She looked half dead.

'Let me *go*.' She heard the sleeves of her smock tearing

as she squirmed, the man's fingers printing bruises all over her upper arms.

'Not until you and your mother have been reunited, child. It won't be long.'

'*Why?*' cried Alyce, eyes stinging again. 'Why *me?*'

There was the sound of footsteps on the staircase behind them, coming down from the basement of the Tower. Mary ignored her question and walked past her to meet the intruders. Alyce was forced around to face the doorway that had led her into the catacombs.

The footsteps became louder, more urgent. Two people, it sounded like, although the echoing made it difficult to tell. She strained her eyes to peer into the gloom.

A figure materialized in a plain white dress, with a face almost the same colour, topped with a mess of rust-coloured hair. Behind her was a tall man in a travelling cloak, his sword drawn. Doctor Dee retreated into the shadows, the look on his face less fear than embarrassment.

'Welcome, Your Majesty,' said Mary, giving Elizabeth a mocking curtsy. 'This is a pleasant coincidence. You're just in time.'

Elizabeth herself didn't take her eyes off Alyce.

'Give her up, Mary.' It was that same melancholy voice Alyce remembered from the night in Bedlam. If only she had gone along with their ruse back then, she could have avoided all of this.

'I'm afraid I cannot do that, Your Majesty. When one has been wrongly imprisoned for nearly ten years, one becomes less inclined to negotiate.'

'I have treated you fairly. I have indulged you. I allowed you, fool that I was, to continue practising your Craft – although I can see it is more corrupted than ever.' She briefly pierced Doctor Dee with a glance. 'Let Alyce go, and we can talk.'

'The time for talking has passed, Your Majesty. For us, at least. For you and Alyce, though, there is plenty to discuss.'

'Mary . . .'

'In fact, now would be a very good time. The girl was just asking: *why me?*' She turned back to Alyce. 'Weren't you? It's a very good question. Perhaps you can answer it, Your Majesty? Why *her*? Why is she so special?'

Elizabeth had frozen. Raleigh looked from one face to the other, his sword point wavering with uncertainty.

'Why did you come down here without the Tower guards, Your Majesty? It would have been easy to overwhelm us. Why would you not want anybody else to be here?'

'Don't listen to her, Alyce,' murmured Elizabeth. 'Her words are poison.'

'Is it because you didn't want anyone else to see you reunited with your illegitimate daughter?'

Silence.

'There,' said Mary, satisfied. 'I said I would bring your mother back, didn't I, Alyce? And I didn't have to use any dark arts at all.'

XXVI

Once, when Alyce was living in Fordham, she had fallen into a well. Not fallen — was pushed, by one of the villagers' children as she reached in for the bucket. She still had nightmares about it — the shattering cold of the water, the slick, black stones that encircled her and reduced the sky to a tiny buttonhole of light. The boys cackling somewhere overhead.

She felt the same now. Just as cold, just as dark. Drowning in air, breathing in and in and in and feeling like her lungs would never empty.

'Is it true?' she whispered.

'Alyce—'

'You are the Bastard Princess of England,' interrupted Mary. 'How do you like that title?'

'Listen to me, Alyce,' said Elizabeth. 'I only wanted to keep you safe.'

'So it's true, then.'

Elizabeth looked at her sadly. 'Yes.'

The world collapsed a little more. Alyce felt like she was sliding away from herself. Her whole life, a fiction.

'Why?' It was all she could think to say. She knew how pathetic she sounded.

Mary laughed again. 'Another good question! It seems callous, does it not, to give up one's own child? But don't worry, Princess. We are going to give your mother the chance to redeem herself. To prove how much she loves you. Master Hopkins?'

She turned and nodded at the witchfinder, who was stood beside her. The man who should have been dead now drew his sword and put the freezing blade to Alyce's throat. Alyce watched Raleigh's fingers twitching on the hilt of his own weapon.

'I wonder,' said Mary, 'whether this time around she will choose her realm over her daughter?'

For a moment, Elizabeth's dry lips moved but made no sound. Then, finally, she said: 'You cannot be Queen, Mary.'

'Then the girl dies.'

Alyce swallowed, and felt the sword's edge graze her skin as it moved. It wasn't fear she felt, though. A silent, hopeless rage was bubbling up from her navel. *Daughter.* The word seemed meaningless.

'No, you misunderstand me,' said Elizabeth. 'Even if I were to hand you the throne, tonight, willingly, you cannot be Queen. Your subjects – *my* subjects – will not accept you, if you show them your true nature. There will be no witch queen, Mary. It is madness.'

'You could have been that queen,' hissed Mary. 'But look at what you've become. You deny who you are. Conceal it from the world, just as I did. You are so suspicious of your own kind you lock me up and you drive your closest advisor into the depths of the earth, to carry out his research in the darkness.'

'What you and the good Doctor practise is not witch-craft, Mary. It is an abomination. A corruption of all we know.'

'*We*,' Mary laughed. 'Who is this *we* you speak of? Most of our kind hate you, Bess, because you do nothing for us. It's as though the Coven doesn't even exist. I will restore us to our *rightful* place.'

'The Coven's rightful place is in the darkness. It is where we belong.'

'In the darkness? Listen to yourself, Bess! You could be the most powerful woman on earth. Aren't you tired of it all? The suitors, the arranged marriages, the advisors speak-ing to you like some idiot girl? Living your life as a pawn of ambitious men? Aren't you tired of *pretending* you're weak?'

'It is the way things must be. It is the way things have always been.'

'Then you are doomed. I have spent enough time being that kind of queen. Being that kind of woman. All my life I have been surrounded by others who have plotted, end-lessly, to use me for their ends. My own *son* conspires against me. In the meantime, everyone I ever loved has died or been killed. Husbands, uncles, fathers. And I am expected to do nothing. To remain *in the darkness*, as you so wisely counsel. Well. I will not suffer it any longer. I will show the world a queen who is truly strong. I will show my people mastery over Death. And they will love me and fear me for it.'

Alyce's frozen muscles screamed at her. Along with the anger she felt at the reappearance of her 'mother', she found herself more than a little persuaded by Mary's words, just as she had back in Doctor Dee's house. Why *should* they be forced to live in the shadows? Why *should* they accept death so blithely, if they had the power to control it?

'Fear,' Elizabeth repeated. 'Yes. That is what it comes down to, isn't it? That is how you will ensure the obedience of your subjects. You will take their fear of death and replace it with fear of *you* – fear that you won't offer them your help, that you won't save their loved ones from death. Or, perhaps, fear that you *will*? Is that also how you will govern? Terrorize your enemies with visions and visitations from the Other Side? Am I close to the truth?'

Alyce's head swam. 'Visions and visitations' sounded a lot like what had happened back in the Great Hall, in the yard of The Swan, on the quayside of the Thames. She'd definitely terrorized the man who tried to rob her. Been proud of it too. So whose side was she on?

Mary smiled. 'You sound envious, Bess. Of course you would be, given how surrounded by enemies you are. Given how much you are hated.'

'Then I am right. Of course. Necromancy will be both the reward and the punishment. How neat. And, I suppose, your followers will administer this justice? Uphold your rule of fear?'

'Our kind will be given the power that is rightfully theirs. The power you deny them.'

'And those witches who do not share your vision?'

'There will be no place for you here.'

'I see. And what of our enemies abroad? Will you send witches into battle for us? Will you conjure an army of the dead to defend us when our shores are invaded?'

'If need be.'

For the first time, Alyce glimpsed the full, horrifying panorama of what Mary might be capable of. And then, somehow more frightening: what Alyce *herself* might be capable of. *An army of the dead.*

Elizabeth laughed, and looked at Mary, Queen of Scots with something that seemed to Alyce like pity. 'Listen to yourself, Mary. You are no fool. You *know* where this will end. We both do. Aside from the oppression, aside from the fear, aside from turning my realm over to tyranny, there is something much bigger at stake here, and you will not admit it.'

For once, Mary was silent.

'You cannot master death,' said Elizabeth. 'No one can. Death will master *you*, if it has not already done so. Every time you summon the dead, you bring our worlds closer together, when our purpose should be to keep them apart. Every one of your black spells rends a hole in the veil that separates us. Now picture your glorious kingdom: hundreds, thousands of witches dabbling in necromancy they barely understand, bringing death into the world on a whim, every hour of every day. Do you really think all of them can control the things they summon? Do you think they can send them back where they came from? Do you think *you* can? What happens to your legions of the dead when you no longer have use for them? You know what lies on the Other Side, Mary. It is not just the spirits of the dead. There are more ancient, more powerful things. They will *use* you. You will open the gates of death, and invite them in to devour us.'

Again, Alyce's innards tightened as she listened. This was what it felt like she'd been doing all along. Opening the gates. Inviting the dead in. Whether she wanted to or not.

Mary sighed.

'You are talking about things you cannot possibly comprehend. It's sad, really. How ignorant you are. How timid. We could have ruled together, you and I, Bess. I considered that once. What was it I used to call you? My *queen sister*? But now we are come to this.' She gave a hollow laugh. 'The funny thing is, if you had even half of my skill, if you had read even a handful of pages from the *Necronomicon*, this situation wouldn't even concern you. You could revive your daughter in a heartbeat.'

'Tell your man to lower his sword,' said Elizabeth.

'No. I need certain assurances from you.'

'I cannot simply *hand* the throne over to you like I'm selling you a horse.'

'As a matter of fact, you can.'

In Alyce's ears, the bitter exchange was slowly being drowned by different voices. The dead were everywhere in the catacombs, centuries of entombed souls. Their resting place probably predated the Tower itself, hundreds, thousands of them. And the fact that Alyce was probably going to join them shortly, with a wound across her throat, had made her sense of them particularly acute. It was as if they heard her worries. Dark, fluid figures bled in and out of the light, encircling her and the two queens like a restless, whispering audience.

'We are not discussing any terms until your men release my daughter.' Elizabeth's voice was vague and watery.

The spectres were clearer now than they had ever been, more present than they had been at The Swan, or on Vitali's stage, or in the Great Hall during the play. More than that: she felt like she *knew* them, knew their lives, could pick individuals out of the dead crowd and speak with them. And, she was sure now, if she spoke they would listen. The Other Side was here, everywhere, hers to command. Queen Elizabeth's warnings seemed meaningless, and untrue.

Alyce made her decision. The only way out of this situation was with the help of the dead, otherwise she would be joining their number. She would have to open the gates.

When she spoke, the cold blade broke the skin under her jaw. The words did not sound like her own. Her voice was deep and ancient, as though coming from a different place and time altogether. The shadows came together and dispersed like a flock of birds, and between the fleeting shapes she could see the looks of shock on Elizabeth and Raleigh's faces, and the horror on Mary's.

The dead heard Alyce, and they obeyed. At once, the

black tide surged towards Hopkins. It licked over him like fire. From the hilt upwards, his sword turned to rust, and then to ashes, and crumbled between Alyce's feet. Before Hopkins had even realized what was happening, Raleigh leapt forward and drove his own sword precisely, almost delicately, into the man's ribs. The witchfinder grunted and slumped to the floor in the dust of his weapon.

Alyce tried to speak again, but felt the masked man's long, inhumanly strong fingers curl around her neck, pressing on her windpipe. With his other hand he caught Raleigh's sword by the blade itself, and Alyce could see it biting through the leather of his gloves and into his flesh, but still he wrenched it from its owner's hand and tossed it aside.

Mary fled.

'*Bring the girl*,' she shouted behind her.

She disappeared down one of tunnels of the catacombs, Doctor Dee by her side.

Alyce's vision became grey and fuzzy as she fought for air. Disarmed, Raleigh lowered his shoulder and drove the masked man back into an alcove, sending the remains of one of Doctor Dee's experiments skittering over the floor. The masked man grasped desperately at the sharp surgical instruments on the table, but Raleigh took a glowing alchemical globe and brought it down on to his adversary's head in a shower of glass and phosphorus. The giant black beak lolled sideways. He didn't get up again.

Queen Elizabeth had not chased Mary or Doctor Dee. Instead, she was strangely still. She began muttering to herself, and then knelt and drew a large circle in the dust of the catacombs' floor.

'What are you doing?' asked Alyce, massaging her throat.

'I'm going after her,' said the Queen.

She scratched several runes around the circumference of the circle with her finger, and continued to chant. The whole design glowed red, as though branded into the earth with a hot iron.

Alyce watched her calmly preparing her escape, and screamed somewhere in the pit of her stomach. She wanted to spit.

'Abandoning me again, are you?'

'Please, Alyce.' Elizabeth turned to face her. She looked so tired and wretched, Alyce's anger faltered for a moment. 'Stay here. Wait for me.'

Then she stepped into the circle. It swallowed her whole, the runes turned dead and cold, and she was gone. Who knew where to. Alyce told herself she didn't care.

Suddenly there was another scratching sound, behind her this time. A groan too. She turned away from the magic circle. Hopkins had hauled himself to his knees. Of course he wasn't dead. He hadn't been alive in the first place.

She ran. Not just from Hopkins, or Mary, but from everything, from everyone. She wanted to run out of the city walls, to the sea, and beyond. She didn't want to be anywhere.

Raleigh's voice echoed after her, but she ignored it and leapt up the wet stone steps leading back to the Tower.

The staircase seemed ten times longer in the opposite

direction. Her legs burned and her head swam from the endless spiralling, and only the heavy tread of Hopkins' boots further down kept her from collapsing against the slimy walls. Everything had become so nightmarish, so unreal, she considered quite calmly the possibility that the staircase would not end, ever, and that she and Hopkins would circle each other into eternity.

Suddenly, a square of dirty red light penetrated the darkness over her head. She had reached the trapdoor. She hauled herself up into the basement of the Tower, grateful for the brief rest she could give her legs. She picked a sharp stone out of the sole of her foot, and then she was up and running again, up the stairs to the Tower's lowest floor, and the way out.

It was blocked. Two of the warders stood slouched and obviously bored in the archway, the torchlight picking out the gold embroidery on their red uniforms. Between their shoulders Alyce could see the outer battlements of the Tower and the deep purple of the night sky, just on the cusp of becoming dawn.

They heard her panting, and just as they turned to investigate she dived through the middle of them, sending their halberds clattering against the door's stonework. She landed off-balance and tumbled down the wooden stairs that led into the courtyard below.

'*Oi!*' The guards came thundering after her. '*You get back here!*'

Alyce rubbed at her twisted ankle, and began limping across the courtyard to the outer ward. After a few painful steps, the sound of the pursuing guards was suddenly silenced. She turned. They were both in a heap on the steps, Hopkins stepping over them, dagger in hand.

Her ankle sent a jolt of pain through her as she tried to run. She hopped another couple of feet, groaned, and fell into the straw and manure among the cobbles. Hopkins' approach was slow, considered, wolf-like. He still clutched at the wound that Raleigh had given him.

More guards were running along the walls and emerging from doorways, roused by the commotion. But among their shouts and footsteps there was another noise. A croaking, and a ruffling of feathers.

In the corner of the courtyard a raven pecked at the dirt, apparently unconcerned by the scene. It stretched its wings and hopped towards Alyce, tossing grass and grit with its beak. Then another one appeared, behind Hopkins this time, and watched him curiously with one beady eye. Two more followed it, and then half a dozen, cawing to each other. Only when another raven descended upon them from above did Alyce look up and see that the walls and the towers were completely fringed with black feathered bodies, hundreds of them, far more than she had seen when Raleigh had brought her in.

They simply sat and watched, in silence, sleek heads occasionally twitching.

Hopkins looked at Alyce, and then back at the rows of birds who were scrutinizing his every move. Then he laughed, swapped his dagger from one hand to the other, and lunged.

The ravens struck up a chorus. A ragged shape plummeted from the sky and into his face, and he growled and swatted it to one side. Another came at the back of his head. Then another, and another. Hopkins stumbled backwards, harried by beaks and claws on all sides, his hat raked from his head and his ruff already in tatters.

Wave after wave of black wings flooded over the Tower's battlements, until the man couldn't be seen for feathers, and his cries couldn't be heard for the birds' cawing. Even after he had fallen to the floor and the wild flailing of his limbs had stopped, they continued to swarm around and over him, heaving like a single entity.

The storm gradually subsided and the ravens took to the air, circling the remains of John Hopkins' body in a broad and slow arc. He was almost in pieces. Then they returned to their places on the battlements and waited, alert to every sound, croaking to each other.

All except one, who sat on the man's torso, and turned to look at Alyce with mismatched eyes, one black, one white. He poked sharply at the man's exposed neck, as though to make sure he was dead, then beat his tatty wings twice and flew to her shoulder.

He stayed perched there while the warders bound her hands and led her away. When she looked into the guards' eyes, she could see they were far more frightened of her than she was of them.

XXVII

At first, Alyce thought she was back in Bedlam. Her cell had the same four grimy walls, the same oppressively low ceiling, the same little wooden door whose spyhole seemed to be watching her even when there was nobody on the other side.

A glittering white figure stood before her. An angel, come to deliver her from her prison, or perhaps to send her down to Hell. She was dead, Alyce decided. Or this was a dream. The angel had a smoky, spicy scent that she found surprising, and not particularly pleasant.

Only when he tried to lift her from the floor, and the pain exploded in her ankle, did she realize that she was very much alive, and very much awake.

'Well, you can *stay* here if you want to, Alyce,' said a voice that didn't sound at all angelic.

The world came into focus, and with it a young man's face.

'Solly?' she said without thinking.

'Sadly not,' said Walter Raleigh. 'Come on, up you get.' She grasped at him to steady herself. 'Careful, this is my favourite doublet.'

Alyce hobbled alongside him, out of the prison cell. She hadn't paid attention to where the guards had taken her, and when she emerged from the staircase into the daylight, nothing looked familiar. The sun had been up for no more than an hour, she thought. Everything inside the inner ward had a misty, subdued feel to it, as though the whole fortress – buildings and inhabitants – was still dozing. A few ravens pecked around in the dew for their breakfast.

They entered the White Tower and retraced their steps to Elizabeth's chamber. As they did, all of the bizarre pieces of the previous night came back to her.

'In future,' said Raleigh, when he stopped to open the door to the bedchamber, 'when I tell you to lock the door, you lock it.'

Alyce stared at her blistered feet and nodded in vague contrition. They entered the gleaming bedchamber and Raleigh closed the door behind them.

'What happened? Where is everyone? Where's . . .' She paused. 'My mother.' The word felt strange in her mouth now, like it were in a foreign tongue.

'We captured Doctor Dee. Our masked friend is now at the bottom of the moat, along with the remains of Master Hopkins.'

'Are they definitely—'

'Dead, yes. Not even Mary Stuart would be able to patch them up again.'

Alyce narrowed her eyes. 'And where is she?'

Raleigh sighed. 'Mary eluded us. Those catacombs go on for miles. Elizabeth – your mother – is contacting our spies. She's had to return to Whitehall. She sends her apologies, again.'

'Her apologies?' said Alyce. 'Does she think that's all I want from her?'

'No. Alyce, try to understand, she is in a very difficult position. An impossible position.'

'My heart bleeds for her.'

'Try not to be too hard on her . . .'

Alyce ignored his awkward attempts at diplomacy. 'How did you find me? How did you know where I was?'

Now it was Raleigh's turn to look at his feet.

'Your friend . . .' he said. 'What's his name?'

'Solomon?' Something kindled inside her at the mention of his name, a warmth that had been absent all night.

'Hopkins and Caxton . . . interrogated him, to find out where we'd taken you. They questioned him rather forcefully.'

The warmth disappeared as quickly as it had come. 'Is he all right?' she asked.

'He tried to warn Elizabeth that the witchfinders were coming for you but her guards wasted a lot of time. They wouldn't let him speak to her. She only came out of her chambers to see what all the noise was, and he was just able to tell her what had happened before he passed out.'

'Is he *all right*?' she said again.

'He is not well,' said Raleigh. His face looked odd when

he was being serious, like it didn't fit him properly. 'He endured a lot for you, it's a wonder he made it to Elizabeth at all. We brought him here afterwards. But we had to leave him to go and find you.'

'Can I see him?' Alyce asked, hardly breathing.

Raleigh nodded. He slipped behind the tapestry into the passage, and she followed him up into Elizabeth's private chamber. The door was slightly ajar. She could see through the crack that the brazier had been lit again, and the room was forge-red.

There were actually two people inside. One was Solomon, lying shirtless on a bench, his skin white as marble. She couldn't work out whether he was dead or not.

The other was Doctor Dee, strapped to a chair, his face wan and drawn.

'Raleigh, listen to me,' he said, his beard quivering. 'Mary . . . the witch. She *forced* me, addled my wits. She has ways of coercing. I had no *choice*.'

'Hold your peace, you dog.' Raleigh didn't even deign to look at him. 'There will be plenty of time for talking later. I'm sure your new Queen didn't leave without telling you where she was going.'

Alyce stood beside Solomon and laid a hand on his forehead. It was feverish, and slick with sweat. The cuts and bruises on his body seemed especially raw in contrast to his pale skin. His eyes were even more sunken and shadowed than usual, the faint flutter of his eyelids the only sign that he was still alive.

She couldn't bear to look at him, but even when she

turned away she heard his strained breathing. There had to be *something* she could do. After all the times he'd saved her, now all she could do was mop his brow. If it wasn't for her he'd still be with Sussex's Men – jesting, drinking, toasting to the next few weeks on the road. It was all her fault.

Dee strained against his bindings. 'Child, listen to me. I can help him. Heal him. Let me show you.'

'We have seen your healing arts,' said Raleigh. 'You're nothing more than a grave robber.'

'I need to see what herbs Elizabeth has . . .' said Alyce, going over to the jars and bottles she'd been perusing the previous night. 'She might have something useful.'

She racked her brains for every lesson in herblore her mother had ever taught her. No, not her mother any more – just 'Ellen', now. But the revelation about her real mother had only made her miss her foster mother more deeply.

She closed her eyes for a moment and tried to focus. *Solly,* she told herself. *Think of Solly, now.* She found thistle, yarrow, goldenrod. No spider's webs, though. Her fingers trembled as she searched Elizabeth's supplies.

Behind her she heard Doctor Dee laugh with contempt. 'The boy is at death's door, my girl. A few dried leaves won't do him any good.'

Raleigh struck him across his face, but it didn't make the words any less stinging. Somewhere inside her, Alyce's own voice was saying the same thing: *This isn't going to work.* And when it didn't work, what then?

'The *Necronomicon*, Alyce,' said the Doctor, spitting blood. 'I know you have it. Why pretend that you aren't tempted? You could choose to save him, here and now. Or you can choose to be weak and ignorant, like your mother.'

'One more word out of you . . .' said Raleigh, tightening his fist around the handle of his sword.

'My notes. I have written a full *commentarium* to accompany the black book. It will explain all. If you'd let me fetch it from the catacombs.'

'That's *enough*.'

Raleigh's threat was suddenly cut short, though. All three of them spun around as the chamber door swung open and a gust of wind sent flames leaping out of the brazier. The smash of the door's iron handle into the wall was followed by long, guttural snarling, like no animal Alyce had ever heard.

They all turned at once. It was Caxton, or what was left of him. His robes were still dripping wet, as though he had only just now hauled himself from the Tower's moat. He had lost his boots, and one of his leather gloves, as well as his mask. His head was even more of a ruin than when they had seen it in Newgate Market. There was hardly any flesh left on it.

'You . . .' was the only thing Raleigh had time to say.

The monster blundered across the room and stretched out his bare, claw-like hand to Alyce's neck, but before she even had time to step backwards, Raleigh was there, sword raised above his head. Caxton caught it and snapped it in two. Then he whirled one half of it around and caught Raleigh on the side of the head with the hilt, sending him stumbling into the chair that Doctor Dee was bound to, and knocking it and its occupant to the floor.

Again Caxton lunged at Alyce. She skipped backwards to the brazier and then swung at him with a poker that had been buried in the fire; it didn't connect, but still flung hot ashes into the man's unmasked face. While he was temporarily stunned, Raleigh raised himself drunkenly on one arm, and charged at him. He threw Caxton into the table, and its legs broke as he collided with it.

Both of men grabbed each other by the throat, Caxton making a horrible, wet hissing noise as he was pinned up against the chamber window. Raleigh's face turned beet-root-red, and it soon became clear that no amount of throttling would cause the fiend to release his own grip.

Alyce saw what she needed to do. She took the poker and hurled it, not at Caxton, but at the window behind him, sending shards of dark glass down on to the cobbles below. Then she struck the man's arms, until Raleigh seemed to be able to draw breath once more.

Caxton flailed at both of them, raking at their clothes and their faces, as they heaved him up into the open arch. Raleigh still had one hand on his throat, while Alyce grabbed one of his legs around the knee. Even when he was halfway out, his head and shoulders suspended in thin air, he continued to grip the savagely sharp edges of the broken window.

Alyce hit his knuckles with the poker once more, and Raleigh hoisted his other leg, and then he was gone, falling the full height of the White Tower down on to the stones beneath. They didn't see him hit the ground, but they heard it.

They peered out of the window. Caxton lay, curled like a sleeping animal, and did not move. The ravens watched and croaked, as guards came running across the lawn.

Alyce and Raleigh looked at each other, too tired and too horrified to speak.

They turned back to the room, and groaned.

The overturned chair was empty. Doctor Dee was gone.

XXVIII

It was dark outside again by the time Raleigh returned. He removed his hat and slumped into the chair that Doctor Dee had been tied to. Somehow, during the day's confusion, he'd found time to change his outfit, which was as fashionable as ever, but didn't stop the man himself from looking worn and tired.

'None of the guards saw him leave. If he went down to the catacombs he's long gone. They stretch outside the city walls. That's how he smuggled Mary in.'

'What about his house in Mortlake?' asked Alyce.

'It's half destroyed. And he'll know not to go back there. We've placed a man to watch it.'

Alyce suddenly thought of Solomon's mother.

'Was there anyone else there? At his house?'

Raleigh looked at her quizzically. 'Like who?'

'Like . . . a woman? Or the body of a woman?'

'There was nothing but ruined books and papers. And a

cage. Nothing in it.'

'Oh.' That was it, then. They'd never know where she'd been laid to rest. Or even *if* she'd been laid to rest. Alyce looked at Solomon, and placed the back of her hand over his mouth. His breath was almost imperceptible. The poultices hadn't had any effect. But there were still other things she could try.

'I did find this,' said Raleigh. He handed her a folded piece of parchment, rain-spotted and begrimed with dust and ash. She opened it. It was barely legible any more, but she could still make out the curls of her own mother's hand-writing. The letter.

'I'd forgotten about it,' she said, not quite believing it was the same artefact she had carried with her all the way to London, that she had rescued from Bedlam all those months ago. She tried to straighten its dog-ears, and looked up at him. 'Thank you. It's the only piece of her I have left.'

They both regarded the letter in silence.

'What does it say?' she asked. She'd never found out. Half of her didn't really want to know. Half of her knew how much it would hurt.

Raleigh looked surprised. 'I'm no expert in the Old Speech, Alyce.'

'But can you understand it?'

'Enough.'

'Well?'

His expression became pained. 'Are you sure? The letter is of no real importance, not now…'

'*No importance?*'

Alyce's face flushed. Raleigh knew he had misspoken. 'Very well,' he said, and plucked the parchment from the palm of her hand. 'I can't read all the words. But from what I can make out it, it says: *Ellen of the Coven to Doctor John Dee. Perhaps the raven has already found you. The worst has befallen us. I go to meet Our Lady Death...*' He looked at her, and she nodded for him to continue. 'There is something illegible after that. Then she says: *I have sent Alyce to you. Look after her with a father's love, until she can be returned to her mother.* And then...'

He paused.

'And then what?'

'And then she says: *I beg forgiveness.*'

Alyce felt the tears come, but was too tired to cry. Too tired to be angry. She took back the letter and scanned the blurred symbols, not finding any of the meaning that Raleigh had found. Maybe one day she would learn how to read them. But who would teach her now? Elizabeth?

She laid it to one side.

'It is Doctor Dee who should be begging forgiveness,' she said. 'Where is he now?'

'Chances are, he's left the country. I'm sorry.' Raleigh shivered. The broken window was letting a fierce draught into the room, and even if they had wanted to cover it with something, Pecke had taken up residence on the windowsill and didn't want to be moved.

'Couldn't *he* go looking for him?' said Alyce, nodding to the raven, who cocked his head to regard her with his good, black eye.

'I discussed it with Bess, but she wants him to stay here. To watch over you. She was sure of that.'

'She could watch over me herself if she wanted to . . .' she muttered.

'Alyce,' said Raleigh sternly. 'You have to stop this. None of it is what Elizabeth wanted for you. Put yourself in her position now. She knows that Mary Stuart wants her unseated from the throne, or dead, and is now apparently able to leave her prison at will. She has been betrayed by her most trusted adviser, and the secret of her daughter is in entirely the wrong hands. Add that to the hundreds of other Catholics, Spaniards, French and whoever else are always trying to kill her anyway. And, on top of all of this, she still has to deal with the business of Court and *rule her subjects*. She cannot simply forget all of that to come and see you at a moment's notice. She wants to see you. More than anything in the world. It is breaking her heart. But she is the *Queen*, Alyce.'

Alyce chewed on her lips in silence. She found it difficult to sympathize with a mother who had been absent for her entire life. But she was starting to realize that, for exactly the same reason, it was difficult to pass judgement upon her. She just didn't *know* her. All she wanted now was to talk.

'Where is she?' she said.

'On her way to the Midlands. To meet with Mary's gaolers. We think we'll continue with the pretence that the Queen of Scots is still in prison – if word gets out that she has escaped, all of her supporters, and I don't just mean witches, will flock to her. We'll have a civil war.'

Just as the couple in The Hangman predicted, thought Alyce.

'Will she be executed? If Elizabeth finds her, I mean?'

Raleigh shook his head. 'That has always been a principle of Elizabeth's. She will not murder one of her own, especially someone she was so close to in the past. I get the feeling that . . .'

He paused.

'What?'

'That Elizabeth still thinks she might be able to bring Mary round. Back into the fold, so to speak. Back to the true Coven. Anyway, executing Mary is just as big an invitation to civil war as letting her go free. Her supporters wouldn't stand for it. It is all devilishly complicated.'

They both fell into contemplative silence. Pecke croaked at them and flew up on to one of the bookshelves.

'And what about me?'

'You?'

'What does Elizabeth want to do with me?'

Raleigh looked at her with that same expression of pity Solomon had once used. 'I don't know. We need to think about that.'

'I've already thought about it,' Alyce said bluntly.

'Oh really?'

'Yes. But I'll need your help.'

'My help?'

'When you brought me here, last night . . .'

'Yes . . .'

'And you were showing off about what a great sailor you were . . .'

'Yes . . .' Alyce could see a glimmer of amusement returning to Raleigh's face.

'We talked about the New World.'

'We did.'

'Take us there.'

Raleigh stared at her.

'Us?' he said. Alyce could see the pity on his face, and it made her angry.

'Solomon will make it. I just need a bit more time with him.'

'Suppose he does survive . . . why the New World?'

'I have nothing to keep me here,' Alyce continued. 'Neither does Solly. It would keep me out of the hands of Mary, out of the hands of the witchfinders. Elizabeth would never need to worry about her daughter turning up unexpectedly. A totally new life. Next time you cross the Atlantic, throw us in the hold with the rest of the cargo. Yes?'

'Alyce, I don't think—'

'I *mean* it, Walter. I don't want to live out my whole life in some English hovel, always fearing the knock at the door. There aren't any witchfinders in the New World, are there?'

'No,' said Raleigh. 'Not yet, at least.'

'Well then.'

A blank look of concentration crossed Raleigh's face, as always happened when he retreated to discuss something within himself. Then, unexpectedly, he smiled. 'Very well. I shall put it to your mother.'

He got to his feet and put his hat back on his head.

'Are you going now?' said Alyce. 'To Whitehall?'

'Not just yet. I need to clear up some business here, first. Not least to try and explain to the guards why somebody fell from the highest window of the north-east turret this morning. But I will ask your mother when the occasion arises.'

'Thank you, Walter.'

He looked over Solomon's body, smeared with unguents and covered in a patchwork of muslin. 'Are you sure you wouldn't like me to stay?'

'It's all right,' she said. 'I think I'd like to be alone with him.'

He smiled sadly and bowed. There was nothing to be said.

As the latch clunked behind him, a strange wheezing noise escaped Solomon's blue lips. Alyce was suddenly on her feet. Pecke squawked plaintively.

'Solomon? Can you hear me?' She soaked the sponge in the bowl again, and dabbed at his brow. 'It's Alyce.'

He gasped, and arched his back.

'Solomon!'

He didn't make another sound. His chest rose and fell, rose and fell. And then just fell.

'Solomon?' Alyce whispered. She rubbed his cold fingers in her own, trying to force the life back into them. Then she laid her head on his chest, and let her tears fall on to his smooth, white skin.

She didn't know how long she stayed like that, but at some point she wiped her eyes and stiffened her resolve.

Calmly, she got up and locked the door from the inside. Then she wiped her eyes, went to the desk, and produced the two books that she'd hidden away behind the Queen's herb stores. One was the *Necronomicon*. The other was Doctor Dee's *commentarium*.

During Raleigh's absence she had found her way down to the catacombs and searched among the debris of the Doctor's grisly laboratory. It had been lying on a workbench, covered with his bloody fingerprints – a book no bigger than a diary, written in both English and his own system of runes and glyphs. In it were all of the secrets he had elicited from the black book. Explanations. Translations.

Her heart was beating fast, her chest light and airy. She tried to shoo Pecke away from the bookshelf, but he simply hopped to one side. He cawed at her, and nipped at her hand, as though he knew exactly what she was going to do.

But she didn't have a choice, she told herself, over and over as she took her seat next to Solomon.

Again the raven called out, louder than before.

She ignored him, and flicked through the blackened pages of both books until she found the spell she needed. She rested them on Solomon's motionless ribs, and then set to work.

P L Y M O U T H
One month later

Alyce had never seen the sea before. Something about the salt in the air, the creak of the galleys and the bustle of sailors brought blood to the surface of her skin, and made her hairs stand on end. Beyond the lines of masts and rigging, the gulls hovered idly over deeper waters, calling back to those on the shore, daring them to join them. Alyce felt like their cries were for her, and her alone.

It was a grey, gusty day, but she could have stayed out on the seafront for hours. As she stared out to the horizon she felt a hand upon her shoulder, which then slipped down her arm and entwined with her fingers.

'Come on, it's freezing . . .'

She turned around to see Solomon's face, pink from the cold wind, his eyes and nose running a little. To look at him, no one would have any idea of what he'd been through. Just like he had no idea.

'I like it out here,' she said, and faced the sea again. Rationally, she knew there was no reason to feel guilty. Solomon was alive and well. That was all that mattered. Why did her belly squirm so much, then?

He unclasped her hand. 'Suit yourself. But Walter says the ship's crew won't be ready until midday, and he's buying us all drinks.' He smiled and sniffed loudly.

'I'll join you if you stop doing that . . .' said Alyce.

'I'm sorry. Handkerchiefs were not top of my list of things to pack for a voyage to the other side of the world.'

Alyce fumbled around in the folds of her dress – a present from Raleigh – and produced a delicate square of lace, which she thrust under his nose.

'Oh. Thank you.'

Solomon sneezed loudly, and when his face came back up to meet hers it was contorted in pain. He put a hand to his heart.

'Still hurts?'

He nodded.

'Let's get you some wine then. The stuff here works more wonders than any potion I could brew for you.'

The pair of them turned their backs on the wharf and wandered across the street, dodging the horses and carts and bands of rowdy sailors, until they reached the door of the Mermaid Inn.

The common room of The Swan had been fairly sedate compared to this place. It was still morning, but the watering hole was full to its low warped rafters with men of fortune, and plenty of ill-fortune, who seemed to have started drinking the previous afternoon and never realized that the night had come and gone. Every face was weathered or scarred in some way, even among the cabin boys, who were younger than either Alyce or Solomon but looked at least twice as old.

The timbers resounded with songs and jokes, and in the

corner Alyce spotted Walter Raleigh laughing uproariously with an old seadog whose shirt was spattered with ale, and whose nose looked like a giant, withered plum. In his sleek grey doublet, pearl earring gleaming beneath his curls, Raleigh could not have looked more out of place. And yet the patrons of The Mermaid didn't seem to care.

He spotted them, made his excuses to the salty old gentleman, and ushered them both over to a table by the window. Thick and dirty as the panes were, Alyce could still watch the ships bobbing gently in the bay from where she sat.

Raleigh left them for a moment and then returned with three cups of wine.

'Savour this. Most wine has turned to vinegar by the time it's crossed the Atlantic.' He raised his cup in a toast. 'To new beginnings.'

They each sipped in silence.

'How long will we be at sea?' asked Solomon.

'Ten weeks,' replied Raleigh. 'Maybe more, depending on the winds.'

There was something odd about the way he looked at Solomon, Alyce had decided. Had he guessed something? Or was she imagining it? As far as he was concerned, Solomon's recovery must have seemed more than miraculous.

Solomon gulped down his wine and pulled a face, which might have been in reaction to the taste, or to Raleigh's answer, or both. But then his face brightened and he leant in conspiratorially.

'We *do* have a witch on board, though,' he said. 'I'm sure

she can conjure us up some favourable weather. Yes?' He turned and raised an eyebrow at Alyce, who looked back at him wearily.

'I would keep sorcery to a minimum, young lady,' said Raleigh. 'Sailors are almost as superstitious as actors.'

Alyce tried to change the subject.

'When we arrive,' she said, 'what will you do?'

'Stay for a little time. There are some of the Coven established there already. They will want news from Elizabeth. And of course, they will want to be in my charming company for as long as possible.' He flashed her a smile.

'But then you'll return to England?'

'Yes.' He paused. 'I will return when I can, but I suspect I will have to spend more time in London, now that Doctor Dee has all but exiled himself. I can foresee your mother and me working much more closely together. Perhaps, one day, she will make the journey to the New World with me.'

Alyce nodded and stared out of the window at the dark slate of the sea.

'It's going to be strange, leaving without speaking to her.'

Raleigh didn't answer, but just stared into the depths of his cup.

In the month since the events at the Tower, Elizabeth had not once managed to come and see her. Perhaps, she thought, that was something to be thankful for. She was sure Elizabeth would have known what she had done. Would have sensed something about Solomon. Or would have simply read the guilt on Alyce's face.

No, Alyce told herself, *there's nothing to feel guilty about.*

Solomon is alive and well. I had no choice. And then sometimes she'd catch herself echoing Mary Stuart's words: *It's not unnatural. We define what is natural*.

When Solomon was fully recovered, both of them were smuggled out to a country house somewhere south of London. And still her mother did not visit.

Alyce had also paid a visit to Mrs Thomson before leaving the city. Their farewell had been brief and awkward, since Alyce could tell the old innkeeper so little about what had happened to her, and where she was going. Martha, she was pleased to learn, had been given a whipping and then been dismissed from her employment, after it became clear she had betrayed Alyce to Hopkins and Caxton.

Hopkins and Caxton. She shuddered to think of those two again. Raleigh had not deemed them worthy of a burial. He had ordered their bodies be wrapped in chains and thrown in the Thames — and this time made sure that Caxton wasn't still breathing.

They finished their drinks and talked of lighter matters, and Raleigh invited the plum-nosed man over for a game of cards. After an hour, they pushed back their stools and headed out to the wharf. Alyce's stomach turned a small somersault when they reached Raleigh's ship.

The *Gloriana* was a small but beautifully formed vessel, with three masts and an extensive, ornately decorated sterncastle. As Alyce approached, the weathering and the damage to the carvings became more apparent, but she only found this more endearing.

Way above them, looking ruffled and frozen at the top of

the main mast, Alyce could see Pecke watching them come aboard. The raven had followed her everywhere since she had left the Tower. She couldn't put her finger on it, but something about the way he shuffled around on the crow's nest made it look like he was rather embarrassed to be sharing his perch with a ragtag band of seagulls.

Raleigh shouted up to a man on deck, who seemed to Alyce the only person in all of Plymouth as well dressed as Raleigh himself.

'Sir Humphrey! I have our two stowaways!'

The older gentleman came to meet them as they came up the gangway, swaying a little with the rising and sinking of the ship.

'Well met, Walter. Crew's all accounted for, baggage and provisions are stowed, wind's moving south-west. We're just about ready.'

Alyce turned to Solomon.

'Are you sure you want to do this? You're leaving a lot behind.'

'Like what? Master Adams? Can't imagine I'd be wanted back in the company after what happened at Whitehall. My father? He made it clear he never wanted to see me again years ago. And I feel like if my mother were around, she would approve of it. In fact, she'd insist on it. I could marry into royalty. Even my father couldn't have a problem with that.'

'Um. Who's getting married?' said Alyce.

'No one.' Solomon pulled at his ruff. 'I just meant . . . It was a joke. I think.'

Alyce laughed.

Once they were on deck, Sir Humphrey took Raleigh to one side and they exchanged some words that Alyce couldn't hear. Then he went up to the bows of the ship to oversee the rigging of the sails, to the obvious annoyance of the sailors hauling at the ropes.

Raleigh turned back to the two of them, an odd look on his face.

'The captain would like to speak with you in his quarters. He would like to get to know the character of his passengers.'

Alyce and Solomon looked at each other and frowned. 'I thought Sir Humphrey was the captain . . .?'

'His cabin's at the back,' said Raleigh, ignoring her query and pointing. They both started off across the deck, but he put out an arm to stop Solomon. 'Just Alyce, I meant.'

Confused, she went to the door of the sterncastle, opened it, and stepped into the darkness beyond.

The captain's cabin was lit with a pair of oil lamps that hung from the rear wall and clinked softly on their chains as the *Gloriana* rose and fell. In the middle was a large desk covered with maps, a globe, compasses, sextants and other nautical apparatus, and behind it sat the captain himself, his head obscured by a broad, feathered hat, poring over the material in front of him.

Alyce cleared her throat.

'You wanted to see me, sir?' she said.

The captain looked up, and Alyce nearly choked. 'I don't know how you managed it,' said a voice she had never expected to hear. 'These breeches are just impossible to wear.'

Looking back at her was the same white face that she'd last seen in the depths of the Tower, the same dark, sad eyes.

Queen Elizabeth got up out of the chair and revealed her outfit in its entirety: a battered leather jerkin, a broad, black leather belt, some heavy-looking breeches that looked as though they were made of some sort of untreated animal hide, and a pair of knee-high boots.

'Not very convincing, is it? You pulled it off much better, I think.'

Elizabeth stepped forwards until she was in the lamplight, and Alyce saw her mother's face clearly for the first time. Her skin was bleached and drawn, smallpox scars too deep to be concealed under make-up. She looked beyond weary, like poor old Master Makepiece, only more dignified. Alyce found herself pitying her, unexpectedly.

'Forgive me,' said Elizabeth. 'For everything.'

Still Alyce didn't know what to say. She wasn't angry any more. She didn't know what she was. Maybe just a little sad, for both their sakes.

Her mother took her hand. 'You are brave. Braver than I am.' Then she pushed a red curl out of Alyce's eyes. 'I wish my hair still looked like this.'

'What would you have chosen?' said Alyce.

Elizabeth looked surprised. 'What?'

'When Mary asked you to choose — between me and the throne. What would you have chosen, if I hadn't escaped?'

'You, Alyce,' she said. 'You, a thousand times over.'

'Why did you give me up, then?'

Elizabeth took her daughter's hands. 'I didn't give you up, Alyce. I had to keep you safe.'

'Couldn't I have lived with you in the palace?'

'What, as a princess? Forever on show, forever having to conceal who you really are? I would not wish it upon anyone. Suppressing the Craft is dangerous. Far easier, far safer to be a witch away from Court, away from the city.' She sighed. 'Not safe enough, though, it would seem. Even with faithful old Pecke watching over you. Even with Ellen.'

Alyce thought back to her cottage in Fordham, watching her mother feeding the scruffy black bird with scraps. Yes, she still thought of Ellen as her mother – couldn't un-think it, even with her real mother standing right in front of her.

'I still miss her.'

'I know.'

'Mary said that she could bring her back. From the dead.' Only as the words left her mouth did Alyce realize she was talking more about herself than about Mary. It almost felt like a confession. Would her mother know, if she saw Solomon?

'No doubt she could. Witches like her have spent centuries trying to defeat death. Dee was intent on the same thing, and you saw what that led him to do. You saw his laboratory. Bringing Ellen back would have been an abomination. It is the one thing we must never do, as members of the true Coven. We communicate with the Other Side, yes, and we may banish it wherever and whenever it spills over into our world. But that is all. We are here to ensure balance. Death is death. It is the end. And all things need to come to an end, at their proper time.'

Alyce swallowed hard.

'I was tempted,' she said, as though that were at least halfway towards an admission of guilt. 'To take Mary's deal. To join with her.'

'Of course you were. Who wouldn't be? Death is with us from the moment we are born, whoever we are. The Great Shadow is always there. But we have to decide whether we treat the shadow as an enemy pursuing us, or merely a friend accompanying us. If you choose the first, then you will spend your whole life trying to outrun it, trying to defeat it — and you will never succeed.' She paused. 'I pity her. Mary. She has lost a great deal. And necromancy promises so much.'

Elizabeth went back behind the table, and from under a pile of sea charts brought out a charred, leather-bound book.

'We found this in the Tower,' she said, handing her the *Necronomicon*.

It hadn't burnt, Alyce realized with horror. She shifted the weight on her feet nervously. The *commentarium* had gone up in flames as soon as it was in the brazier, but the black book had survived somehow.

'Where did you get it?' asked Elizabeth.

'It was Solomon's. His mother had it.'

The Queen nodded. 'I know of Anne Harper. I know she was deceived by Mary, like so many others.'

'It scared me,' said Alyce truthfully. 'I just wanted to get rid of it. So I put it in the fire. I know it's forbidden.' And then she lied. 'I didn't use it.'

'Good.' Elizabeth took the book back, and stared at her long and hard. 'You wouldn't need it, though, I suspect.'

Alyce sensed things beginning to unravel. 'What do you mean?'

'You can do things, can't you? Without the book. I saw it in the play. And I saw it in the Tower. You can call upon the dead. You can make them influence the things around you.'

The boat creaked in the pause.

'I don't know . . .' said Alyce. 'Yes. Sometimes. I'm sorry.' She didn't know why she was apologizing. 'I don't mean to. I don't know how I do it.'

'It is a gift,' said Elizabeth, and although she smiled, her face seemed full of pity. 'But it is one you must use with the utmost respect. Do you remember what I said to Mary? At the Tower?'

Alyce nodded.

'There is nothing wrong with speaking to the dead. But allowing them back into our lives is dangerous. Every time it is done, the boundaries between this world and the next are weakened. And at a certain point, those boundaries will cease to exist, and the Other Side will overwhelm us. This is what Mary would do – flood our world with the restless dead, and all the other strange creatures that come with them.' Alyce swallowed dryly. 'Besides, the dead are not our slaves. We cannot force them to do our bidding. They only desire—'

'Our company. I remember.'

'Did Ellen tell you that?'

'Yes.'

Elizabeth smiled. 'She brought you up well. Better than I could have.' Her eyes shone for a moment, and she blinked hard a couple of times. 'Remember what she taught you, Alyce. And remember to listen. To the great pulse of the world. Sunrise and sunset, summer and winter. Everything living and dying, always and for ever.'

There was a chorus of shouting from outside the cabin.

'I must go, my love. If this ship sets sail with me on board, the consequences do not bear thinking about.' She kissed her daughter on the cheek, and embraced her tightly.

Alyce didn't know what to feel. She tried so hard to imagine it was her mother holding her, but it still didn't come easily. Her face flushed, but she was unsure whether it was from embarrassment, or sadness, or affection, or some strange mixture of the three.

'Is there no way you could come with us?' she heard herself saying.

'No way in the world,' said Elizabeth, smiling sadly. 'Mary is still alive, if not hale and healthy. Doctor Dee will no doubt try his luck again at some point in the future. There is too much to be done here.' She paused, and tears welled in her eyes. 'Forgive me,' she said once more. 'I hope we shall see each other again. In the meantime, I know you cannot love me. But think better of me.'

And then she was gone, and Alyce was left alone with all the questions she knew she should have asked. She waited a few minutes, thinking, swaying gently with the ship.

Her father. She hadn't asked about her father.

Alyce ran out of the sterncastle and out on to the deck, hoping she could still catch her, perhaps on the quayside.

There was no sign of her. Only the crew, and Solomon, waiting under the mainmast.

'The captain just left the ship,' he said, a baffled expression on his face.

'The captain? Oh . . .' So her mother had managed to fool him. 'That wasn't the captain.'

Together they walked to the front of the ship, as the gangplank was removed, the mooring ropes cast off, and the sails unfurled. The sailors bellowed to each other, and Alyce and Solomon spoke in quiet voices about what had taken place in the cabin.

Soon the *Gloriana* sailed out of the bay, gulls circling her topmast, bow cleaving the black waves.

'You know those books you gave me?' said Alyce, when they were clear of the harbour.

Solomon frowned. 'Yes . . .'

Alyce thought about telling him everything, but changed her mind at the last second. 'Well . . . I lost them.'

'Oh. That's fine.'

'Is it? They weren't mine, really.'

'What are you talking about? They were a gift. No matter. That reminds me, I've got you something else . . .' He looked over his shoulder to see if any of the crew was watching, then rummaged in the satchel that hung from one shoulder. From it he produced another little straw doll. 'I made this when you went back to say farewell to Mrs Thomson. From memory. I know you lost yours.' He fiddled with his ruff. 'I had to take a piece of your hair to make it. You were asleep. Sorry.'

Alyce took the mommet very gently. 'Thank you, Solly,' she said. She looked down at it in the palm of her hand and remembered the last time he had handed her a straw figure, back at The Swan, a lifetime ago. 'It does still look a bit like a worm.'

'Well, I tried my best.' He smiled sadly, and she kissed him.

The wind was picking up now, and swept their laughter all the way to the back of the ship. They huddled a little closer together for warmth, and fell into contented silence. Pecke flew down from the crow's nest, and perched right on the tip of the ship's bowsprit. England disappeared behind them, and with it the shouts of the crew, until it felt as though they were completely alone on the prow.

Neither looked back as they were borne, hand in hand, over the deep.

HISTORICAL NOTE

Alyce's story takes place at a moment of huge change and upheaval in the history of Europe. Turmoil in the Christian church, advances in science, mysterious corners of the globe discovered and mapped and brought to order: all these things prompted more and more people to question the truth of the world and their place in it. The witch-hunts were at the centre of this uncertainty and anxiety. European societies needed someone to blame, and witches fitted the bill – in many ways the sufferings of women at the hands of witchfinders were the birth pangs of our modern, 'enlightened' Western world. This was a time before magic, science and religion could be easily defined as separate things.

Witchborn is the story of what *might* have been happening in the background. Queen Elizabeth I and Mary, Queen of Scots, as powerful women, were both subjected to accusations of witchcraft, as were their mothers. Elizabeth really was advised by Doctor John Dee – astronomer, astrologer, alchemist, philosopher and mathematician extraordinaire, who claimed to be able to speak with angels and the dead. Even Sir Walter Raleigh (not yet a 'Sir' at the time of this book) was implicated in the 'School of Night', a supposed secret society of atheists and occultists. Did Elizabeth, the Virgin Queen, really have an illegitimate daughter? Well, there is no evidence to suggest as much, and it would be very difficult for her to hide the truth both during and after her pregnancy. But then, if she *were* a witch – and a witch queen, at that – she would no doubt be able to cover her tracks in ways we couldn't imagine . . .

ACKNOWLEDGEMENTS

Thanks to the following, and apologies to all those I have inevitably missed out:

Alice Glover, who started all of this; Julian Dickson, the first person to think the thing was worth reading, and the only reason I carried on writing; my agent Jane Willis, for her wisdom, support and kindness; Naomi Colthurst for invaluable editorial advice in the very early stages; all the Chickens for their enthusiasm and faith in the project, but in particular Barry and Rachel, for taking a chance on me, and my editor Kesia, for getting all my *Star Wars* references and being more in tune with the book than I ever could have hoped for; Tuulevi, Sandra and Andrew, Titus and Carrie, who all let me write in their houses; readers and general supporters Joelle, Vic (sorry you nearly went blind), Ben, Anna, Emerald, Chris, Will L, the Bunhill Massive (Will D, Mary, Dave, Sarah) and the brothers Bowling for their thoughts, ideas and camaraderie; and Steph, the world's greatest critic and proofreader, who read it more than anyone and was there in good times and bad.

Writers and other clever people who I have drawn upon for the historical side of things are too numerous to mention, but constant companions have been Catherine Arnold, Antonia Fraser, Ian Mortimer, Liza Picard and Anne Somerset. This book would have been impossible without their (much more scholarly) work.